PENGUIN METRO READS
ONLY THE GOOD DIE YOUNG

Akash Verma is the co-founder of a fashion start-up centred around Indian designs, www.chokore.com, and a national bestselling author. Akash has more than twenty-four years of experience in the FMCG sector and media, at senior levels with companies such as Coca-Cola, Red FM, Big FM and the *Times of India*. His work has taken him across the country, and he finds this experience very relevant while giving shape to his stories.

Akash has authored four books till now and been covered by the national media, in publications such as the *Pioneer*, the *Times of India*, the *Hindustan Times* and *Financial World*.

Akash lives with his family in Gurgaon, Haryana. His parents are eminent and award-winning Hindi writers.

He can be reached at:
Mail: akash.v1970@gmail.com
Facebook:https://www.facebook.com/Akash-Verma-595364230638661/
Twitter: https://twitter.com/akashvermanow
Instagram: https://www.instagram.com/akash_verma_now/

ONLY THE GOOD DIE YOUNG

& I'm not a saint

AKASH VERMA

Penguin
metro reads

An imprint of Penguin Random House

PENGUIN METRO READS

USA | Canada | UK | Ireland | Australia
New Zealand | India | South Africa | China | Singapore

Penguin Metro Reads is part of the Penguin Random House group of companies
whose addresses can be found at global.penguinrandomhouse.com

Published by Penguin Random House India Pvt. Ltd
4th Floor, Capital Tower 1, MG Road,
Gurugram 122 002, Haryana, India

First published in Penguin Metro Reads by Penguin Random House India 2021

Copyright © Akash Verma 2021

ISBN 9780143450122

Typeset in Adobe Caslon Pro by Manipal Technologies Limited, Manipal

Printed at Repro India Limited

www.penguin.co.in

This is a legitimate digitally printed version of the book and therefore might not
have certain extra finishing on the cover.

Vengeance is in my heart, death in my hand, blood and revenge are hammering in my head.

—William Shakespeare

Prologue

December 2015
Lal Tibba, Mussoorie

The sky is so pitch-black that it's like an impervious, impenetrable blanket. It looks ruthless, this darkness of it—like there is no escaping it, like it is the final frontier. You could try. You could try to touch it, poke it and try to find an opening, but it won't let you go. There are no stars because it has swallowed them all up. Will it swallow me too?

Am I going to die?

Am I cursed to stare at this shroud of a sky till my last breath?

No, I won't let go. I've not learnt to let go! My parents . . . Ma, taught me to never give up.

Or to forget . . .

And that means you, A.

You did what you should have never done.

You knew I had big dreams to chase. You were a part of them. There was no one as good as me—Sid, a fuckin' gift from God!

But then you had to go and mess it all up, bitch!

I'd hate it if I were to die. Death doesn't suit me, this insipid state of lifelessness. It seems to cling to me like ill-fitting, borrowed clothes. Uncomfortable. I want to shrug it off and wear my old comfortable clothes. I want my old life back. But is that even possible now? I lie here, like a crumpled piece of shit, over this heap of glass shards. All bloodied and wounded.

I can't feel any sensation, but my body feels like dead weight. My mind is numb. My face too. Rivulets of blood are seeping out of the punctures in my skin. Blood seems so eager to leave my body and render it lifeless. Bloody fuckin' renegade! Now I have to wonder whether the smell of my blood will draw the predators on the mountainside.

I can't breathe deeply; I'm unable to. My chest won't allow the expansion. Hell, I'm not sure if it's that or I'm incapable of taking a deep breath—no sighs for me.

Just an endless wait for death.

Once again, it's the sky. Just the sky and me.

What a destiny! I'm injured, wounded, broken—you pick the word. You, whose face I can still see peering out of the window. A faint shadow of relief in those big eyes.

I'm not supposed to die! I'm only twenty-six, dammit!

Yet here I am, trapped between life and death. In a limbo.

All because of you.

All because you didn't want me to succeed.

All because you had to put yourself before me—you had to, you selfish bitch!

I'm too young to die!

Only the good die young—that's what they say.

But I am not good. And not a saint.

1

Dhruv

3 October 2017
Domestic Terminal, Mumbai

Mumbai has unnerved me every single time I've set foot here in the last few months. It wasn't like this before. It used to be like any other city. Just that I frequented it more as my advertising agency, C&M, is headquartered here. But now, since you have been here for about a year, coming to this city has never been the same. Work still brings me here—a couple of times a month at least—for a sales review or a client meeting. But every time I am here, I feel like running to you first, clasping you to my chest and not letting you go. Yes, that's what I still feel, Anuradha, after pushing you so far away from my life. The first few months after you left were tough—to come to work each day with you not being in office; to live without you in Gurgaon; not hearing your voice; and not feeling your touch. Despite having Shalini and the kids back in my life, there was this one large gash in my heart. However hard I tried, it refused to heal. It stayed there, untended and bleeding. My head feels heavy with the weight of a sack inside it.

'"Don't do it!" didn't we warn you?' the pebbles inside the sack which rests in my head scream in unison. 'You can't love two people at the same time.'

'I didn't do it knowingly. It wasn't in my control,' I protest.

'Oh, come on! Liar, liar, pants on fire!' squeals one. 'You had a rock-solid marriage, a lovely family. Didn't you know what you were getting into?'

'I know. All my fault. I thought I could handle it. I loved them both, you know. I just couldn't stop.'

One of the pebbles has a throaty voice. It's smaller than the rest. 'Look where this "love" has led you to. No one's happy. Neither Shalini, nor you and I guess not even Anuradha.'

'Well, who knows?' I say. 'Maybe she has found someone. Why "maybe"? I am sure she has someone in her life by now. She is young, beautiful, successful . . . she can easily be happy. Don't you think so?'

The pebble glances at me, scrutinizing me. 'Yes . . . maybe. Will you be happy if she has found someone?'

I clear my throat, 'Why not? Yes.'

'Sure?'

I nod. 'Yes. I will be happy as long as she is.'

'Do you want to meet her?' the pebbles chorus.

'No. It's over, isn't it? Why would I want that?'

'Ah, come on,' one of them says. 'It's what you want the most. To meet her. Isn't it?' I fumble for an appropriate answer. Unsuccessful. I go quiet, then.

The plane has landed. I get out of the airport and spot the driver holding a placard with my name on it. I purse my lips and force a smile; a familiar weakness sweeps over me. He signals to me to wait and hurries off to get the car when I nod. I glance at the passengers leaving the airport, people gathered around the arrival gate, greeting incoming passengers: relatives and friends. *I wish you too were here, waiting for me, Anuradha . . .*

Such feelings seem even more unreal after the way our relationship ended. But then how is one supposed to conceal one's true feelings from oneself? How can I hide that I love you? Even after you lied to me. Even after I promised my wife, Shalini, that our affair happened in the heat of the moment and was well over. How can my feelings for you ever cease to exist? Maybe I really am the asshole that the people I love think me to be. Shalini and you. Maybe I don't deserve love from either of you. My relationship with my wife will never go back to what it was. I have done enough to scar it and I don't know if those scars will ever fully disappear.

'We have struck a compromise for our children, Dhruv,' was what Shalini told me at the dinner table one day when the kids were asleep. 'It can never be the same again,' she had said. Shalini is a headstrong, self-made woman who sticks to her word in her personal life as much as she does when treating her patients. So, over the last one year, she has immersed herself totally in her work and the kids. I have been left alone and miserable, switching silos within my heart—trying to fulfil my familial responsibilities in one of them while trying to drive away your memories from the other. So far, I have not had much success in doing either.

The driver honks from the parking bay and signals to me to get in the car. I know what you would have felt after our last meeting in that café at Christmas last year, when I ended our relationship abruptly the way I did. I admit I have been the selfish one in our relationship. I wanted to have both, have my cake and eat it too. My family and you. And I thought I could manage it all, like the clients that I simultaneously juggle in my professional life as the Delhi branch head of C&M. How insanely wrong was I! But then you weren't completely honest with me either, Anuradha. You hid your past from me about Sid, that fucking monster boyfriend of yours. I shudder to think how a woman as smart as you could fall for a pervert like him and then go on to do all those stupid things. But then love can do that. Love can push us to make stupid mistakes. But you went a step further after that. You fell for a married man. Me.

Love, every time it strikes, can turn one insane. Who knows that better than us, Anuradha?

2

Sid

December 2015
Lal Tibba, Mussoorie

'My spidey sense is tingling,' said the American superhero, Spiderman, when he had a bad feeling about something. I have the same terrible feeling rocking my insides, although things have eased a bit. I am a bit more in control of myself. I was lucky that I fell on this mound of glass that took the brunt of my fall. If it had been the hard, rocky ground of this hill instead, I would have been gone. Out in a second. I can hear the wind whistling through the trees, my own breathing and the chirping of crickets. Occasionally I hear a distant howl. There could be a jackal around somewhere and if the guy were to come across this piece of dead meat lying here . . . it'd be party time for the little fellow. I shudder. My body being torn apart by an animal is not what I should be thinking about in my current situation: helpless and totally fucked. All thanks to you, bitch!

I have been lying like this, on blood-splattered glass, for quite a while. My body has regained some strength, but I still can't move. I am not confident enough to risk moving my body lest I stumble and end up hurting myself even more. A wretched state to be in. I hear the grass rustle somewhere close by. A snake? Could be a deadly cobra. Just one kiss from the bugger and that's it. The end.

No wait, it isn't an animal. I can hear the sound of footsteps. Is there someone around who can help me? A human being! I want to scream as loudly as I can. But I can't. This fucking glass all over my face has made it impossible for me to move my facial muscles. The shards have pierced and lacerated most of my skin. I try shouting with all of my energy, but only a muffled whimper comes out. The footsteps come closer and in a matter of seconds, the person arrives, next to my motionless body. A stranger's hand touches my shoulder. It is gentle at first, but then it grabs me hard and starts shaking me. Stop it, asshole, it hurts. Soon, one hand gives way to the other and I can feel my body being turned over by this stranger. I am able to open my eyes a bit and see a drunken man looming over me. He has a thin moustache, a bulbous nose and his face is pitted with pockmarks. I can smell the cheap whisky flowing in his dirty veins. He stares at me, his eyes roving over my face, trying to figure out whether I am dead or not. What's the verdict, asshole? Oh no, he's spotted my expensive designer watch. It's a gift, you bastard! Don't you dare! He grins and quickly relieves my hand of it. He leers at the watch and then his eyes start travelling again, across my dirt-stained, blood-soaked denims. They stop at the bulge of my front pocket where my wallet rests. He clumsily gropes inside my pocket and extracts the wallet that is filled with banknotes. Fuck, Fuck, Fuck! Not the money too!

What have you turned me into, bitch? A fuckin' vegetable!

The bugger doesn't want to stop there; he rifles through all my pockets and then yanks out the gold chain around my neck.

It's a thick one that Mom had gifted me on my twenty-fourth birthday. Another one and a half lakh gone.

Then, he pulls out a bottle of country liquor tucked beneath his shirt and takes a long swig. He puts the bottle aside and once more scrutinizes my body carefully.

I feel violated!

He pulls out my hand that rests under my thigh and sets his eyes on the last of the valuables left on my body—the blue sapphire on my finger, worth more than a lakh. He sniggers and mumbles something. I think he's thanking his God for leading him to this godforsaken trail tonight. He tries to slip out the ring from my finger. It doesn't come out. He tries again, pulling at it with all his strength. My fingers have swollen up with the pain. Fuck, it is killing me! I howl, and this time I am able to unlock my throat muscles. The sound escapes my mouth as a small cry. The stranger is shocked to hear my voice and looks at me like he has seen a ghost. He retreats a couple of steps and stops, looking at me, figuring out his next move. What will it be? Will he run away or kill me and then take the blue sapphire ring?

I can hear his heavy breathing in the quiet of the night. He walks around me, without taking his eyes off me and then picks up a boulder. Not too big, but well-rounded and just heavy enough to fully kill a half-dead man. He hunches over my body, the boulder clasped in his hand tightly. My heart starts thudding again, kicking my rib cage violently. I can't help but laugh at the irony of the moment. It isn't you who will kill me, bitch, but this drunken petty thief! He glances at me once before pinning my hand—the one with the sapphire ring—firmly to the ground. He raises the hand holding the boulder. Then it dawns on me! The bastard has no interest in my life, but only wants to break my fingers and slip out that damn sapphire! I have to do something exceptional. This is the moment. My nervous system kick-starts and is set on fire. My other hand moves all by itself and picks up a large piece of broken glass, and, before he crushes my finger wearing the sapphire, the glass ruptures the skin of his neck and pierces his jugular vein. The impact is instantaneous and blood from his neck gushes out. With one hand on his neck, the stranger falls to the ground without a sound.

Here I lie. No more a victim, but a killer. My first murder was to save myself but all the others that I will be committing in the future will be for revenge. Revenge for what you did to me. I want to live, I really do. I don't want to die here, alone and helpless, having been tossed out of a window like a piece of trash. All alone. I know what the world will assume: a failed businessman; hounded by his creditors; jumped out of a window and committed suicide. So many of them do that and that's exactly what my death would be interpreted as. Just another bloody coward! A failure! If that's what the world wants to believe, so be it. If you think you have killed me, bitch, I will prove you wrong. And then I will come for you.

I move my arms over the rough ground to grip something that will help me get up and my fingers fold around the country liquor bottle belonging to the idiotic bugger who's drawing his last breaths a little further away. Yes! I put it to my parched lips and take a few quick swigs. It tastes awful but warms my chest and belly. Two more swigs, and a plan starts taking shape in my head. By the time the bottle is empty, I have enough strength, or perhaps I am sufficiently numbed, to put my plan into action.

I have been counting the seconds in my mind to keep a tab on the time. It also makes me think of something other than my broken bones. I count close to nine hundred seconds before I rise up like a staggering drunk. I retrieve my watch, wallet and gold chain from the thief before pushing him back on to the pile of glass, with his face down, where I lay a moment ago.

I scan my surroundings. It's all trees enveloped in darkness and mountain rocks. Beyond this, is an expanse of land that stretches for about two hundred feet, and then a sheer drop into the valley. I inhale the cold mountain air deeply and a sharp pain in my chest makes me double up. Slowly I rise again and start to put my plan into action. I hunker down and unbutton the dead man's shirt to exchange it with mine. Luckily, he is nearly as tall as me but a bit on the heavier side. His shirt falls loosely over me. Slowly and steadily I work with him and by the time I am done, I am exhausted. I think it takes me about thirty minutes. It's far into the night and the chill is now settling into my bones. The effect of the cheap liquor is wearing off, so I'm guessing I can't stay here for much longer. I glance at his baggy and crumpled chequered trousers that I have to swap with my Gap denims. Damn. If exchanging a shirt was tough, this exercise is going to be a nightmare. But then what option do I have?

I can hardly stand when I zip up his trousers on my waist. I lean against the mountainside over which the Jawahar Bungalow stands tall. I was meant to be dead tonight after being pushed out of one of its windows. Instead, I live.

After having switched clothes, I consider my plan for a moment. Merely exchanging clothes is not going to be enough. More needs to be done. I stuff my wallet with a few currency notes and put it into the stranger's pocket along with my various identity cards and my driving license. The rest of the cash finds a place in the pocket of his trousers that I am wearing. I sigh deeply. It's time for the grand finale. I pick up the same boulder that was meant to break my hand. I take a deep breath once again, before slamming it with force on the dead man's face.

A squelching thud. It's like cracking open a coconut. His face bones rupture instantly and blood spills out like coconut water. I feel a rush of adrenaline as I bludgeon his face two more times. Good! His face is beyond recognition now and I turn him around and dump him on the mound of broken glass. I walk around hundred feet towards the cliff and, using all my strength, hurl the boulder into the valley. It vanishes without even a sound.

I repeat the loser story in my head: Sid was running away from his creditors, couldn't take any more shit and jumped out of the window to fall on this heap of glass bottles. The steep fall, the stones and the glass pieces disfigured his face and took away his life.

I have killed myself!

Fuck!

I have successfully killed myself!

I walk back to the dead body and gaze at it. The wallet with all my identity documents is in his pocket, the clothes on him are mine. So, it's all fine up to there. But wait. You need something to seal the deal really. Something that everyone close to me would know is definitely mine. My blue sapphire ring has to be on this dead man's finger. If this is found, no one would have even the faintest shadow of a doubt that Sid committed suicide. I hunker down and slip the sapphire on to his dead finger. What this asshole couldn't take from me while he was alive, he is now wearing as a dead man.

I search the pockets of his trousers that I am wearing. A ten-rupee note and a visiting card. In the faint light from the Jawahar Bungalow above us, I can barely see what's written on the card until I bring it close to my face and then I am able to read it. I am certain that lady luck is on my side today. Despite everything. In spite of you wanting to murder me, I am not going to die today.

The visiting card belongs to a doctor: Dr B.D. Banerjee, BDS. The address on the card is in Lal Tibba, so this must be somewhere close by, and it includes his mobile number. I need to call him. The thought reminds me of my iPhones. I had two of them: one was in the room above, where I was staying, and the other was with me when I fell down. Fuck. It must have dropped out of my hand when I fell. I can look around for it, but there is no point. There's no way I can find it now in this darkness. I will have to come back here later to look for my phone if I want those videos back. Videos: the one with which I was blackmailing Hemant Tiwari and the others that were recorded by the hidden camera in the room above. I wanted that concealed camera to record my conversations with Hemant Tiwari and then with Anuradha. But do I really need my mobile phone now? What will I do with Hemant's video now that I am 'dead'? I can't blackmail Hemant Tiwari any more! And I can't be punished for it. And even if someone found out about the hidden camera in the room above, what would they get from it? A few of my other videos, including the one of that bitch pushing me out of the window, and my chat with her last evening. That's good, no? Why should that bother me? She's the one who killed the bad guy. She's the one who'll be punished for murder, even if the person she killed was blackmailing her . . . hell, no. I don't want that! I don't want anyone else to punish her but me.

Let me think about the cell phone and the hidden camera later. First, let me save myself. Both gadgets were of use to Sid when he was alive. Now, he is dead. Let Sid remain dead. I have to reach this doctor's house without being seen. As fast as I can, before the morning sun rises. I pick up the last item of clothing that is lying on the ground. The dead man's muffler. Suddenly I realize that it's cold. Biting cold. The throbbing pain from my wounds is coming back. I touch my blood-soaked, badly-wounded face. The skin is severely damaged and from several places pieces of glass stick out, caked in dry blood. It feels as if I have a new face, a glass-encrusted face. But this is good—what with Sid gone, his face is gone too. I cover my face with the muffler and I start trudging up a narrow path that runs towards the main road.

3

Dhruv

3 October 2017

Domestic Terminal, Mumbai

'Sir ji, Powai?' the driver asks, glancing at me in the rear-view mirror. I nod. I am heading straight to the Mumbai Advertising Federation Awards Night, being held at a suburban hotel, from the airport. My flight landed at 5 p.m. A large gathering of advertising professionals in Mumbai has always given me the jitters because the chances of bumping into you goes up. We still have common ground—advertising. You may have switched agencies, but we work in the same field and hence the probability of the odd encounter is always there. The mere thought of it is enough to set my pulse racing. I take a deep breath. *Calm down.* It was okay to watch you from a distance after you moved here. I did that once: watched you covertly, just to confirm that our lives were finally separate. But meeting you face to face can turn a bit awkward. I don't know how we might react. Will we rediscover the attraction we once felt for each other? The thoughts in my head are crammed together, like small pebbles in a sack with a rope tied around it.

'What if she is there at the event today?' a pebble raises its tiny head.

'I don't think she will be. But even if she is, how does it matter?' I say.

'Mister, stop fooling us. We know you inside out,' another one mutters, irritated. 'Stop acting "cool".'

'He has no clue how he will react if he bumps into her,' yet another gibes.

'Shut up, will you?' I say, blocking out their irritating voices.

~

The Renaissance Hotel stands tall on the banks of the artificial Powai Lake. The cab drives up the winding hotel driveway that leads to its entrance. It is past 7 p.m. when I enter the hotel premises. The lobby has started to get crowded. People from the advertising world are here for the most coveted event of the year, an event that celebrates the advertising fraternity's most distinguished talent. For the younger agency crowd, it's plenty of exotic food coupled with free-flowing alcohol. It's a night to go wild. I spot a few familiar faces at the security check. We exchange pleasantries and walk along the meandering pathways towards the lakeside lawns. The organizers have given a sublime touch to the surroundings with a stream of lights that flank the pathway. The trees are dimly lit, giving a celebratory ambience. I inhale deeply, breathing in the fresh air and nature's fragrance, something that can only be found in an oasis such as this within the parched metropolis. I enter the main arena through a decorated gate manned by ushers who welcome the guests. I look around for some known faces from C&M. I spot Rachna, my branch's creative director, surrounded by familiar people from the Delhi and Mumbai teams.

Rachna spots me, breaks the circle and rushes towards me. 'Hi, Dhruv. How was your flight?'

I half smile. 'It was good. Except for the evening madness on Mumbai roads.'

'Eh! Sounds familiar, no?' Rachna quips. She is right. We have the same thing to say about the Gurgaon traffic every day. Mumbai is no exception.

I nod. 'Have the others come?' I ask, glancing at the small group of C&M associates walking towards us.

'Yeah, Mudit should be around. Besides him, only Pooja is here from the Delhi team. I thought it would be a good opportunity for her to meet and interact with the Mumbai creative fraternity.' Mudit is our strategy head from Delhi and Pooja our new creative head. She is the one who came into Anuradha's role after she resigned that night. Seeing Pooja enter my cabin every time brings back memories of Anuradha walking in through the very same door. My heart cringes every single time.

'Hi, Dhruv,' Mudit pats my shoulder. I acknowledge his gesture and then we go on to meet up with the others from the Mumbai C&M team.

'Isn't Vikas coming?' I ask Virag, the national creative director based at Mumbai. Virag is Rachna's functional boss, a balding, bespectacled guy in his mid-thirties who can always be found whistling a tune. 'I don't think boss is coming. He's entertaining some guests from Hong Kong.'

I nod. I was expecting him, my boss, to be here. But then Vikas is *the* boss. He can afford to not be here. I look at my watch and then at the huge, dimly lit stage lined with an array of lights that stand unlit, waiting for the grand spectacle to unfold. I spot the emcee for the evening standing in the aisle talking in whispers to a couple of people gathered around her. Last-minute prep, I guess.

'Should we get seated?' I ask the C&M bunch.

Rachna nods, looking at me, and then her eyes jump to Virag. 'Yes, we should.'

Virag lets out a snorty chuckle. 'I am sitting next to you, lady, because you are nailing it for Mojo tonight,' he pats Rachna's shoulder. The group resonates with laughter. Mojo was an energy drink launched by the global beverage giant, the Unicola Company, last year. We bagged that account after a lot of grind, the clincher on the deal was an outstanding pitch made by Anuradha to the global heads of Unicola. How happy I was after we snagged that account, my first win as the Delhi branch head. That was the cusp from where our relationship soared. Anuradha had done all the initial spadework on Mojo and had created this first campaign that was launched just after she left. It was a breakthrough campaign that had made the industry sit up and take notice. Today it was the frontrunner for the 'Campaign of the Year' award.

The stage lights up just then, displaying its splendour and magnificence. The emcee yanks the mic close to her face and, after an initial welcome address, announces that the bar is open and that the awards would start soon after a performance from a well-known Indian fusion band. The C&M group rushes towards the bar and drags me along. We have one drink there and carry another one to a corner where all of us sit, huddled together. By then, the fusion band has started its repertoire, its easy Western rhythm melding seamlessly with the Indian orchestra, creating a harmony that enthrals the gathered crowd. Sometime towards the end of the performance, I feel it—a sudden tug that grips me once and then leaves me cold. Like a sign that portends what lies in store. Its sudden manifestation makes me nervous and I cast a sidelong glance at the aisle a few chairs across from me. Her olive skin glowing under the artificial lights and her hair drawn back, Anuradha sashays past me, at that very instant. My heart stops beating for a second just as it had when I had seen her for the first time. My eyes follow her as she walks away to my extreme right and sits down with another group. I have always believed that Anuradha and I have a karmic connection—a bond that defies time and space. We may go our own separate ways, but it will always remind us of its presence. Like it is doing today, after almost an year. Once again.

The performance ends and the awards ceremony begins after the customary vote of thanks by the committee chairman and the keynote address by a young corporate honcho, the co-founder of an Internet venture, a virtual marketplace for millions of products. Theirs was the first company to use kids in a television campaign that was very successful. As he speaks at length about how using children in a campaign helped them break advertising clutter on television, my mind mulls furiously over what would happen if Anuradha and I were to bump into each other. My mind draws up various scenarios and plots my response to each one of them. But deep in my heart I know: all this planning would come to naught if we even come face to face tonight. The awards presentation ceremony has moved ahead by this time, but I can barely focus on the happenings on stage. I glance at the C&M gang sitting beside and behind me. A few of them are already holding the trophies they have won, which means that a lot has transpired while I was caught up in my own world. *I was so lost, I didn't even realize we had won some awards!*

'And now for the campaign of the year award. The nominations are . . .' the emcee virtually screams into the mic. The commercials start playing on the giant side screen, one after another. The first one is the children's ad from the company whose co-founder spoke a while ago. I can see him whisper excitedly to the woman sitting beside him. I know her; she is the managing director of his ad agency; a mini, page-three celebrity. The next ad is of a private bank that showcases how banking has become one of the simplest things today—very high on emotional quotient. The third ad that plays is Mojo, our brand, based on insights gathered by Anuradha and the team. The copy of this ad was written by her. Even after watching it millions of times on television, watching it here gives me goose bumps once again. I wonder what she is feeling at this moment, looking on at her creation.

There is silence after the ad spool finishes. The emcee adjusts the mic and after a dramatic pause, speaks, painfully enunciating every word, 'And the award goes to . . .' she glances at the beaming presenters and hands them the cordless microphone. Both of them are doyens of the advertising world: one of them has made his mark by venturing into Bollywood while the other is the grand old daddy of the fraternity. There is pin drop silence; no one speaks, no one moves; all waiting with bated breath. Virag, unable to control his excitement any more, gets up, despite Rachna's unsuccessful attempts to restrain him.

'Moo . . . jooo!' he shouts at the top of his voice.

'Who said that?' one of the presenters peers at the crowd, a cheeky smile lighting up his face. I feel a sudden rush of blood. Excitement grips my entire being. *We can win this . . .*

Even before I can complete the sentence in my head, the other presenter screams, 'Yessss . . . Mojo it is!'

It is as if a volcano has erupted. We can no longer stay in our seats. The bunch from C&M jumps up in the air, following it up with happy hugs and lots of fist-pumping. We're the cynosure of all eyes. I glance at Anuradha. Although it is dark, I can make out that she is looking at us. However, I am not sure if she has seen me.

Rachna nudges me. 'Let's go, Dhruv,' she says looking at the stage and the applause that awaits us there. I nod and step aside, making way for her to walk ahead.

'It's your baby. You have to hold it first,' I say. Rachna punches me lightly on the shoulder and smiles before leading our group. All of us walk swiftly towards the lit-up stage. Something strikes me.

'Rachna,' I yank her arm.

She is puzzled with this sudden gesture. 'What?'

'I saw Anuradha just now. She is here,' I whisper into her ear.

'Let's go . . . let's go . . .' Virag urges us on impatiently.

'Is she?' Rachna stares at me momentarily and halts at the foot of the stairs that go up to the main stage.

'We have to call her, Rachna. She was as much a part of this campaign as you and I.'

'But, Dhruv, she is no longer working with us,' she whispers, ascending the stairs.

I am adamant, 'We can't take the award for Mojo with her sitting as a mute spectator. It will be grossly unfair. She was a part of your team when you guys created the campaign,' I say firmly.

Rachna nods, pursing her lips. 'Okay. I think you are right.'

We shake hands with the presenters, the younger ones in our group are waving at the crowd that is up on its feet. A standing ovation is expected. Rachna borrows the mic from one of the presenters and looks at the cheering crowd.

'Wow, what a night! Today is the best night of my entire creative career but this award wouldn't be complete if we don't invite a special person on to the stage. She is no longer with us, as in with our agency, C&M, but is still one of us for sure,' she laughs. 'Anuradha, where are you? Can you come up on stage, please?'

I look towards her. She has covered her face with her hands, overwhelmed with the suddenness of this invite. She is so goddamn pleased that she can't stop smiling, and that warms my heart instantly. She stands up and walks slowly to the stage, shaking her head disbelievingly. I steal a glance at her, at my sizzling, amazing soul mate, Anuradha. How I loved and lost her is a terrible story of the past. But, at that moment, I realize that I can never stop loving her. I look down at the ground then and when I look up, I see her hugging Rachna on the stage. We don't come face to face. She doesn't seem inclined to approach me as we stand at either end of the group. The photographers click pictures of us with Rachna, Virag and Anuradha jointly holding the trophy. I am happy standing at a distance, looking at her wrapped up in adulation and glory, cheering with the C&M gang.

We meet finally when I am at the bar. Someone taps me on the shoulder from behind. It is Rachna with her arm wrapped around Anuradha's slender waist. Both of them have a glass of champagne each in their hands.

'Look, Dhruv, I've got your rock star back.'

No escape is possible now and frankly I don't want one either. All my people-pleasing morals leave me as soon as I lay eyes on her standing close to me. Both of us are prisoners of fond memories as well as deep scars, and I am unsure, out of the two, what she is left with. The latter seems like the firmer possibility.

'Hi, Anuradha.' Suddenly, I feel unsure about how I should be talking to her.

She nods, smiling tightly. 'Hi, Dhruv. You haven't changed much.'

Rachna looks at her with a teasing smile. 'What, dude? It's been just a few months since you left. Dhruv wasn't going to go ancient in that time.'

'If I haven't then that's good. How has Grassroot been treating you?' I ask. Grassroot is the agency where Anuradha currently works, a ten-year-old company that was taken over three years ago by WPP, a global media conglomerate. So, flush with funds, the agency is on an upscaling mode, strengthening its presence nationally. I like the work they do for their clients but one of their co-founders, Ram Walia, is an asshole. An egoistic creative professional and a terribly horny man. The industry grapevine is rife with his sordid exploits.

'Nothing to complain about. It's been good so far.'

Rachna raises an admonitory index finger at her, 'Don't tell me that it's a better place to work than C&M.'

'I didn't say that. I just meant that it's the people who make an organization. I've been lucky to work with a good bunch here.'

Rachna smiles. 'Ah . . . there you go, diplomatic girl. Don't worry, I'm not your boss any more and by the way, has Ram stopped leching at anything that walks around with a pair of tits?' It's obvious that his reputation has spread like wildfire among the women.

Anuradha snorts with laughter. 'You know the answer, Rachna, don't you?'

'Yeah, yeah, don't we all?' Rachna says shaking her head and then all of a sudden locks eyes with her. 'Don't turn around, but the man himself seems to be heading our way.'

I flick a glance behind them and see Ram Walia, a short bulky man with a French beard, a completely shaven head and glinting earrings, walking swiftly towards us. I half smile, acknowledging him; he shakes my hand firmly, not returning my smile, with a moronic expression on his face.

'Well, congratulations, Dhruv. You won because there was hardly any competition this year.' His remarks put me off completely. I know he has this incorrigible skill of irritating people around him all the time, but I don't have any patience today, and especially not now, when I am in a completely different frame of mind. The last thing I want to do is pick an argument with this asshole.

'I don't know why you feel this way, Ram, but we'll see next year. Hope you guys at least qualify for the awards,' I say impassively. He didn't expect this comeback and glances at the others, nodding mockingly. Rachna looks at him enigmatically, trying to hide that she is pissed with this rowdy intruder, while Anuradha is looking the other way.

'Was Dhruv your boss at C&M?' he looks at Anuradha.

'No, Ram, he was the branch head. Rachna was my boss.'

'I see,' he pauses dramatically. 'I see. So that's why they called you on to the stage. But did you work long enough on Mojo before you left C&M?'

'Of course,' I snap at him, 'why else would we invite her? She was part of the core team.' *Why don't you just disappear, asshole?*

He nods. 'Yeah, I get that. And see you next year, Dhruv. I won't forget what you just said.'

'Then we'll see you next year, Ram.'

He glances at Anuradha. 'How are you going back? I can drop you.'

She smiles. 'I'm good, Ram. I have my car.'

'Sure?' he raises his eyebrows.

'I'll be fine, thanks,' she replies. He walks away and merges into the crowd.

Rachna makes a face after he is gone. 'Phew! What a moron. How do you tolerate him every day, sweetie?'

'I am compensated well enough for putting up with all of this. I negotiated hard for my salary when I joined them,' Anuradha smiles.

'Bitch,' Rachna slaps her shoulder. 'Anyway, my glass is empty. I am going for a refill. Anyone?' she glances at us.

Anuradha shakes her head. 'I had better get back to my gang over there. You guys aren't paying my salary any more. You are here, no? I'll call you tomorrow,' she says looking at Rachna.

She shifts her gaze to me, 'Bye, Dhruv. Thanks for remembering me up there.'

'Any time, Anuradha. It was your hard work anyway.'

4

Sid

October 2016

The Bengali doctor saved me. B.D. Banerjee—the alcoholic Bankim Da. I landed on his doorstep in the wee hours ten months ago and collapsed on the threshold. I was so bloody fucked up. All I remember telling him was: *Do not let me die. Do not tell anyone that I was here. Do not ask me any questions.* In return, I promised to pay him handsomely. Then I had passed out. The greedy Bankim Da kept his word. He did save me—for money, of course. I had an expensive Rolex, enough cash and my thick gold chain. Still. All of it put together came to a few lakhs, which was enough for me to survive in this godforsaken hamlet in the hills for at least a year with the bachelor Bankim Da. I couldn't have asked for more when I realized that he lived all by himself, occasionally visited by his few patients, and in the company of alcohol. Bankim Da was nearing sixty with greying curly hair, receding at the hairline. He was of medium height and had a slight bulge around the middle. I remember this soap opera that Mom used to watch on YouTube. It was from the eighties. *Hum Log*. There was an erstwhile big star who made an appearance at the end of each episode. Ashok Kumar.

Yeah, Bankim Da bore a strong resemblance to a fifty-year-old Ashok Kumar.

All said and done, he was a good doctor, although, due to his alcoholism, he wasn't actively practising any more. So, he took good care of me. He took me in and treated me, and as I drifted in and out of consciousness I remembered his concerned face peering at me.

When I opened my eyes on the hard bed of a modest room a couple of days later, my face was completely bandaged, except for my eyes, nose and my mouth. My body felt heavy and terribly weak. Bankim Da sat on a chair with a glass of whisky in his hand, gazing at me. He raised the glass as soon as he saw my eyes open.

'Cheers. Ma Durga *tumake bhalabase. Apani anyathya marta chila.*'

I considered him. 'I don't understand Bengali,' I said in a raspy voice. It hurt when I spoke. My throat felt completely dry.

Bankim Da chuckled. 'It means, Ma Durga lobes you. She has brought you back from the dead.'

'That calls for a celebration,' I whispered. 'Which means even I get to drink.'

Bankim Da sniggered, looking at the bottle. 'Bloody, smart rascal. What about the medicines that are being given to you?'

'Don't worry. Ma Durga is there, no, doctor da? She'll take care of me.'

'You can call me Bankim. Bankim Da,' he smiled and rose from his chair, holding the bottle of alcohol. That night, Bankim Da spoon-fed whisky to me as I lay bandaged on the bed.

Then, a month and a half later, he removed the bandages from my face. My body had regained some of its old strength and the wounds had healed. Bankim Da had been emitting warning signals for a week before the day he freed my face of the bandages. I was certain that something was wrong with my face . . . but then, how bad could it be?

This shit can't be real! was my first thought when I saw my hideously disfigured face in the bathroom mirror. I wanted to look at it alone without anyone knowing how I felt when I saw my ruined face. There was nothing left of it but flakes of crumbling skin zigzagging all across. The healthy skin, the chiselled features, the handsomeness that I once possessed were all gone. I looked like the hero from the movie *Deadpool*, without the mask, grotesque, with all his ugliness exposed. But, unlike him, I had no superpowers to boast of. I had nothing left. No identity, almost no money and now . . . no face.

All thanks to you. The only thing left was my unbridled hatred towards you. The only thing that I wanted at that moment was your destruction. Slow and excruciating.

With my face gone, Sid had ceased to exist. Whenever we needed money, I sold off another one of my precious belongings. After the cash got over, the Rolex sustained us for another six months and only last month did I let go of my gold chain. Bankim Da was fine with the arrangements. He didn't need much to keep his mouth shut. Alcohol, good food and a little money for his daily expenses were enough. With money coming in freely, he had further limited his clinical practice. I never ventured outside and no one knew that there was a 'dead man' living in the house. Bankim Da's old computer, with an Internet connection, was my only window to the outside world. Through local newspaper clippings on the Internet, I came to know that the story of my 'death' had played out exactly the way I had wanted the world to see it. So, that was one good thing that emerged from this whole painful ordeal. My account on Facebook was deactivated. I am sure my mother would have asked someone in the family to do that, as they do when one is dead. I created another account with a fake identity that I am now using to stalk you. Not a day goes by when I haven't looked at your profile. You have moved on to a new agency, C&M, and made new friends. You have forgotten me as well and seem to be completely content with your new life. *How can you do that, you fuckin' murderer?*

This world of movies, I tell you! They are the ones that can give wings to your desires. They can make the unimaginable seem possible. The only things that helped me pass my time during my self-imposed exile was watching films on Bankim Da's late-nineties television set and surfing the Internet. Then, one day, while watching a Hollywood movie on HBO, I got an idea. The channel was showing the entire blockbuster series of *Mission Impossible*, the high-octane Tom Cruise thriller in which he plays the secret agent, Ethan Hunt. One of the key tactics that he uses to trump his enemies is disguise. Ethan Hunt is a master of disguise, and the ease with which he changes his identity, film after film, with the help of hyperrealistic masks, is mind-blowing. It also seeded the idea in my head. *Switching identities.* Is that even possible in real life? From here began my quest to explore such a possibility. If not here in this country, then somewhere else perhaps?

My second pastime, the Internet, opened up a world of possibilities. It introduced me to the world of silicone masks. According to the Internet, these very realistic masks have the ability to fool ninety-nine people out of a hundred in real time. When I explored some more, I found out that silicone, being a synthetic polymer made up of silicon, oxygen and other elements, most typically carbon and hydrogen, has the ability to look lifelike if moulded properly. As a mask, it is flexible, like rubber, with low toxicity and high heat resistance. In a nutshell, it is the ideal ingredient to create masks that look and feel absolutely real. This technology was developed for folks from the film industry so that Hollywood superstars, like Tom Cruise, did not have to sit for hours having their make-up done. Now with these super masks on their faces, they were ready to go in a matter of minutes. A plan had started to take shape in my mind and the only thing left was to test one of these masks.

To test a mask meant sourcing one. I spent hours going through websites of companies worldwide that made such masks. Unfortunately, no one in India manufactured these. Hours of hard work yielded a result I could work with: one company that specialized in such lifelike masks was based out of Florence in Italy, Creativefix. An apt name. They had made a mark by supplying their customized silicone masks to top-notch Hollywood studios, with their website boasting of a few Hollywood stars sporting masks created by them. The cost wasn't prohibitive to start with: 1000 euros for a good silicone mask, while a very fine quality one would cost about 1600 euros. I decided to go for the low-priced option as it made sense to test one of them first and see if they actually delivered. Also, my resources were dwindling and the day when I would run out of all my money was not too far. There was also the added responsibility of Bankim Da. He had become used to the freeloading and the moment the funds ran out, I was sure he would try and blackmail me. Sigh. These things needed to be sorted!

After fixing an appointment over an email and having a couple of long-distance calls with the company, Creativefix, in Italy, I was convinced that they were sound enough to create something satisfactory. How good a job would they do? Would it be good enough for my plans? I could only hope till I saw the final product. I had to send them some specifications about the customized mask that I wanted: description and usage requirements (where and how I would want to use it), my head circumference and a picture of the person who would wear the mask—which meant *my picture*. And lastly the picture of the character that was to be created. I wrote to them saying that I had suffered traumatic injuries to my face due to an accident and wanted to hide my ugliness under the mask that I was asking them to make. So, I sent them the pictures. The picture of my disfigured face along with Bankim Da's pictures. His close-ups from various angles. He had to be cajoled like a kid, but I had to give a reference and since I didn't want to send them my earlier photographs, I had to use Bankim Da's face. This was important for my plan. I sent Creativefix several pictures of Bankim Da, saying that that was how I had looked before the accident. They sent an email back saying that they were very sorry to hear about my accident and would do their best to make a mask as close to the picture as possible. Frankly I thought the company didn't really give a rat's ass about whose mask they were creating—Brad Pitt's or Bankim Dutt Banerjee's. Only the money had to be right. The night they confirmed the project, I got Bankim Da drunk with a bottle of Black Label. Whatever apprehensions he had about sending his pictures melted along with the ice in his glass of scotch. After a week I found myself wishing that I could fast-forward the remaining six weeks that were left before my master key arrived.

January 2017

My new silicone face arrived a couple of days ago and it was quite stunning with the face, the mop of curly hair receding at the hairline, a stubbly beard and eyebrows! Clearly the sympathy angle had worked! See, that's the thing about people abroad, they are compassionate. In India, there are just too many people and there's hardly any room for compassion!

I couldn't wait to try it on. When the courier landed at the house and Bankim Da took its delivery, I didn't open the parcel in front of him. When he asked me questions, I just said I was trying to see if I could look better.

Then, as soon as we'd had dinner and he was knocked out in his bedroom, I took the box and locked myself in the room in which I had been hibernating for several months now. And then, in front of the mirror, I opened the box. The slippery silicone mask emerged. It was bigger than the actual size of my head. With a pounding heart, I held it in my hand and felt it quivering in my palms. My new skin! A super stretchy jelly with openings for eyes. There was a pen-drive that came along with it, highlighting the dos and don'ts about handling and wearing the mask correctly. I went through the instructions once. They were fairly simple. I had to first cover my hair with a net, apply a lubricant and once that dried out, I was to apply a powder all over my face. All this was in the kit. And then I was ready for the mask. I held it in my hands in front of the mirror. It felt odd to see Bankim Da's face in my hands and my own distorted face in the mirror. I took a deep breath, thoughts running amok in my head. I held the back flap of the mask, stretched it open with my both my thumbs and slid it over my head. Immediately, it felt like I had literally slipped into a different identity.

The only thing that I had wanted from life at that moment was to make this thing work. Somehow. I had nothing else to look forward to.

I raised my head slowly to look in the mirror and instead of my disfigured face, I saw someone else staring back at me. Bankim Da! Fuckin' unbelievable! My heartbeat was chugging like an engine in overdrive as I moved my palm and adjusted the silicone nose over my nose and the lips over my own parted into an artificial smile. The most eerie bit were the eyes—it was like someone else had taken over. I tried to recall Bankim Da's face and his expressions. It was important for me to recreate them for the transformation to be smooth. It was too good to be true. Joy erupted like a volcano in my heart.

Now I had to set the wheels of the next part of the plan in motion—in Mumbai. Somewhere close to Anuradha. I looked up her Facebook profile yesterday. She has moved to Mumbai now. She will go wherever it profits her, that bitch! No loyalty!

But before I did that, I had a small task to complete. Mumbai is an expensive city and I needed money to start with. So I had Bankim Da call my mother the previous day. I needed to tell her that I was alive if I wanted to get money from her. I made Bankim Da tell her that he was going to visit her with some critical information about me. I didn't want him to tell her that I was alive: Mom just can't keep a secret. I had decided to tell her that myself and then swear her to secrecy. I was sure that she would acquiesce. To her, nothing was more precious than her only son's life. So, I was off to Lucknow the following day.

Just one small task remained though, before I left.

This time I wanted no loose ends.

I am about to leave in a couple of hours for the railway station. My train to Lucknow is at 9 p.m. from Dehradun. We are having our last few drinks together, Bankim Da and I. He has raced ahead and become melancholy. He is slurring, addressing me as his younger brother. I promise him that I will keep sending him money. He chuckles and says I will have to, because he is the keeper of my secrets. *Greedy bastard*. He doesn't know this but I ventured out yesterday wearing his face to the local market. Everyone on the streets greeted me as Bankim Da. I reciprocated with the wave of my hand. Still not sure if I can impersonate his voice. So had to be careful. From the only medical shop in the vicinity, I purchased rat poison and while doing so I made sure to tell the shopkeeper that it was for the rodents in the house. I told him that they were way too many for comfort.

It's time for me to leave. I get up and pick up my small bag which has my clothes and the silicone mask. Bankim Da has disappeared inside the bathroom once again. He is constantly cribbing that alcohol has screwed up his digestion and how he has to answer nature's call so many times during the day. All his troubles are about to end soon. I quickly empty the bottle of rat poison in the bottle of whisky. He is drunk enough not to notice anything. Even if he does, he will still polish it off. A greedy bastard is what he is. Bankim Da will be discovered dead in the morning after consuming the rat poison that he himself purchased from the local pharmacist. Lonely, drunk and depressed human beings in desolate hill towns do end up taking their own lives sometimes. Like Sid also did. I snigger. I have been careful enough to remove the traces of my presence from the house. But even if they do find something that belongs to me, how does it really matter? It is impossible to link it to a man who is already dead.

After bidding goodbye to Bankim Da for the last time at the same door where I had landed a year ago, I cover my face with a muffler. Bankim Da quickly goes inside the house, eager to have his next drink that will push him a few steps closer to death. I leave the house and walk for a few minutes to reach the bus stand. I locate a public toilet and enter it. It stinks of piss. I get inside one of the stalls and extract my mask from the bag. I quickly put it on. I come out and check myself in the dirty mirror above the washbasin. Perfect. I step out wearing Bankim Da's face. I feel alive with this new face in the old world.

5

January 2017
Lucknow

The cell phone buzzed discreetly on the bedside table. The old woman sleeping on the bed was jolted out of her slumber at the very first beep. She had hardly slept. She grabbed the phone and muted the alarm before it disturbed her husband. She sat up hunched on the bed, her eyes travelling up the wall to gaze at the clock. 1 a.m. *It was time for her to go.*

She sighed and turned to find her husband wrapped up in a quilt, only his forehead visible, snoring gently.

Grief, her constant companion over the last year, swooped down at her again. She felt its intense overwhelming sadness pulling her into its depths. *My son* . . . Sleep, just like happiness, had deserted their lives. Her husband was sleeping with the help of pills and she . . . she spent every night tossing and turning until she woke up to the following day's inane drama of life.

She switched on the zero-watt bulb and adjusted her saree in the mirror, glancing at her wrinkled face: she looked older. Much older than her sixty-five years. She picked up the woollen shawl that had been tidily folded and placed on one of the side tables and walked out of the bedroom. The living room was draped in the light of a night lamp. She glanced at the wall to her right—at the garlanded picture hung on it. It was the picture of her son, their only son: Siddharth, or Sid, as they fondly called him. Siddharth smiled naughtily down from the frame at her, long curls framing his face, eyes radiating warmth and glowing skin that was never meant to burn on a funeral pyre so early in his life. He was just twenty-six when he died. *Just twenty-six, for heaven's sake!* the old woman muttered under her breath for the umpteenth time, as her eyes began to turn moist again. This was not the time to cry, the voice inside her head said.

She looked out of the window, at the road bathed in the diffused light emanating from the street lamp. She could see an approaching headlight and hear the faint rumble of an engine. Raju had arrived with his autorickshaw. She heaved a sigh of relief and opened the main door. The old woman felt a sudden chill in her ageing bones as she stepped out into the small garden of her single-storeyed, three-bedroomed independent house in Gomtinagar. She wrapped the woollen shawl around herself over her sweater, pulled on a woollen cap and locked the door behind her. She had never been out of the house alone at this hour. But this opportunity was rare and she couldn't let it slip away. Her husband would never find out that his wife had gone missing at this hour—his sleeping pills would be at work and she would be back before he woke up anyway. She glanced at the nameplate on the door: Amrit Mathur, Sarla Mathur and Siddharth Mathur, it read. They had kept it as it was, even though one amongst the three would never again cross this threshold. *Ever.*

But then that phone call had come two days ago and ignited her heart with fresh hope. It had re-energized the old woman. The caller had said that he was a doctor and went by the name of one Bankim Banerjee. The call had come from Lal Tibba, the same monster of a place where her son had been hiding out from his creditors. The same place where he had committed suicide by jumping out of a window. A suicide—she could never figure out why. She knew her son very well and like every Indian mother, she had been there for him no matter what he went through. She had always been ready to help him. What else was there in a parent's life?

The doctor said he knew something about Sid that would make her happy. *What could possibly make her happy now that her only son was dead?* She sighed once again.

'*Mataji*, are we going alone? Sahib?' Raju, the autorickshaw driver asked, a tad surprised. She nodded before getting into the auto.

'Yes, Raju. Sahib can't come with us; he is unwell,' she lied.

'Okay. But I've been wondering where we are going at this hour,' Raju yawned. He ran all their errands. Her husband had stopped driving after Siddharth's death—he said he was too nervous to drive.

'Take me to Hazratganj.'

Raju turned around and gave her a look of disbelief. 'Hazratganj? At this hour, Mataji? There won't be any shops open at this hour.'

Sarla Mathur could feel the skin on her face hardening, her gaze turning cold. 'Let's go, Raju. We don't have much time.'

Raju gave her a curious look, but then shrugged his shoulders and started his auto.

Settled in, Sarla retraced her memory back to that phone call. Bankim, the man on the phone, had told her that he had a message from Siddharth, her son. When she had asked how that was possible because Sid was long dead, he had laughed. And then, in his thick Bengali accent, he had said: 'It happens sometimes that the dead come alive.'

She had been paralysed for a moment, but, before she could ask the next question, the line had gone dead. She had been there when Sid's funeral pyre was lit. It had happened before her very eyes. Sid was dead. But. Even then. She had agreed to meet Bankim in Hazratganj. However ridiculous it may have sounded to someone with a logical head, to a grieving mother that one tiny shred of hope was like a lifeline.

Lucknow was deep in slumber and the auto raced freely on the wide road that ran parallel to Lohia Park. Sarla, wrapped in her woollen shawl, glanced impassively at the darkness outside; at the occasional burst of light from streetlamps, that stood like sentinels, and the stray vehicle passing by.

It's been more than a year since you took your life, Siddharth. There has never been a moment when I haven't thought about you, my son. I wish I could do what you did. Take away my life if I couldn't deal with my problems. But is it so simple? Leaving one's responsibilities behind, just to get rid of one's pain? How could you be so selfish, Siddharth? How come you didn't think about us, your old parents? Did we fail you?

Tears rolled down her eyes unheeded and settled at the edge of the shawl that partially covered her face. The auto breezed through a dead Hazratganj that was waiting to come alive in a few hours and regain its normal buzz. She asked Raju to stop the auto in front of St Joseph's Cathedral. The old woman muttered a small prayer to herself as she got out of the auto.

It was a magnificent stone building that stood tall and splendid, housing both a school and the church inside. The church complex was well lit, with a bright white orb of light encircling the tall statue of Jesus Christ that stood on top of the semi-circular arch above the entrance gate. Christ's arms were outstretched, welcoming people to this holy sanctum.

She looked around the gate. Not a soul to be seen. She walked along the boundary wall of the church that turned at a ninety-degree angle at the corner after a few metres. She heard the sound of approaching footsteps before a man emerged from around the other side of the corner. The stranger smiled at her from a distance. *What could this man know about my son that I don't?* Sarla thought, looking at the curly-haired, bearded man walking towards her. His gait and the way he swung his arms as he walked seemed familiar. A strange sensation ran through her body, electrifying her. Alarmed, she looked at his face. It was a stranger's face. Rather plasticky, she thought. His pace dropped when he was a couple of steps away from her and then he stopped. Sarla scanned his face, his hair, the clothes he wore. It was all unfamiliar. Yet there was something about him that screamed familiarity. Sarla couldn't *see* what it was, but the mother in her could sense it. She got all her answers when she uttered the first sentence.

'Is that you, Dr Banerjee?'

The stranger took a step forward and then his lips moved. What Sarla heard next was a miracle.

'Ma . . .' Sid said.

It seemed to her like the moment had frozen. She was rooted to the ground; her body numb, her mind laboriously processing what she had just heard. It *was* him. The face was somebody else's, but it was him! The overwhelmed old woman, unable to withstand the sudden emotional turbulence, clutched the sidewalk railing lest she keeled over.

Tears glistened in her eyes before breaking free and running over her lined cheeks. 'Siddharth, my son. Where did you go?' she whispered.

Sid spoke slowly, enunciating each word, 'I had a horrible time, Ma. It wouldn't help even if I give you the details.'

'Both your father and I have also been suffering every second since that day when we found that body. He was wearing your clothes and had your wallet and even that sapphire ring that you always wore.'

'I know, Ma. I know everything,' Sid said. 'It's a long story and I don't have that kind of time right now to tell you everything.'

'But why couldn't you tell us that you were alive, Siddharth? How could you let your parents suffer like this? We could have helped you.'

'You couldn't have, Ma. No one could have,' he said coldly, his face impassive.

Sarla hugged him, crying uncontrollably. 'You could have told us just once. We are your parents, and nothing is more precious to us than you.'

'Then help me now, Ma. Your son is back from dead, so help him.'

Sarla felt a palpable shift in her son's demeanour. He didn't look emotional, but rather detached, to meet his mother. Almost as if he were here for a reason.

'And your face, Siddharth? How has this changed?'

'Same long story, Ma. Will tell you when we meet next.'

'You aren't answering any of my questions. What happened to your face?'

'You really want to see, huh?' Sid asked, locking his gaze with his mother as anger flashed across his eyes.

She nodded slowly and her son lowered his head and slid both his thumbs beneath the back of his neck. In a couple of seconds, he peeled off a jelly like substance from his face. It looked like some sort of a mask. Sarla shrieked when saw her son's mutilated face.

'Oh my god, Siddharth, what is this?' she exclaimed, horrified at the sight of the ruined face of her once handsome son.

'This is all that is left because of what happened in Lal Tibba. The world thinks that I am dead and so let that be, but I wanted you to know that I am alive.'

Sarla sniffled. 'But why do you have to hide it, son? Why not tell the world?'

'I am carrying a lot of baggage from my past, Ma. They won't let me live if they find out that I am alive. You are the only one who knows my secret. No one should know, not even Dad. You will have to swear that you will not tell anyone.'

Sarla nodded, tentatively touching his face, the crumpled skin. 'At least tell me where you are going? And what happened at Lal Tibba that led to this?'

'Mumbai. To get a new face. It's possible, Ma; all sorts of facial surgeries can be done these days. I can't have my old face restored due to bad repercussions, but I can have a different face and a new identity for myself,' Sid said.

He would have to manipulate his gullible mother for the money. He looked at his watch; it was another two hours to the scheduled departure of the Mumbai-bound Udyog Nagri Express from the Lucknow railway station.

'Mumbai? Anuradha has also moved there, her mother told me. Maybe she can help you.'

Sid scoffed. 'Anuradha? That bitch is the fucking reason I am—' he held back his words.

'Did you just call her a "bitch"? What does she have to do with this? I thought you guys had broken up a long time ago.' Sarla was old but not dumb. She knew her son well enough to realize that there was something he wasn't telling her.

Sid couldn't tell his mother that Anuradha was responsible for the situation he was in and that revenge was the sole purpose of his existence now. He couldn't disclose to his mother that the reason why Anuradha had pushed him out of that window in Lal Tibba was because he had been blackmailing her with her sex video. That reason might make his mother empathize with that bitch. He didn't want that. He considered his mother irrational and stupidly righteous in matters such as these. To her, principles and morals were everything.

That bitch Anuradha is guilty and she has to be punished.

'Nothing,' he shook his head. 'But that girl is the last person who should know this. And now, Ma, I need your help. I need some money.'

Sarla nodded, digging in her purse and taking out a bundle of banknotes along with her debit card. 'Here. This is all the cash that I am carrying at the moment and here is the card for our joint account. This will have a few lakhs. The pin number is 6386. In the meanwhile, I can use your father's card. If you need more, let me know. I have some savings and jewellery that can be sold off, too. I will keep depositing money into this account as and when you need more.'

'Thanks, Ma.'

Sarla pursed her lips. 'You don't worry, son. Get your treatment done and bring your life back on track. That's all we want. And come back soon.'

A warm gesture was required at that moment, Sid thought and hugged his old mother. 'I will, Ma. I will come back.' He was done with this task.

Sid left Sarla with an uneasy feeling. He had come back a year after the tragedy and behaved as if he had been on a tour, and yet she couldn't help but feel sorry for him. Her son . . . he had probably been through hell, the accident, losing his face at this young age—it must have taken its toll. And at the same time, she knew that her son had changed. He seemed hostile, angry, bitter . . . why was he so angry with Anuradha? Something was not quite right here and yet, as she walked back and instructed Raju to take her home, the fog of sadness had lifted! She was happy again.

6

Anuradha

3 October 2017
Renaissance Hotel, Powai

I went numb when I saw you on the stage, Dhruv. I never
wanted to see you ever again in my life. You ended it so abruptly,
so suddenly, without thinking for an instant about how I would
feel. How would I live thereafter? As if everything were my fault;
loving Sid was my fault; loving you, an even greater sin. Is it my
destiny to remain unloved after giving away all I can, all I have?
Yes, I did lie; but it was to protect you and me, to protect us! It
made me vulnerable to be exposed to you as the person who had
killed Sid, but that was self-defence and you know it. Was that
any reason to leave me and walk away? Why was it so easy for you
to do what you did? Could you have done that to your wife? No,
you couldn't. You were shitting bricks when she walked out of
your house. But leaving me alone, stranded in our relationship,
came so easily to you. What if I had not walked out of it? What
if I had stayed behind to claim what was mine? You were mine;
your love was mine. But, stupid me! I just resigned that night
and left Gurgaon a couple of days later, not knowing where to
go and what to do. I was in a daze for a month, heartbroken

and crushed. That's what I was. A lifeless piece of shit who kept thinking that her married lover ended a sizzling extramarital affair with his mistress after squeezing everything out of her because things became too hot for him to handle. That's what I thought of myself, your convenient mistress, ready to warm your bed any time you wanted me to.

But then, as time went by, my anger and the singeing hatred inside me subsided. I remembered all the time we had spent together. Every moment of it steeped in such passion and warmth. We were fiercely in love, and I knew neither of us could have faked it. What prompted you to take this harsh decision of breaking up, Dhruv? A decision that changed the course of my life yet again. I never asked you for commitment even though I did long for it. I dreamt of a life with you, but I always refrained from talking about it, knowing fully well that it was impossible for you to part with your family. If both of us knew the outcome of this relationship, why did we get into it in the first place? This baffling mother of a question kept hounding me until I got the answer. It was a karmic connection, a bond that defied logic, status and time. We were prisoners of our karmic destiny. However hard we may have tried to break away from it, we couldn't have, unless one of us decided to walk away out of his, or her, own free will. *Like you did.* I didn't have the courage to leave you despite knowing you had a family you would never leave. Only after we separated did I realize that I loved you so much it had turned me weak. I had to then get a grip on my life if I wanted to go on living.

I did everything I could to distract my mind from this love. I read, went to the gym, travelled to various places on my own and gave my all to my work at Grassroot. It helped. I couldn't erase your memory, but I could dim its intensity. Until today.

And then look what you did. Appeared before me unannounced and acknowledged my talent publicly by calling me up on stage to receive the award for Mojo. A brand for which I had worked my ass off. It was my sweetest memory ever, because I fell in love with you while working on it. It was special that you regarded my contribution. Who does that in today's world where everybody is vying for a place in the spotlight? But you're different; you're not one of the herd. And that's why I love you. I was speechless when Rachna called for me from the stage and then later, when she told me that you had insisted on it. All my emotions came rushing back then. I wanted to hug you and hold you close to my heart when I met you today. I don't know if it will ever be possible or appropriate to do that, now that you have drifted so far away.

~

I glance to my left, towards the bar. I see you standing there with the C&M bunch, some of whom I had worked with when I was in Gurgaon. How our worlds have changed, Dhruv, over this last year? What used to be mine not so long ago, has drifted so far away from me today.

But then I can't let you go away. Not just like that. I have so many questions for you. But. Will you answer them? I look at you again; you have put your glass away and it looks as if you are bidding goodbye to your colleagues. I drag my attention back to the group from Grassroot, busy bitching about the people who have won the awards tonight, getting their malicious kicks by ridiculing others. When I steal another glance, I see you walking towards the exit. I need to leave now. That's how I've always been—I don't stay at parties. I need to get back home.

'See you guys, I have to leave,' I say.

'So early? I thought the night's just begun,' says Ash, a senior copywriter with Grassroot who turns musician by the night. He is quite a hit in Mumbai's EDM (electronic dance music) circuit and his cuteness adds to his charm. Lots of women in the office really dig him. As luck would have it, I think he harbours a secret crush on me. He resembles a young Matt Damon from one of my favourite films, *Saving Private Ryan*.

I make a 'sorry' face. 'Sorry, Ash, I need to leave.'

He nods. 'Okay, then. By the way, I believe you are looking for a new place to rent. I can help you.'

'Can you? Thanks so much. I'll talk to you tomorrow. See you,' I say, before turning away.

I am almost running on the pathway before slowing down to a sedate pace as I enter the hotel lobby. Outside, beyond the giant glass doors at the entrance, I can see you speaking to someone on the phone. I catch my breath and walk through the door, looking away from you, hoping you will notice me. And then I glance at you.

'Leaving early?' I ask. What a stupid question that is!

You nod. 'And you? Can I drop you somewhere?'

Yes! I do a fist-pump in my head. *He wants to talk for sure.* 'I have my car,' I say, controlling the surging excitement within.

You look surprised. 'Oh! You've started driving? Back then, you never drove.'

'A lot of things have changed since then,' I hear myself say. Shut up, Anuradha! Don't let your rant fuck it up. Not now. 'I can drop you instead. Where are you staying?' I say hastily, trying to undo my last statement.

I peek at your vulnerable face. Dhruv, you could never mask your emotions. You are caught again, between what your heart wants and what your mind tells you to do. Thankfully you choose the former.

'Well, I . . . I'm not sure, Anuradha. I am staying at Lands End, Bandra,' you say hesitantly.

I smile. 'Bandra is home. Let me drop you,' I say, handing over the car's key card to the valet.

7

Sid

3 October 2017
Renaissance Hotel, Powai

I see you now. So clearly. Once again. After such a long time. You look engrossed as you talk to this man whom I've never seen before. The way you flick strands of your hair away from your face reminds me of our courtship days. I know you do this when you are conscious about yourself. Self-conscious about creating an impression. But why do you want to impress this man? Who is he?

You look better than before. At least that's what I see. There isn't an iota of remorse on your face or any anxiety regarding the crime you have committed. Knowingly. With your own hands. How can you behave like that? Like you are innocent. Untainted.

You haven't realized as yet that I am staring at you. Standing outside this cab, wearing a driver's uniform and this ugly face, sweating in this muggy heat of Mumbai, all for you! Even if you did catch me gawking at you, you wouldn't know it's me. You wouldn't realize what *I* have gone through to come back. My hatred for you exceeds the suffering that I went through when I was wounded and bedridden. That hatred has kept my soul alive. And now that I am back, my soul wants something in exchange for all the beating that it took. It thirsts for *revenge*.

When I landed in Mumbai nine months ago, wearing Bankim Da's face, I knew no one here except his renegade brother, Golu Da. I telephoned him and went to stay with him in Borivali. I could not have met him with Bankim Da's face, so I had to show him my real face—the ruined one. Golu Da was horrified to see it initially but calmed down eventually. I had an alibi. I was a patient whom his brother had treated when I was about to die after a terrible accident. It worked, my lie. But more than that, the alcohol and cash that I splurged on him over the next few days did the trick. Golu Da, in a matter of days, was living off my money. Freeloaders, both fuckin' brothers. He learnt of Bankim Da's suicide in Lal Tibba a few days later. We drowned our sorrows in alcohol that night, singing Hindi songs that Bankim Da loved. Within a matter of a couple of months, I turned him into a hardcore alcoholic who would start drinking from the time he opened his eyes. It suited me just fine. He was easy to support as I had enough money coming in from my mother. In the midst of all of this, I took to tailing you in Golu Da's taxi, which he seldom drives now. I drive it wearing Bankim Da's face, keeping a close tab on you. Watching your every move.

While I drive around in his taxi, Golu Da is fast asleep, inebriated, in his single-roomed house. How can anyone stay in that stinking pit? Along with a chronic alcoholic? I am doing it. I couldn't have ever imagined living a life like this. But then, stark vengeance has made it possible. Revenge has many similarities with love. Revenge can also make you do extraordinary things.

What do I see now? The two of you are getting into your car. Why is this man tagging along with you? I need to find out.

In fact, I need to know everything that transpired in your life after that evening in Lal Tibba. After you left me to die.

You are sobbing at the steering wheel of the car. I can see your shoulders shake. This guy must mean something to you. I can't make out what is happening as I glance at you from my taxi across the traffic when our cars draw abreast. Both of you seem to have some common ground. I have lost out on so much. I have quite some catching up to do and quickly. If I don't, this whole exercise of having taken so much trouble to come back into your world won't serve much purpose.

It's so easy otherwise for me to exact my revenge. Do exactly what you did to me. Return the favour. I can do it right now if I want to; but that's not what I want. I am not going to make it so easy for you. The end of your story isn't going to be as abrupt as mine might have been. It will be a saga of pain. Of suffering. I will turn your life into a living hell—little by little—before I put a full stop to it.

I have to be close by, in your vicinity, if I have to write such a story. I will have to know all these characters who have mushroomed in your life, after I disappeared from it. They are important because only through them will I be able carry out my plan. I can't be sitting in this cab and spying on you from a distance. I will have to be in your car, in your home and in your surroundings.

I am going to do that pretty soon, darling!

8

Anuradha

It's an odd feeling, with Dhruv sitting next to me as I drive. Images of umpteen rides in his car flash before my eyes. It seems as if it were in some other lifetime.

'New car?' he asks, looking around.

It's a Honda City that I bought a few months ago. 'Yeah. Pretty new,' I say switching on the car stereo.

'*Baahon main chale aao . . . Humse sanam kya parda?*' (Come into my arms . . . Why should there be this distance between us?)

The seductive song opens a floodgate of memories. Big, big mistake to have switched on the radio! What were the chances? But now that I have, I don't want to switch it off. I want to see how Dhruv reacts.

'Wow! Remember this song?' he exclaims.

I nod. How can I forget? You had turned into a peeping Tom that night and saw me naked for the very first time. I quiver from within, wanting to tell him. I don't.

'Yes, we had won the Mojo pitch that day. And that celebratory party that followed was so good.'

He nods slowly, takes a deep breath and looks away, gazing out of the window. We have crossed Godrej Memorial Hospital and the car races away on the Eastern Express Highway. It's past ten and the traffic has thinned on the roads; Mumbai traffic is much more predictable than Delhi's, where it can come to a standstill at any time of the day or night.

'We used to play that game, didn't we?' he says.

How can I ever forget our silly little guess-the-film game as we listened to songs across various radio stations?

'Yeah,' I smile, 'and I beat you every single time.'

He nods and then falls silent. It's not until we reach the Western Express Highway that he speaks again.

'Do you miss Gurgaon sometimes?' he asks.

Why can't he say what he *really* wants to instead of beating around the bush? Can't he just say: do you miss me?

'Not after what it did to me,' I say quickly, as anger seeps into my voice.

'You hate me for what I did, don't you?' he says.

I glance at him. Our eyes meet. 'What's the point in asking me now, Dhruv? You did what you had to without even bothering to hear my side of the story.'

He goes quiet again. 'I was terribly upset about being kept in the dark, Anuradha . . .'

And that is just enough to make me fly off the handle. 'Just fuck it, Dhruv. Sid was not some goddamn saint whose autobiography you had to know. Did that one piece of truth I hid from you give you the right to leave me high and dry? Kill me once again like Sid did? Is everything my fucking fault, Sid and then you?' I howl and the pain that I have buried inside crawls out through my tears.

'Anuradha, I . . .' he stammers and then reaches for me and massages my shoulder. I feel his familiar warmth on my skin.

'It was crazy with all that was happening around us that time, Anuradha. That bloody Hemant who had wreaked havoc in our lives, the search for that goddamn video of his and then there was Shalini who had driven me crazy by leaving the house with the kids. I mean it was insane,' he hangs down his head, gripping it between his hands.

It angers me further. 'So just because your wife walks out on you, you stop loving me and throw me out of your life? How convenient it is for men like you, Dhruv Saxena! Fuck me as long as it doesn't inconvenience your personal life and then I am the first to go,' I say sharply.

'Stop it, Anuradha? I love you, goddammit! Watching you go killed me as well,' he says impulsively but without raising his pitch. He has never done that to me, ever . . . however unreasonable I may have been in the past.

'Huh. All you cared about was your family. All your claims of caring about me and loving me look like a big sham in hindsight,' I retort. We are close to the hotel entrance at Bandra. You grab my arm.

'I want to talk, Anuradha. Our conversation is far from over. Come with me, let's talk.'

I look into your moist eyes; they don't hide any deceit. I give in.

'Not here,' I say, fearing spectators to our drama.

I pull over to the side of a road in Bandstand, a kilometre away from the hotel, along the sea. Beyond the cemented jogging path, lies the calm Arabian Sea with its waves lapping against the rocky coast. Had we been here earlier in the evening, these rocks would have been dotted with couples, restless to get cosy. I come here quite often in the evenings for a run or a quiet walk and have always ended up thinking about Dhruv beside me, laughing, talking . . . You never walked out of my heart, Dhruv: it's just that now that you are really here, sitting next to me, I am hating you for never doing that.

'I am sorry, Anuradha. I really am.'

'Saying it now doesn't mean anything. You made your choice, moved on and left me behind.'

He sniffles. 'I was a broken man, left without his family, and the only other person I loved was feeding me lies.'

'So?' I flare up. 'I wasn't hiding anything else in our relationship. Sid was a tragic experience for me. I was scared of the truth leaking out even though I knew it was the right thing to do . . .'

He looks at me. 'But there was no need to hide your secrets. I never kept anything hidden from you, Anuradha.'

'Ha! You spoke the truth only when you were in bed with me,' I burst out. Damn! I never should have said that.

He grips my shoulder tightly. 'For God's sake, Anuradha, is that what you think of me? I slept with you because I loved you from here,' he places his hand on his chest. His voice is shaky, his eyes filling up with tears. I have never seen him like this before.

'The way you left me, or rather "dropped" me, I can't help but think that you used me, Dhruv, as long as it suited you.'

He nods slowly, looking away, dabbing at his eyes with the sleeve of his black jacket. 'You have every reason to doubt my intentions. I have only myself to blame.'

I shake my head. 'Come on, man! You don't have to play the victim card to me. You have a wife and two lovely kids waiting for you at home.'

His voice quivers. 'When Shalini went away I knew she would never come back into my life again, in the real sense. And that's just how it happened. We live under the same roof but in separate cubicles of life.'

I am stumped to hear it. So, if he knew how his relationship with his wife was going to be, why didn't he choose me? I cry out from within as another mound of pain erupts.

'Why did you let me go then, Dhruv? Why couldn't we have been together?' I almost scream.

The silence hangs between us for a while.

'Because I couldn't do it. I could not get myself to build a happy new life over the ruined debris of the old one.'

'So that means you screw up two lives instead of one? It was both your wife's life and mine versus only your wife's, if you had decided otherwise. What sort of logic is that?'

'Anuradha, you still have a life ahead of you. You have not made your choices already, like I have.'

'So, it's you who gets to decide what I should be doing with my life. Now that you have gone away, I should find another man, push myself to fall in love with him and think of a life with him. And what if that doesn't work out either? Find another man and start all over again . . . and again? It's my heart, Dhruv, that we're talking about, not some fucking client proposal template that you keep sending to different clients after changing its title,' I burst out.

'It was a mistake. That's why I decided to end our relationship,' he replies.

I snort. 'A mistake that screwed up my life.'

Now that your wife doesn't want to be with you, why can't you and I be together? I want to ask you, but now is not the right time. Despite my rant and all the hatred I spew, I still haven't been able to move on like you, Dhruv; I still love you.

'You ended it when you wanted and in the way you wanted. You also threatened me by keeping a copy of that video lest I ever decided to show up in your life again.' Our conversation in Café Bisque last December plays like a film reel before my eyes.

'I never kept a copy. The one that I gave you was the only one I had.'

I am stunned at this confession and speak after a while. 'Why did you lie then?'

'I wanted you to go far away. I never wanted our paths to cross again.'

I sigh. 'I wanted that as well. I unfriended you on all my social media platforms after that.'

'Yes, I know,' he says sombrely. 'Both of us wanted to flush each other out of our systems.'

It is strange, but my heart starts warming up once more to the only man I have ever loved deeply in my life. It starts healing again as Dhruv sits beside me—aching, heartbroken, just like me.

Suddenly I hear a screech of tyres behind me. I turn on my driver's seat and see a taxi pulling up next to my car. It's a bit odd to find a black-and-yellow taxi halting here at this hour. The cab driver seems to be fiddling with something. Loud English music plays in the cab. I recognize the song, 'Paradise', a Cold Play song. A cab driver playing an English song. Doubly odd.

I shift my gaze to Dhruv. 'So, what do you want now?'

'Can we become friends at least?' he asks tentatively.

He looks cute, unsure of himself.

'Friends? What is that supposed to mean?'

'I have tried everything to keep you out of my mind, Anuradha, rather unsuccessfully,' he says with a nervous smile. 'Maybe by becoming friends we will be able to deal with our emotional stress.'

In my mind I am not opposed to the idea. Who knows where that will take us? The decibel level of the music playing in the taxi has gone up by several notches. I crane my neck to look into the taxi and now I see the driver, quite clearly: *a middle-aged, curly-haired man, looking directly at me.* He resembles the yesteryear actor, Ashok Kumar, but more than that there is something different about him, something scary. I'm glad Dhruv is with me. For a moment, my eyes lock with the stranger's before I break away. He wears an inane grin on his face as he peers into my car and glances at Dhruv.

'What?' I gesture with my hand. Fuckin' freak. He shakes his head, the ugly smile still pasted on his face as he reverses the taxi. The weirdo drives away then.

'What an asshole!' I mutter.

'Who was that?' Dhruv asks looking towards the cab that is now speeding away. I shrug.

'Fine, Dhruv. Let's try to be friends,' I smile tightly.

He looks relieved. 'Thanks a lot, Anuradha. I am sure we can be great friends,' he holds my hand gently, looking into my eyes. I don't think I could have resisted if he had decided to kiss me at that moment. Maybe that's what I want deep in my heart. But then he doesn't.

'It's getting late. Let me drop you home,' he says.

'My apartment is quite close, I will manage. Why don't I drop you to your hotel?'

'I want to see where you live. Don't worry, I'll walk back. It's been a good day and a walk will help,' he insists.

He wants to see where I live . . . maybe he wants to come up . . . maybe stay.

We are in front of my seven-storeyed apartment building in ten minutes. I park my car outside the main gate before we walk towards the building.

'Nice,' he says, taking in the old Bandra building packed with twenty-eight miniature flats.

'It's an okay place. Anyway, I will be shifting soon. My lease ends in a few days and the landlord doesn't want to extend it.'

'Zeroed in on something?' he asks.

I shake my head. 'I have to start looking; hopefully in a day or so. Friends at work will help—'

'Let me know if I can,' he butts in.

I nod. 'Want to come up?' I ask.

'No, thanks. Some other time. I'd better get going,' he says quickly. I can see it on his face again, the tussle between his head and his heart.

'Okay. Some other time, then. Are you here tomorrow?'

He nods, smiles and then walks away. I sigh once before entering the building gate, pondering over one of the better days of my life since Dhruv left me alone in that café last Christmas.

What I don't notice is the same black-and-yellow taxi parked a few feet away from my building; its headlights are switched off and the driver looks in my direction with an impassive face, watching my every move.

9

Anuradha

I am at my work station, gazing blankly at the green wall of my office, thinking about last night. The way we warmed up to each other once again. With time, our relationship status has changed: from lovers, we are back to being just friends. Friends? Not really. Dhruv and I can never be *just* friends. There is a reason we met yesterday and poured our hearts out, there is a reason both of us feel for each other the way we do. We are meant to be together, that's what my heart says, although I don't know how or when. Does Dhruv feel the same? Does he want to be with me too? But then why the hell can't he make it happen, despite knowing that Shalini doesn't love him any more? Why? *Wait!* Don't be so hasty and greedy, girl. Dhruv is like that—a man with morals, someone who wouldn't break one relationship to find happiness in another. Don't push him. Not now. This is not the right time. Let him settle down, give him some time. Then, let him figure it out himself. I inhale deeply and nod.

'What's got you thinking so hard, honey. New love?' someone taps my back. I find Anna peering at me with a raised eyebrow.

'Naah,' I laugh. 'Not so lucky as yet,' I say before getting up.

Anna D' Souza is the creative director and my boss at Grassroot; light-skinned, five feet six, bob cut, with dimples to die for. Anna is quite a head-turner.

'Too bad. Why don't you do something about it, Anuradha?'

Suddenly Anna is all excited. 'Do you know who is coming over?'

I look at her with questioning eyes.

'Aman Bhalla! The man himself. Can you believe it?' she giggles like an excited teenager.

Aman Bhalla—AB—is known to be one of the most eligible bachelors of Mumbai: successful, gorgeous and articulate; he is said to have a good head on his shoulders. His picture is splashed across *Mumbai Times* every other day, hobnobbing with the who's who of the city. Grassroot handles the account of his chain of upmarket cafés in Delhi, Mumbai and Bangalore.

'Why? Isn't Vishal looking after his day-to-day operations?' I ask. Vishal is the CEO of his company who is responsible for running the business. I have seen him often, interacting with the Grassroot team, although I have never worked on that account.

Anna whispers to me. 'I think AB sacked him after their Bandra and Lower Parel property revenues tanked over the last six months.'

I nod thoughtfully. 'So, will he be taking over until this is sorted?'

'Yeah, I guess so. I wish he takes over forever, no?' Anna swoons. 'So much better than that nut, Vishal.'

She snaps out of her trance after a few seconds. 'There's news for you too, honey,' she says, 'you will be working on this account from today.'

So that's the reason she has been acting all sugary. Smart bitch.

'Oh no, Anna! I already have too much on my plate,' I scowl.

She pats my cheek. 'Come on, girl, you'll be meeting Aman Bhalla often now. Isn't that a big incentive?'

'It's not that, Anna. I have other accounts to handle and with this new one, I will have a shitload of work.'

'I get it, sweetie,' Anna nods. 'But Aman is insisting on a new team, so both Ram and I think you will be perfect. Let's look at it as a short-term assignment.'

I snigger. 'Short-term? Come on, boss, you know there is nothing "short-term" in advertising. Do I have a choice?'

'You can talk to the boss. He won't agree, though. He wants you there.'

'Okay,' I sigh after a minute. 'When is the client coming over?'

~

It's late in the afternoon when I meet Aman Bhalla in person along with Ram and Anna. I actually go weak in my knees when I glimpse him for the first time. The man is so goddamn hot. Anna was right; meeting such a good-looking man is truly motivating. He's a Hollywood's-George-Clooney-meets-Bollywood's-Rahul-Khanna kind of a man: he has a chiselled bearded face, straight hair and a smile that cuts deep dimples into his cheeks. He is tall at about six feet. He is wearing a blue-chequered linen shirt over a pair of skinny denims and tan loafers, and I can smell the fragrance of his cologne as he walks over to my desk with the others.

'We are giving you our best creative brain, AB. Meet Anuradha!' Ram announces boisterously, pointing at me. I stand up almost mesmerized by his magnetic personality.

'Good to meet you, Anuradha,' he stretches out his hand. I grip his broad palm. Also, his eyes are a warm honey-brown.

'Glad to meet you, Mr Bhalla,' I say.

He gives me a lopsided smile. 'Do I look that old? Please call me Aman or AB like everybody else.'

I nod, smiling. 'Okay. Aman.'

He looks at Anna. 'So, she is the one everyone's raving about?'

'You'll find out for yourself pretty soon, AB,' Ram butts in, hard-selling me. I don't like it when expectations are built so high at the outset. I would much rather let my work speak for me than Ram.

'Great. We have a good thing going then,' Aman says gazing at me. I feel his eyes stay on me for a few extra seconds.

'Are we having a briefing now?' I ask.

Aman smiles mildly. 'Not today. Today was only meant to meet you guys. We start working very soon, but be prepared, I am known to be a hard taskmaster,' he says, maintaining his smile.

'Don't worry, we'll be ready, Aman,' Anna says.

Aman nods. 'Good, I will see you soon then.'

Anna gestures at me with her eyes to accompany Aman to the reception. I follow them along with Anna. Ram and Aman walk ahead. I can't help appreciating his tall, muscular torso, his confident stride, shapely legs and ass.

'It's a nice office you have here, Ram. It's a pity I didn't come earlier,' he says, as we reach the reception.

'Well, now that you are here, you can make up for it by coming by more often,' Ram quips. Ram is so goddamn dramatic that it's not funny any longer. He has smart one-liners for everything. Simple words have no place in his vocabulary.

'I will, I will,' Aman says, his eyes flirting with mine. I like it, this attention from a man as attractive as him.

We are at the office reception. Grassroot is on the ground floor of the building. The walls on both sides of the reception are green, while the front is made up of transparent glass. One can see people from the other offices in the building, rushing in and out, visitors waiting at elevators on the other side of the oval building complex. A few kiosks, set up outside, sell juice, tea, coffee and snacks to the office crowd. It's almost four in the afternoon and people have started crowding around them.

'Can I ask you for a favour?' I hear Aman say to Ram.

'Anything for you, AB,' Ram says.

Aman signals at someone seated on the reception sofa. He rises instantly, a nondescript man with a pencil-thin moustache.

'I have a property that's available for rent. Can I put up this advertisement on your boards here and expect some like-minded professionals to show interest?' he asks, glancing at the two soft-boards on either side of the reception desk.

Ram looks eager to please. 'Well, of course you can, AB. In fact, put them on the boards outside our office as well, to attract traffic from the other offices in this building.'

Aman gestures at his sidekick who jumps to it immediately and starts pinning the advertisement flyers on the noticeboards. Ram tells Varsha, our receptionist, to obtain the keys of the noticeboards outside our office too.

'You are in Bandra, no?' Ram asks.

'Yeah,' Aman says. 'Very close to Bandstand. Cedar Grove.'

Ram nods, 'Isn't this the apartment that you want to rent out in the same building where you stay?'

'Yes, adjacent to mine. A few years ago, I had bought two apartments on the tenth floor of the building. We made structural changes to the whole damn thing then. A part of it is available for rent, and I'm kinda picky, so don't want this to go to just about anyone,' Aman explains.

The Grassroot office boy has arrived with the keys. Ram signals to him to unlock the noticeboards outside the office. We move out along with Aman and Ram. Renting an apartment is on my mind too. I only have two weeks to vacate my current one.

Ram looks at me and says as if he's read my mind, 'Weren't you looking for a place to rent, Anuradha?'

I don't think I'll be able to afford a place in Bandstand. Why does he want to embarrass me in front of Aman?

'Is that so?' Aman looks surprised. 'Where do you stay now?'

'In Bandra, close to Linking Road. But this flat . . . I . . . I mean yours, won't fit my budget,' I say hastily.

'Have I quoted you a price yet?' Aman asks.

'No, but . . . but I know the rentals around there,' I fumble at his directness and look away at his sidekick, engrossed in pinning the advertisement on to the board. The ground floor of the building is buzzing with people, a small group has already surrounded the board, peering at it.

'Come, let me show you the ad. We haven't fixed a rent yet,' he says as we move closer to the noticeboard.

I look at the advertisement:

> *1 BHK, tastefully furnished, available for rent.*
> *More than the rent, what we need is a good tenant. Rent, however,*
> *is negotiable.*
> *Cedar Grove,*
> *Bandra West.*
> *Contact Shiv: 9892547878*

'Smart line,' I can't help but smile.

'A good tenant is what you need these days. A few thousands here and there don't really matter,' Aman says, his calm gaze fixed on me.

Ram chuckles. 'Of course, AB, why would it matter to you? Money is for ordinary mortals like us.'

'Oh, come on, Ram! You are too well funded by WPP to say this.'

I see Ash walk out of the office. He looks at us. 'Hi, AB, what brings you here?' he says.

Ram looks surprised. 'How do you know him?'

Aman half smiles, he looks so cute. 'He stays in the same building as I do, plus he plays with his gang sometimes at our café in Bandra and Town.'

'AB will be looking into Café Maximum directly from now,' Anna says. Café Maximum is the chain of cafes that AB owns.

Ash shrugs. 'Well, good then. We'll get to see him here more often than at Cedar Grove.' Aman laughs, his dimples are striking. Ash looks at me. 'One of the apartments I was talking to you about last night is the same one in Cedar Grove. Though I don't know about the rent AB is expecting.'

'Isn't this a really small world?' Ram says.

'I don't think I'll be able to afford it, Ash,' I repeat reluctantly.

'Come and have a look. That may help you make up your mind,' Aman says.

'But . . . but . . .' I hesitate.

Ash pats my shoulder. 'Come on, Anuradha. No harm in having a look. Maybe AB is willing to offer a hefty discount to Grassroot employees.' The group breaks into laughter.

Aman glances at me. 'So . . . are you coming to have a look at the house?'

'Okay,' I nod, 'if you insist. But I'm telling you now, it'll be futile. I won't be able to afford it.'

'That we'll keep for later. Call Shiv when you want to go over and he'll be happy to show you around,' Aman says, pointing to his assistant. They leave then.

Ram chuckles after they have left. 'He likes you. I'm telling you he'll give you that house.'

'Oh, come on, Ram, for heaven's sake! We've only just met,' I say shaking my head, but feel strangely happy. From the corner of my eye I catch a weird expression on Anna's face. She looks jealous.

We walk back into the office. I am in two minds, wondering whether I should call Dhruv or let it be. But then, if I don't after what transpired last night, he might think I am no longer interested in keeping anything alive between us. Even friendship. I play with the thought in my head for a moment and then pick up the phone.

10

Sid

Things are falling into place. I will soon be where I ought to be. Near your inner circle. Closer to you, around you, in your surroundings. Now my eyes will always be trained on you. *All the time.* I was in your office building today, pretending to be a courier guy when I saw you come out. I saw two new faces today. The rest of them I knew. I have been stalking you for months now, so I know who they are—Ram, Ash and Anna. Aren't you careless about your privacy settings on Facebook, dear?

After you guys dispersed, I checked out the flyer on the noticeboard that I had seen all of you looking at. It turned out to be a rental ad. Are you thinking of moving?

I want to come closer to you now. I need a new face to pull me into your world. And once I am there, I will destroy it. Piece by piece. But right now, I am going to stay put. Wait for the right moment.

Your finish line isn't too far . . . and your time starts . . . now! Soon, you will be in your own hell. It's all your own doing. You'll be in exactly the place you ought to be. If you thought I wasn't a good man back then, you'll be shocked at the monster I have turned into.

Getting close to you would mean that I can peek into your life any time I want to. I'll know exactly what's happening in it. All these guys who are a part of your world will have a role to play in your story. I'm going to decide their roles and also how your story will end. How cool is that? I am going to start writing your story as soon as I enter your world.

It'll be an unbelievable story, I promise.

11

Dhruv

Anuradha called at last. I was uneasy the whole day as our conversation from last night played on a loop in my mind. She was hurt and she had every right to be. The way I ended our relationship was so sudden that it gave her virtually no chance to explain her side of the story. She is right. Sid was no fucking saint, and then, after what he did, he didn't deserve sympathy. She wanted to hide it from me at any cost. When the truth was uncovered, I was broken. The reasons for my state of mind at that time were many: anger, for not being privy to the truth; sadness, because Shalini and kids walked out on me; guilt and even fear of letting this relationship continue. I had been totally overwhelmed by the situation and the complexity of all those emotions. That's when I decided to end our relationship. I loved her, yet I let her go. I could have continued, chosen to overlook her one indiscretion. But then, deep inside, I was also scared of continuing our affair. Perhaps because of the moral code that we are forced to live by, the way this society expects us to lead our lives. That's what we just keep doing, even ignoring what our heart truly wants. Keep living a lie. Because you can't *do what your heart wants*. You can't do that, you can't trample on others as you walk towards the one you think is meant for you.

I couldn't do that to Shalini and the kids and, in the bargain, I ended up messing up my life totally. Each one of them was truthful about their feelings except me. Shalini loved me as a wife does, Anuradha loved me and wanted a life with me. Although I loved both of them, I chose to disappoint both, and ended up screwing up my relationship with both. *Maybe it's me who is the asshole here.*

But then why do I want her in my life as a friend now? I don't know. Maybe I can't let her go; maybe having her as a friend is some kind of atonement, proof that she has forgiven me for breaking her heart. The mere thought eases the turbulence inside me. I know I can't set things right with Shalini now. She knows about my affair, about Anuradha. I had confessed to her after Anuradha moved to Mumbai, because there was no way to get her back without telling the truth. She knows about it, but what she can't gauge is the intensity of the feelings I have for Anuradha. I sigh and take a deep breath before looking at my watch.

It's 7 p.m. as I enter Monkey Bar in Bandra West. It's close to Anuradha's house and she told me over the phone that she would be coming here directly from her office in BKC (Bandra Kurla Complex). It's pleasant outside so I decide to take one of the tables near the wall in the veranda of the restaurant. Being a weekday, and slightly early by Mumbai standards, the bar is not very crowded. Loud eighties English music plays inside the bar, its volume diminishing as it wafts outside to the porch, where I sit. Anuradha enters the bar through its wooden gate, wearing a sleeveless floral blue dress, looking as ravishing as ever. A couple of heads turn from the neighbouring tables, as I wonder when I had last kissed her.

'Have you been waiting for long? I am sorry. There was an unplanned client visit, so the entire schedule went for a toss,' she says apologetically before drawing up a chair.

'No, that's all right. I just got here. How was your day?'

'Oh, it was fine, and yours? Met Vikas? He must be happy with the award your branch got last night.'

Vikas is my boss at C&M, based out of the company headquarters in Mumbai.

'Vikas is doing fine. He was happy that you were also there to take the award with the team last night,' I say.

'That was a really sweet gesture, Dhruv. There wasn't any need for it, though.'

'You were instrumental in getting us Mojo, and with you sitting right there, there was no way we were accepting it without you.'

She nods. 'I know. Rachna told me you insisted. I felt good.'

'Let's order something,' I pick up the menu from the table. I signal to the hovering waiter.

Anuradha looks at the menu. 'I have tried this cocktail before, it's nice. Vodka-based.'

'Which one?'

'Mangaa—the one at the top,' she says.

'Okay. We'll have two of these,' I tell the waiter. 'Something to munch?'

She shakes her head. 'Not really.'

'That'll be all for now,' I say to the waiter.

We sit in silence for a while, listening to the music, perhaps wondering what to say. It's strange sitting like this with her, a woman who was an integral part of my life just about a year ago.

'So, how have you been all this while? Forgot to ask you yesterday. It was mostly I who did the talking last night.'

'Miserable, to tell you the truth. But have been better since yesterday,' I reply.

She nods and then smiles wryly, 'Don't tell me I have that kind of an effect on you.'

'You have no idea what kind of an effect you have,' I say.

'I felt good, too. Perhaps everything here,' she indicates her chest, 'found a vent.'

I nod and fall silent for a while. 'The two of us were living with the same pain all this while, in our own shells. Coming together and sharing, helped.'

The drinks arrive. She picks up her glass and takes a sip.

'You blocked me on all the social platforms, no? Facebook, Twitter, Instagram,' I say.

'I did. I thought I hated you . . . until yesterday.'

'And, look at me! I could never muster the courage to call you even once after that day last year,' I say. 'Sometimes we end up becoming prisoners of our own thoughts and in the bargain, we suffer even more. I think that's what we've been doing.'

'And?' she asks.

'If we can't be lovers, we can at least try to become best friends again,' I suggest.

'Can you do that, Dhruv? Become just my friend?'

'I can at least try, Anuradha.'

'And what if you fail?' she asks, locking eyes with me. I go blank. My mind searches for an appropriate answer desperately. 'Don't worry,' she says, putting her hand over mine, 'I won't push you.' I quiver at her touch and smile uneasily. She clinks her glass against mine in a toast, 'To our friendship, Dhruv.'

'How do you like working at Grassroot?' I ask after a moment.

'It's a smaller setup than C&M, but work is fun. We spend more time in getting new clients than servicing existing ones. It's not as cushy as C&M,' she winks at me.

I nod, smiling. 'But Grassroot is doing pretty well. One of the fastest growing agencies in the circuit. How is the crowd there?'

Anuradha takes a sip of the cocktail. 'Anna, my boss, is smart, like Rachna, and the crowd is sweet.'

'And Ram?' I laugh softly.

She chuckles. 'He is fine to work with. It's just that he always seems ready to drop his pants.'

'Trust me, the entire advertising world is aware of Ram's special trait,' I say, signalling to the waiter.

I order another round of cocktails and a plate of popcorn chicken. Between sips of the cocktail, Anuradha talks about her last one year in Mumbai, her time at work, new friends, what she does over the weekends, her gym routine, her house and the short vacations she has taken within the country and abroad. I realize she has packed in a lot within this last year, while I have nothing to tell her except the regret of letting her go. This journey has been equally painful for both of us, but she has managed to move forward, one step at a time, even though the pain has remained in her heart. While I am still there, holding on to my bag of pain, rooted to the same spot. I realize that meeting her today has given me fresh hope, it has truly refreshed me.

I look at my watch. 'It's time for me to go. My flight is at 11 p.m.'

'Oh, it's already eight! I didn't realize that. You should be going,' she nods.

I signal to the waiter to get the cheque. 'When are you shifting?'

Her face lights up suddenly. 'Have you heard of Aman Bhalla?'

I jog my memory; I have heard that name. 'Yes, of course. The owner of Café Maximum, no?'

She nods. 'He's our client, you know. He was at our office today and owns a space which is available on rent. He wants me to see it.'

'So . . . go and see it,' I say.

'I won't be able to afford it, no?' she says making a face. She looks so cute, I wish I could kiss her.

'Where would this Aman Bhalla get such a charming tenant?' I say, alcohol once again has liberated me from my inhibitions.

She smiles. 'You are right, he won't. Although Aman himself is no less. What an awesome looking man!' she says animatedly. I feel jealous for an instant but before it shows on my face, I dab away the emotion. *Don't say anything stupid, Dhruv—you promised to be her friend. Only friend. Don't you dare go down that other path again*, my heart says.

'I hope you get that place, Anuradha.'

She points a finger at me. 'Next time, you are coming to my new home, okay?'

In the last one year, I had never imagined that we would be sitting together like this again someday. But then life has a way of revealing its mysteries in the most unexpected of ways and at the most unanticipated of times. The waiter gets the cheque and I take out my wallet to pay.

'Shouldn't we go Dutch,' she asks, '. . . now that we are friends?'

I look at her, a smile plays on her lips. I know it's a teasing one. 'There will be more to come. You can pay the next time.'

It's time to say goodbye as we stand outside the bar. The traffic is still heavy on the road, but the honking has gone down, like the diminished energy levels of people getting back home. My taxi waits on the other side of the road.

'It's been my best trip to Mumbai ever,' I say slowly. It hurts; leaving her is still painful. But at least I can look forward to seeing her soon.

'I am glad we met,' she says, grinning. Anuradha has one of the best smiles in the world.

'Yeah. We'll meet again very soon.'

She nods and steps forward and before I know it, she hugs me tight. 'Have a good flight, Dhruv.' Her touch carries me in its warmth all the way to Delhi.

12

Anuradha

I get off the cab at Cedar Grove, a twelve-storey building on Bullock Road near Bandstand. I have finally made up my mind to check out the flat even though I'm pretty sure I won't be able to afford it. Ash has come along as he stays in the same building. He said he was done with his office work for the day. It is Friday, and he has a gig tonight. I know Ash likes me. He has never actually said so, but I know he does. It's sweet of him to accompany me. I had fixed a meeting with Aman's assistant for 6 p.m. He was being overly courteous to me on the phone, almost as if I were a special guest of his boss. Ash knocks on the metal gate of the building and within seconds a small window opens, through which a watchman identifies him and then nods. The door is automated and unlocks with a clunk. We walk swiftly towards the elevator.

'Which floor are you on?'

'The eighth,' he says, pressing the button on the elevator panel.

'And Aman?'

'AB is on the tenth floor,' he says, humming under his breath.

We get into the elevator. 'Do you share your flat with others?'

'Yeah, there are two of us in this one BHK.'

The lift goes past the eighth floor. I look at him. 'Aren't you getting off?'

He half-smiles. 'It's your first time here. I had better show you around. Maybe we'll become neighbours.'

'I seriously doubt it, Ash,' I say yet again.

~

I ring the call bell of Aman Bhalla's apartment. A copper nameplate hangs on the wall by the giant door with his initials 'AB' inscribed stylishly on it. This guy certainly has flair, I say to myself. The door is flung open and Aman stands in front of me, smiling warmly. I am taken aback, not expecting him here. I had expected some flunky of his to show me around. He looks gorgeous, fresh out of the shower, the fragrance of his cologne filling the air. He is wearing a V-neck white T-shirt over faded blue denims, the classic American look.

'Hi, good to see you here,' he extends his hand for a handshake.

I feel a little nervous at this unexpected encounter. 'I thought I might as well see the house once before letting it go because I can't afford it,' I say clasping his hand.

'That's a good decision, Anuradha,' he says and looks at Ash. 'Hi Ash, what a nice surprise to see you here!'

'Just giving her company as I was coming home anyway,' Ash says getting the hint that Aman wasn't expecting him.

Aman looks at him briefly before looking away.

'Come on in, guys,' he moves aside, and ushers us in through the dimly lit passage. I realize that his home is fabulous as soon as I step into his huge living room, perhaps twice the size of my current apartment. Right from the décor, to the deep brown wooden flooring, paintings and objets d'art hanging on the walls, and elegant cabinets and side tables. Everything is perfect. The look on my face is a dead giveaway.

'I hope you like the house,' he says. I smile.

'Of course. It's lovely!'

He pushes a button on an automated sensor on the wall and the curtains go up to reveal the gigantic wall-to-wall windows. The view is breathtaking. Some distance away, between two buildings, I can even spot the sea.

'You get a better view of the sea during high tide. The other part, the one we want to rent out, has the same view but you don't get the sea, I'm afraid,' he says.

I shake my head. 'This is beautiful as it is.'

'I had bought two houses: one was a four BHK and the other one a three BHK. We didn't require so many bedrooms, so I converted three of them into this huge living room. Now we have three bedrooms in this house and another large living room with a bedroom in the other.'

'Smart customization!' Ash whistles appreciatively.

Aman nods. 'Hmmm . . . the unit that I want to rent out is the same. It's just that it's smaller. Coffee? Or do you want to look at the other house first?' he asks.

The house first, because if it is even half as good as this, it's much better than all the other apartments that I have seen so far. But then . . . the rent? I still don't think I can afford it. But no harm in taking a look.

'I am keen to see the house first, if you don't mind.'

'I knew it, let's go,' Aman smiles and gestures to us to follow him. His assistant, Shiv, comes out from one of the rooms, Aman signals him to come too.

I fall in love with the house at first sight. The living room is similar to Aman's, with the same view, but much smaller in size. Sheer red curtains with an abstract pattern hang over the glass windows, which means the room gets a decent amount of sunlight during the day. The kitchen is modular, and the bedroom is cosy. An inbuilt wardrobe with a sliding door makes the room spacious. The bathroom is modern, although the space for the mirror is vacant. Overall the house exceeds my expectations many times over.

Aman is watching me keenly. I look at him and then at Ash.

'This one's so much better than my pad,' Ash says enviously.

Aman glances at me. 'So, what do you think?'

Now that I like the flat, we need to talk about the rent. I am nervous. 'It's quite good,' I mask my enthusiasm. 'I don't know if I could afford it.'

'What's your budget?' Aman asks.

I am in a state of indecision, not knowing what to quote. My budget is about 50k, 55 tops, but I am sure this will be nowhere close to what he would be expecting.

'It's 50k,' I say hesitantly. Aman looks away. 'That's fine, Aman,' I quickly say, 'please don't feel pressurized to give me the flat.'

'It's a deal. Done. You are my new tenant,' he says, handing me a bunch of keys.

It's so sudden, this rather dramatic episode, that it takes a few seconds to sink in. My biggest worry of finding a decent place in this city has been resolved in a jiffy in such an unbelievable manner. And, I get this house at an incredible price. I find it hard to believe. I look at Ash. He looks stumped too.

'Thank you. I hope all single women in this city find a landlord like you,' I say, laughing. I am still in a daze with the deal that I have just sealed.

'I hope you enjoy your stay here. These days it's tough to find a good tenant like you,' Aman says.

'I hope this is not a ploy to get me working overtime on your brand,' I quip.

'You never know,' Aman says and we laugh together. Ash has gone quiet; in fact, he seems to be sulking.

'Please let Shiv know if you want anything extra done around the house,' Aman says. Shiv nods, standing behind him.

I glance around the house and then at Shiv. 'I won't require anything special, except a recheck of the electrical fittings and a new mirror in the bathroom.'

'I'll get that done, madam,' Shiv says politely. He has a long gentle face with protruding eyes.

'Just one more thing,' Aman says as he walks towards the common wall that separates the two flats, Aman's apartment and this one, in the living room. He draws one side of the L-shaped curtain that extends beyond this apartment's living room windows, to reveal a door behind it.

'Before we customized this house, this used to be a door to one of the bedrooms. It can be locked on both sides. I will hand over both sets of keys to you. You can lock it from this side as soon as you move in,' he says and gestures to Shiv.

'That's fine, Aman. You can keep these house keys with you for now; I will move in next Sunday,' I stretch out my hand with the house keys he has just given me.

'We have an extra set that we can use to get the work done while you are not here. You can come by at any time with your stuff. This house is yours from today as far as I am concerned,' he says.

Aman's graciousness and charm has bowled me many times over. 'Thanks, Aman. I owe you a big one for this.'

'A housewarming party when you move here? But now . . . some coffee,' he replies.

I nod and we head back to his house. We discuss work over coffee, about how he is looking to rejuvenate Café Maximum. Aman comes across as a sharp thinker, someone with an astute understanding of the hospitality sector and also of the consumer he wants to target. It's always a pleasure to have an intelligent client on board, one who is eager to dissect the problem, accept suggestions and work together with the team. It seems like it's going to be great fun working with him, for he has loads of both effervescent charm as well as brains. Ash has been unusually quiet over the last few minutes. I decide to ask him the reason as soon as we get going from here.

'Can I use the restroom?' I ask after I finish my coffee.

Aman nods and points to his right. 'Go straight down that corridor.'

The corridor is dimly lit and as I am almost at the bathroom door, another door to my right opens and an old man comes out suddenly. I gasp and leap back to avoid bumping into him.

'I am sorry to have scared you, dear,' the old man apologizes.

It takes a moment for my racing heartbeat to settle down. Aman has heard the commotion and walked over.

'This is my dad, Anuradha,' he says. His father looks gentle. Aman has his face, but has darker eyes, I think.

'I am sorry, sir, I should have been careful,' I apologize as well.

'That's all right,' he says and glances at his son. 'She is . . .?'

Aman clears his throat. 'Our new tenant, Anuradha. She works for the agency that handles our account.'

His father's face turns impassive and hardens. Aman doesn't look him in the eye. His father nods slowly and then turns away to go back into his room.

A few minutes later, we are saying our goodbyes. We have exchanged numbers, and I have told Aman that I will be making the advance rental payment along with the deposit during the following week.

'Thank you for everything. It couldn't have been easier than this, thanks to you,' I say, feeling light inside. It's a tick against a really huge task on my to-do list.

Aman gazes at me intently. 'It will be wonderful to have you here. I'm looking forward to it.'

~

'Do you want to drop by my place?' Ash asks as we enter the elevator.

'Some other time, Ash,' I say pressing the ground floor button. 'I feel so relieved that I just want to get back home and start planning my shifting.'

His face falls, but he nods.

I smile at him. 'Now that I am going to be your neighbour, there will be many opportunities to get together.'

'Yes, there will be. But why did AB drop the rent so much for you?'

'Because he is a good man from here,' I say, tapping his chest. We get out of the elevator on the ground floor.

'He dropped more than half his rent because he is a good man?' he says sceptically.

'What!' I am surprised. 'I know he quoted a low rent, but is it really less than half?'

'Do you know how much I pay for my one BHK that is smaller and not as good as your apartment?'

I shake my head, 'No idea.'

'About a lakh. Your house at 50k is a fuckin' steal. I mean why would one do that without a motive?'

'What motive?' I scoff. 'Money is no big deal for him, Ash. Aman is a good man who wants a good tenant. Not everything one does has a motive behind it.'

Ash smiles wryly. 'I don't want to upset you, Anuradha. I am happy that you got it so cheap.' We gaze at each other for a few seconds.

'I'd better leave now. See you on Monday,' I say.

He purses his lips and turns around without a word to walk towards the elevator.

I look up at the glittering building that stands majestically before me: Cedar Grove is my new home.

13

After saying goodbye to Anuradha, Aman Bhalla was deep in thought as he walked to the centre of his living room. He felt light inside; happy that his new tenant was moving in. He stood there for a few minutes, multiple thoughts running through his head, in a maze, at lightning speed.

'Shiv, are you there?'

The assistant emerged from one of the inner rooms, 'Yes, sahib?'

'The mirror needs to be fixed next week. You know, no?' his gaze turned hard as he faced his assistant.

'Yes, sahib, I'll get it done.'

'Buy it from the same guy,' Aman said. Shiv nodded and went back inside.

Aman took measured steps to the gigantic windows of his apartment. They were soundproof and none of the traffic noise from the busy Bullock Road penetrated within.

Aman's father was pacing his room in restless circles, extremely agitated with what he had just found out. They had a new tenant now. The expressions on his face changed with every passing second. He broke his path and walked to the window overlooking Bullock Road. He gripped the iron grill of the window so hard that it left red marks on the sagging skin of his palms.

~

Ash entered his flat looking sullen. He locked the door and sat on the couch in the living room, staring at the wall blankly for a few moments. A sudden wave of terrible suspicion singed his insides. This flat for 50k? Impossible! AB was not the man Anuradha thought he was. He had a hidden motive and it was only a matter of time before it was revealed. He had heard rumours about Aman's dubious character. He vowed to find out if there was any truth behind them. Ash rose and peered out through the window that overlooked Bullock Road.

~

Anuradha, happy after having finalized the house deal, was waiting for her Uber to arrive. Sid was at the bus stand on the opposite side, amongst a small crowd of commuters waiting for their bus, looking at her intently. He read the name of the building again: Cedar Grove. It was the same name that was on the rental ad. By now, he had found out that the dashing new guy in Anuradha's life was Aman Bhalla—a hotshot entrepreneur and a bachelor to boot. Had Sid continued his entrepreneurial journey, he would also have been one like him. But. The woman standing opposite him had trampled all over his plans and fucked them all up. What was she doing here? Was she looking to rent the place? Was Cedar Grove going to be her new address? From the smile on her face, it looked like she was coming back. Sid knew her well enough to gauge that. Sid had to now find a way to be inside Cedar Grove. With a new face. Sid had to place an order for it soon. He had already decided on his new look. His new identity. The only task left was to get all the pictures of it. The new character that he had to play. To get the new silicone mask in less than three weeks, he would have to pay a premium. A hefty one. But that was all right, for he couldn't waste any more time. He had already spoken to the mask creators in Italy about his urgent requirements and was going to wire them the money so his mask would arrive in less than three weeks. As soon as he had it, he would step into her life. Her payback would commence.

14

Anuradha

Our Grassroot team is huddled together in the conference room along with Aman. It's our first team meeting with him to decide our POA (plan of action) for the following year for the brand Café Maximum. Aman has jotted down key problem areas on the whiteboard and has given everyone ten minutes to think about each one of them. There are four of us from Grassroot: Anna, Ash, Mohit from client servicing and me. Anna has pulled in Ash as well into the new team to work closely with Aman in getting the brand back on track. I glance at the whiteboard, at the circled words on it: *low alcohol consumption, low table turnover rate, consumer* and *brand messaging*. Aman looks at his watch and gets up.

'So, as I said earlier, these seem to be the four core issues that are pulling the brand down. Revenues from the Bandra and Town outlets, which were our hottest joints, have been declining month by month.'

'Table turnover rate?' I ask. This is my first brush with the food-service sector, so I need to warm up to the lingo.

Anna considers me. 'It means how often the tables in your restaurant are occupied by customers. A higher table turnover rate means more number of customers, which means good business, while the reverse is obviously not good.'

I tap my nose with a pencil. 'Got it. Low alcohol consumption would also be a function of that; less people hence less alcohol consumption.'

'Not necessarily,' Aman intervenes. 'Some places, with the same number of tables as us, have a different business model. Their walk-ins are similar to ours, yet they consume much more alcohol than our customers.'

'So,' Ash says, 'basically you need the right people to come into your café. It doesn't matter how many. Right?'

Aman nods, slowly. 'Well that's one way to look at it. But what you need is a perfect mix: you need the right kind of people in good numbers coming into your café all through the day.'

'So why aren't we getting these people?' I ask. 'Sorry, but I'm oversimplifying this a little.'

Everyone in the room goes quiet. Aman takes a deep breath and smiles mildly. 'Well, that's why we're here, aren't we?'

Anna nods, reciprocating his smile. 'I wish we knew, Anuradha,' she says, 'we'd have fixed it then.'

Ash and Mohit snigger while Aman keeps a straight face.

They may laugh at my question, but I do have a special knack that others don't; it's called 'using my common sense', which is rare these days. Looking at things from a different perspective, not getting distracted by the way other's think, that's my forte.

'No, seriously,' I say impassively. 'What Aman has jotted down are the symptoms. We need to find the cause to get to the root of the problem.'

Aman nods, looking impressed. 'She has a point, guys.'

'Can we look at the creative done for the brand over this past year? The local creative for these stores versus all the others?' I ask Mohit.

Anna speaks in a restrained manner. 'Where are we going with this?'

'Let's look at them together. Maybe we'll find something there,' I say tentatively, glancing quickly at everyone. Aman nods.

Mohit plugs his laptop to the projector and clicks open the annual creative review for Café Maximum. It's a PowerPoint presentation. It's a thirty-slider and we spend about a minute on each.

'So, what do we have now?' Anna asks and looks at me after about thirty minutes. I prolong my silence.

'They look almost identical,' Mohit says.

'There's a difference. Can we go to slides ten, fourteen, nineteen and twenty-three?' I ask.

This time we go through the four slides slowly, spending more time on each one of them.

Aman sniffs. 'Our focus has been specifically on families for the Bandra and Town outlets. Everywhere else we've positioned it primarily as a young, cool and fun place to hang out with friends.'

'Exactly,' I say snapping my fingers. 'Family brunches, family meals, family discounts, entertainment for kids, even birthday parties.' I run those slides once again. 'So, over time, it has become a place for families to hang out. Families, as we all know, spend more time in the outlet, opt for value meals and also share food orders . . .'

Ash butts in, 'Yeah like in a family of four with two kids, they will go for three dishes.'

'The man doesn't drink as much as he does when he's out with his friends,' Aman says, looking at Anna.

Anna purses her lips. 'That can explain low alcohol consumption and low table turnover rate.'

I get up and stand next to the whiteboard, facing the group. 'I am sure over the weekends the restaurant looks full with families, but then they don't move out quickly. They don't order enough alcohol, nor do they order too much variety from the menu.'

'And the perception that has been built over time is that Café Maximum,' I add, 'is a place for families. If you have spelt it out so clearly in your communication, then you haven't given others, except families, a good enough reason to go there.'

Aman looks sternly at my boss, Anna, 'Why did we do that?'

Anna looks nervous suddenly. 'Ummm . . . Vishal wanted it that way. He said it would work and that he knew his business.'

'Oh . . . come on, Anna, this can't be your stance,' Aman throws his hands up in the air, looking far from pleased. 'Classic client-versus-agency debate. You could have brought it up more strongly. Don't you have my number?' he argues aggressively, picking up his cell phone.

Anna's face has turned pale. I have to do something to save my boss.

'The situation is not that grim. I think if we work towards it, we can turn it around quickly,' I cut in. Thankfully, Aman is all ears. I glance at Ash and Mohit. 'We can start with a series of corporate events with celebs. Can you get us some artistes, Ash? All of them know you so well.'

'Yeah, done deal. I'll confirm the names tomorrow.'

'Why don't you guys make a weekly calendar? I'll rope in a few young film stars too,' Aman says.

'That will be great. No?' I glance at Anna. She still looks tense.

'We need to do both. Make the café happening for the young and if we get in the older family crowd as well, it's a bonus,' I say.

'Sounds like a plan. Now let's get cracking on it and we'll review our progress every week,' Aman says.

Ash and Mohit exit the room, leaving the three of us behind.

Aman side-hugs Anna who still looks despondent. 'Cheer up. Sorry to have upset you, but you know I am not a blame-game guy. If there's an issue that you need to flag up, trust me, I am the first guy you should call.'

Anna looks at him and smiles tightly, 'I get it.'

Aman smiles and raises a fist at me. I bump it lightly with mine.

'You were right, Anna. She is a rock star,' he says. I'm thrilled to bits to hear it. He smiles and walks away. He stops at the door of the conference room.

'When are you moving in?'

'Day after. On Sunday,' I reply.

'He's such a chilled-out guy,' I say after he has left.

'So, you are moving into his house on rent, eh?' Anna asks. I nod. 'That's why all this bonhomie, no?'

I don't like the sting in her voice. 'I don't think so,' I say before stalking out.

~

November and December are the best months to be in Mumbai—especially for a north Indian girl like me. There's a definite nip in the air and the humidity, that drags its feet most of the year, finally leaves the city alone for these couple of months. Christmas and New Year festivities bring along a celebratory mood in Bandra, where a sizeable Christian population flourishes. Fairy lights brighten up buildings across the suburb as the city waits to welcome the new year.

I am at Cedar Grove, engrossed in the arduous task of shifting my stuff to my new flat. I didn't disturb Aman today when I came in. I asked the tempo guy, who ferried my stuff here, to bring along two boys for help. It has taken me the entire afternoon to bring my stuff upstairs through the service lift, unpack it and put the basic furniture and kitchen essentials in place. As soon as the kitchen gets going, one starts warming up to the new surroundings.

Ash is away in Pune for a gig. He told me he was disappointed for not being around to help me while I shifted. It was a sweet gesture, even mentioning it. Having managed the reins of my life on my own so far, shifting is just one piddling little thing. It's past seven in the evening when I take a break to glance at the living room. It's almost done, just a few paintings and picture frames need to be hung up. The kitchen is ready, the cutlery is in its place; the clothes have been put away in the cupboards in the bedroom; and the books are out, placed on the shelves in the book racks. *I can also be a bloody efficient homemaker*, I say to myself and smile, although I'm not sure when I will actually become one. That role has eluded me so far. I think of Dhruv. I wonder what he's doing at this moment. Perhaps hanging out with his family. I take a deep breath; the refrigerator is empty. It needs stocking and dinner needs to be organized. The thought makes me realize just how hungry I am. There are apples in one of the bags that should be enough to satiate my immediate hunger pangs. I look away from the window, nibbling on an apple, feeling good about the new house, thinking how far I have come from a cocooned and sheltered life in Lucknow to being here, alone in what they call the big bad city.

~

Within an hour, I am back at Cedar Grove after my grocery shopping, and just as I am about to enter the gate, I hear Ash call out to me.

'Hey, welcome to Cedar Grove,' he says, squeezing my shoulder.

I turn around, happy to see a familiar face in this new place. 'Hi Ash, how was your show?'

He shakes his head, 'Oh, it was crazy, man. The crowd wasn't letting us go. We played till five in the morning.'

'That's good. Well, from today I'm officially your neighbour,' I say, swinging my grocery bags.

'Damn,' he purses his lips. 'I wish I could have helped you. I feel bad.'

'Don't. You couldn't help it. Maybe you can cook me dinner one day soon,' I say, pressing the elevator button.

'Why not today?'

'I'm too tired; I won't enjoy the meal. Maybe some other day,' I say, stepping into the elevator.

Just as I press the button for the tenth floor someone puts their hand between the doors and they reopen. I find Aman standing there scratching his forehead; his assistant is beside him.

My heart rate jumps. 'Hi Aman,' I say, smiling.

'Oh, hi, Anuradha. So, you've finally moved in!' he says, glancing at my grocery bag.

'Yeah, this morning. Were you out of town?'

He nods. 'I was in Bangalore for a new store opening. Hi Ash, what's up?'

Ash smiles. 'All good, AB. Just back from a gig. I was telling Anuradha maybe we could get her dinner tonight. It's her first night here.'

'Well, I am not so sure she's up to it,' Aman nods, looking at my face.

I half smile, not wanting to refuse Ash again. He gets the message.

The elevator stops at Ash's floor. He bids us goodbye and walks away.

'So, all settled in?' Aman asks, as we get off on the tenth floor.

'Yeah,' I nod. 'Pretty much. Whatever is left will get done over the week.'

'Let me know if you need any help. I'm just next door,' he says, gazing at me intently.

~

I am about to go for a shower when the doorbell rings. I am pleasantly surprised to see Aman at the door, with a bottle of wine and two glasses.

'Hi there. Hope I didn't invade my tenant's privacy,' he says, smiling.

'Not at all,' I move aside giving him space to come in. 'As a matter of fact, the tenant is pleased to see the landlord,' I say dramatically. Both of us break into a laugh.

'I thought the first day for my new tenant has to be a bit special,' he says, placing the bottle and the glasses on the table.

'I am glad you thought that, Aman. A glass of wine would be just the thing for now,' I say.

He opens the bottle of Chardonnay and pours out some into both glasses. 'I have ordered pizza; it should be arriving soon,' he adds.

I am floored by his gesture and wonder why he is going out of his way for me. But it feels good to be cared for like this. It's been quite a while. To top it all, being taken care of by an absolutely smashing man like Aman.

'The house looks pretty settled,' he says, glancing around the living room.

'I don't have much stuff to do up the house,' I say, taking a sip, 'so it didn't take much time.'

Aman nods appreciatively. 'No, but this looks neat.'

'So, it's just you and your dad here?' I ask diverting attention from myself.

'Yes, it's just us. And, what about you? Where are you from?'

'Lucknow, my parents are there. After that, I worked in Gurgaon for a while and then here, in Sin City.'

Aman laughs mildly. I like the way he controls his smile to make it look sexy. 'You've been in advertising all along?'

'Pretty much,' I nod. 'Why? Do you want to hire me?' I ask, the wine loosening me up a bit.

'Nah,' he shakes his head. 'You are doing a much better job for me by being on the other side.'

'You bet,' I laugh. 'Can I ask you something?' I say.

'What's stopping you?' he says.

'How does it feel to be one of the most eligible bachelors?'

'Ah . . . that's all media bullshit,' he gestures with his hand. 'They keep writing whatever's convenient for them to make the headlines.'

I want to know more. 'So then?'

'I've been in relationships, some of them were plain shitty, while others, the ones I really wanted, just didn't work out,' he says.

'Well, really? I pity the women who couldn't make it work with a man like you,' I say, genuinely surprised.

He sniffs, picking up the glass and taking a sip. 'When one invests so much in a relationship and it doesn't work out, it breaks one up,' he pauses, thinking. 'In my case it never worked out.'

'I know what you mean. It makes you extra cautious and cynical about getting into another relationship.'

Aman looks at me with questioning eyes. 'You too?'

I laugh a little. 'Everyone is hiding a broken heart here!'

We break into laughter again. It's nice to see a bit of his real side. He's a different person from what he is made out to be. The doorbell rings.

'Must be the pizza guy,' Aman says, readying to get up.

'Hang on,' I say, 'I'll get this.'

I yank open the door and find Ash standing there with a casserole. 'Hi, I made stir-fried chicken noodles. Got some for you.'

I remember his dinner invite and then Aman coming over unannounced. I could have called Ash over as well, but I didn't. Did I really want to? The idea of spending alone-time with Aman was exhilarating.

'Well . . . ummm,' I am a bit tongue-tied, not knowing what to say, when the pizza guy comes up behind Ash with Aman's associate, Shiv.

'Madam, sahib had ordered this,' Shiv says politely. Ash looks at him, trying to understand what's happening here, before Aman walks out of the living room, holding the wine glass.

'Is the pizza here?' he asks and then catches sight of Ash. 'Hey, Ash.'

Ash looks at him, the glass of wine and then at the pizza boy, understanding dawning on his face. 'Oh, you already have your dinner organized. Umm . . . I thought . . . I thought—' he trails off, still clasping the casserole.

I am in a fix, for he seems to be hurt, it shows on his face. 'Well, Aman just surprised me with this sweet gesture. Why don't you come on in and join us?' I say, looking at his crestfallen face.

'No, no, that's fine. You guys have fun; I'd better get going.'

Before I can stop him, he has already dashed off to the elevator. Aman meanwhile takes the pizza from the delivery boy. I know I have hurt Ash. I'll have to make it up to him tomorrow.

I sip from the glass while chomping on the last slice of pizza. Aman has had some, says he has a salad waiting back at home. I put the plate aside and stifle a yawn. Aman gazes at me once before getting up.

'You must be drained after a long day. Have a good night,' he says at the door.

'Not before a shower,' I say smiling, 'the best healer after an exhausting day.'

He nods. 'That mirror in your bathroom was fixed, I think early this morning. I hope you noticed.'

I am impressed with his attention to detail, or is it because of *me* that he remembers? The thought sweetens my mood that had turned glum after the Ash encounter.

I come out of the door with him. He side-hugs me, by wrapping his strong muscular arm around my shoulders. I can smell the aqua perfume on his skin. I have a quivering sensation inside me.

'Good night. Sleep well, Anuradha,' he says. Suddenly the door of his apartment is yanked open and his father comes out. He looks at us strangely before his gaze jumps to Aman's face. He looks angry. Aman releases me and walks away to his apartment.

~

I think about the way this day has unfolded as I peel off my clothes. I am naked, and I take a hard look at my body in the mirror. I can see myself only till my waist. I walk back a couple of steps to look at my whole body in the mirror. I look for any visible layer of flab mushrooming anywhere. There isn't any.

That makes me happy. I switch on the shower and while I adjust the temperature of the water, I think about Aman, about his gesture today. It was so warm, coming from such a charming man. Some women become their own enemies—how could a sane woman let go of a man like Aman? I muse. The temperature is just right now. I step under the water and it caresses my naked body, running all over it, from head to toe. It intoxicates you, a hot water shower after alcohol, it gives vent to suppressed feelings. I think of Dhruv, his hands on my body, his body over mine, the smell of him, the feel of him kissing me all over. I am aroused and I long for his familiar touch. And just then, Aman's face flashes before me, his tall muscular frame, strong arms, broad chest and the aqua smell of his skin. I can see both the faces flicker before my eyes, one after the other, Dhruv and then Aman. I don't know why this is happening. Why is Aman invading my thoughts in this private moment? Just then my hands slither over my body, provoking it even more, before they go down over my thighs, sliding between them, travelling deep inside me.

I moan softly.

15

'This obsession with pretty women is going to ruin you. Don't you get it?' his father said disdainfully, following him into the living room.

'Why don't you have your medicines and go to sleep? It's late,' Aman said, not meeting his father's eyes.

The old man stepped forward and stopped a couple of feet away from him. 'You had promised me. You had promised that it was the last time.'

'What have I done, Dad? Age is making you senile,' Aman said, his face hardening.

'If my senility can stop you from self-destruction, then so be it,' the old man snapped.

Aman yanked open his bar to fix himself a scotch on the rocks. He downed it in one go. He fixed another one, twice the size of the first.

'Are you even listening to me, Aman?' the old man said breathing hard; the sudden rush of blood was doing no good to his weary body.

'Enough,' Aman raised his hand in the air. 'Go to your room.'

'You are disgusting,' the old man said shaking his head. He then turned away and walked out of the house.

Aman looked at his watch; it was 10 p.m. 'Where has this stupid man gone at this hour?' he muttered before entering his bedroom.

He switched on the large computer screen fixed on his writing table. He typed his password and clicked on a folder titled 'AD'. A smile played on his lips. 'Anuradha Dixit, you are mine now,' he said.

Aman could see her naked in her bathroom. Not one piece of clothing on her bare and mind-blowing body. He took a swig from his glass as she stepped back and her full body became visible; perky breasts, a slender waist, well-rounded ass and shapely thighs, disguising the honey pot that he so craved in that moment. He took another sip as she stood under the shower, jets of water falling on her body, making it taut, her nipples growing firmer as she rubbed her hands all over, and then took them between her thighs. She was pleasuring herself, Aman realized. He loosened his belt and slid his hand inside his trousers.

16

Dhruv

Gurgaon

It is past 10 p.m. when I enter my apartment with my set of duplicate keys. It is bathed in dim light. Today was the day for reviewing our plans for next year. The entire Delhi servicing team was cooped up in the C&M conference room for ten straight hours, except for the odd bathroom break. My head feels heavy from staring for hours at multiple billing scenarios for next year. The Delhi branch contributes about forty per cent to the overall C&M business, so for the company to meet its yearly targets, the Delhi branch needs to get its numbers right. Vikas, my boss, had joined us via videoconferencing and after getting me to agree to a revenue number he had in mind, he was keen that the meeting ended. 'Dhruv, I know, only you can make this number happen,' he had said during our one-on-one talk after the meeting. I wish, like the revenue, I could make things right in my personal life too.

Shalini, who is usually asleep at this hour, is working at her laptop, hunched on the couch in the living room. She looks at me and smiles tightly, quite unlike the huge welcoming grin that would appear on her face earlier, when I would get back home in the evenings.

'Hi. Working late? How was your day?' I ask, putting my office bag on the side table.

'It was good and yours?' she replies mechanically, her gaze shifting back to her laptop.

'Hectic day. Setting targets for next year.'

She gives me a quick look. 'Your dinner is in the microwave. Do you want me to wake up the maid? She has just gone to bed.'

'Don't bother her. I'll have a drink first; it's been a draining day.'

She nods slowly and goes back to her work. This is what our relationship has turned into, purely transactional. Shalini and I used to be so close at one time. All of that changed after she came to know about my affair with Anuradha.

But ever since I met Anuradha in Mumbai two weeks ago, the pain has eased a little bit. Perhaps having her back in my life, even as a friend, is better than not seeing her at all. Sometimes I don't quite understand myself. I push people away from my life and then plead with the same people to come back. I did that with both Shalini and Anuradha. It's quite a lousy thing to do. Anuradha and I have exchanged a few messages since I came back from Mumbai. Just general chit-chat, no personal stuff. I know she has moved into a new house that belongs to the same hotshot entrepreneur we had spoken about, Aman Bhalla. I remember her mentioning that he was generous and damn hot. She had ended that message with a swooning smiley. I had replied back with a smiley, but deep inside, my heart had been singed.

I sit on the chair next to the couch where Shalini is lounging and take a sip of my drink. She isn't facing me. After a while she looks away from the screen and takes a deep breath.

'I didn't want to, but then I guess I would rather ask you straight,' she says, turning around to face me.

I am on guard instantly. Shalini's profession, of a psychiatrist, makes her an incisive and blunt woman. She doesn't like to beat around the bush. I glance at her, not knowing what is coming.

'Did you meet Anuradha in Mumbai?'

It's déjà vu. 'Yes, I did. Why do you ask?' I reply looking deadpan.

She nods. I can make out from her expression that she is a bit relieved with my frankness.

'Why Dhruv? You said it was all over after she left C&M.'

'Shalini,' I glance at her, 'she was at the awards night when we won. Rachna felt she deserved to be on stage with the rest of us when we received the award.' It was one of those impromptu lies.

'You know what this affair of yours has done to us?' she looks at me. 'It has killed me from here,' she puts her hand on her chest and then bursts into tears. Shalini doesn't cry easily, it takes a lot for her to do that.

'Shalini,' I get up and sit opposite her holding her by the shoulders. 'Please don't do this. How many more times should I apologize?'

'Even a billion apologies won't erase what you did. You destroyed everything, Dhruv, my trust and along with that my heart,' she says, her voice raspy.

'It was a mistake, Shalini. I made a mistake once and I have come clean. I have no feelings, nothing for her now,' I assure her. That's another big lie. *For how long will you lie, Dhruv?* my heart cries.

'Why is she your friend on Facebook? She wasn't on your "friend list" earlier,' Shalini looks at me, her crying has stopped.

She was until last year before she moved to Mumbai, after which she blocked me. Shalini wouldn't have bothered to look at my list earlier, she had no reason to before she came to know of my affair. She must have noticed her on the list recently, after Anuradha unblocked me a few days ago.

'She sent me a request and I accepted,' I say plainly, hiding the fact that I was desperate to be back on her friend list again. 'What's the big deal? After all we are in the same industry. Are you spying on me?' I ask in a lame attempt to lighten the mood.

She looks at me sharply. 'You're tagged in a picture from the awards night and it showed up on my timeline. Seeing that girl with you was not pleasant. Will you meet her again?'

'Why would I? We accidentally bumped into each other at the awards night.'

I have told her another convenient half-truth. That makes me feel only partly guilty. Shalini can draw her own conclusions about my affair but they would strictly be her own.

'How would you feel if I had an affair?' she asks. She has asked me this question earlier as well and my reply has always been the same.

'Like shit. Haven't I confessed this? Men are more brazen, stupid and insecure than women.'

'Don't generalize,' she says. 'It's not about "men and women". It's about you and me. How could you do this despite knowing that I love you so much? We have kids, for heaven's sake!'

We are going down that road once more. 'Let's not do this again, Shalini. Please, I beg you. I am not meeting her, period!' I protest. I don't want to tell her about the evening we spent together at Monkey Bar. I will never be able to explain my feelings for Anuradha to her. It's better to leave things as they are. Too many explanations will only complicate matters further.

'I don't trust you after all that I've been through over the last one year. I know it's not just her pretty face for which you risked our marriage, I know you well, Dhruv. That's why it bothers me even more,' she says.

I know that too, Shalini, but it's just that I can't tell you about my true feelings for Anuradha. I really wish I could, but I am helpless.

'It will never happen again, Shalini. I promise.'

She sighs, looking at me. 'If it does happen again, I will know. It will be the final nail in the already sealed coffin of our relationship.'

She gets up slowly, shutting down her laptop. I hold her hand. 'When will you forgive me?' She purses her lips and smiles tightly. 'A woman can forgive, but she will never forget.'

~

I sigh deeply after Shalini goes inside the bedroom, the room that reinforces how we are just two strangers who sleep on either side of the bed. Our lovemaking has become devoid of love. It is now merely an act to fulfil the compelling physical need. I miss sharing a bed with Anuradha, the way we used to; the connection our bodies had and the way it entwined our souls. I am truly remorseful about hurting Shalini, but to stop loving Anuradha was not in my control. From the minute I saw her, the remote control of my life was taken away from me.

I pick up my phone and look at the unread messages that have accumulated in plenty all through the day since I have been busy with the meeting. I scroll down to find a message from her: Hi, Dhruv. When are you coming to Mumbai next?

My heartbeat races: Hi. Sorry, didn't see your message. The ticks under the message turn blue immediately.

I can see she is typing a reply: No worries. A friend can reply whenever he wants to. A smiley comes after it.

I am coming on the twenty-second of this month, I type. The ticks go blue again after which there is a pause.

It's decided then. On twenty-second night, I'm throwing a small party at my house. You have to come.

We can't be meeting again so soon. I don't need any more twists to my already complicated life.

Anuradha, I am looking at returning the same night. It's a Friday. There is a pause again.

A sad smiley face appears on my screen followed by a message: It's my housewarming party, Dhruv. Can't you stay overnight . . . for a friend?

I take a deep breath before typing: Okay . . . fine. I'll come.

Three smileys appear warming my heart: Thanks. Will send you the details on the twenty-second. Goodnight. Then she is gone.

I miss her presence, albeit briefly, and then I get up after deleting her messages from my phone.

17

Lucknow

Sarla opened her eyes slowly after finishing her prayer. The life-sized statue of Lord Hanuman stood imperiously before her. His kind eyes seemed to be fixed on her. She brought her head to the ground, touching it reverently, seeking clemency from the deity for the billionth time. She had been on a sin spree over the last few months—committing one sin after the other, ever since the day she had met her son. She had not broken her promise to him about not telling anyone that he was alive. That he had a ruined face and was now determined to hide his identity. That he was not what he used to be. That she had a bad feeling about him now. Not even her husband knew that their son was alive. She knew it was unfair on him, but she also knew that telling him was not an option.

It was early afternoon and the Hanuman temple on University Road was sparsely filled with devotees. 'Lord of the Lords. Saviour of ignorant mortals. Guide me towards the light, O Lord Hanuman,' she muttered under her breath. Striking the bell once with her trembling hands, the old woman turned around and walked out of the temple. Siddharth needed more money after cleaning out her account. He had asked a few times over the last seven months. He never responded to her questions over the phone whenever they talked. Almost as if his old parents meant nothing to him. *Where was all the money going and what was he doing holed up in Mumbai?* Siddharth never answered. The only thing that he said was to give him time. He said he was working on a plan. *What plan?* God alone knew.

Then, a couple of days ago, he said something out of the blue. He said that Anuradha had moved house. When Sarla asked how he knew . . . had he met her in Mumbai? He denied it. He said he had been keeping a track of her whereabouts. Sarla thought he was drunk that night. Now why would Siddharth track Anuradha? They had broken up before he had met with that accident in Lal Tibba, so how come he was still tailing her? But she had an inkling that something was not quite right ever since that night when she had met Siddharth. The brazen contempt that had flashed on his hideously scarred face upon hearing Anuradha's name was enough to tell her that something was wrong. Terribly wrong.

As the days passed, her suspicion turned to conviction. Siddharth was in Mumbai because of Anuradha. He was up to something sinister. She, Sarla, had to do the right thing.

18

Anuradha

Finally, the house is ready for the housewarming party. I glance around feeling satisfied with all the hard work I have put in for the party over the last two days. I mentally do a last-minute check: food, done; snacks, done; booze, done; fairy lights in the living room, done; washroom, all tidied up; bedroom, neat and cosy. Yes—*everything* is done, I exclaim, looking at the clock. It's 6.30 p.m. and people should start arriving in an hour or so. I have kept the gathering small, limited only to the people I know well: Ram, Ash, Anna, Aman and Dhruv. Aman, who is away on work in Delhi, is coming directly from the airport, while Dhruv will be coming from the C&M office. I hope everything goes well today. I am looking forward to meeting everyone, especially Dhruv.

Anna and Ash are the first ones to arrive, together. I had apologized to Ash the very next day after the incident on the day I shifted. I had explained to him how Aman had arrived unannounced and considering my equation with him now, I couldn't say no. Ash understood. I felt he wanted to tell me something about Aman, but he kept it to himself. I was grateful for that. Anna has been acting a bit strange since the day Aman called for the brainstorming meeting in office. The first thing she asked me when I invited her over was if Aman was invited too. When I nodded, she said, 'Well then, it's going to be a no-holds-barred night.' I couldn't fully understand what she meant, but then I just let it be. 'I'll play it by ear,' I thought.

I hug Anna at the door as she hands me a pretty bouquet of oriental lilies.

'I hope you're not expecting gifts from neighbours,' Ash says, holding out his empty hands. I laugh and step aside. 'Not at all. Please come in.'

'Nice, that's a pretty good pad you have here,' Anna says looking around. I can see a streak of envy flash across her face again. She is wearing a black satin evening dress with a deep V-neck.

'How much did you say Aman gave it to you for?' she asks, looking at me, checking out my ivory-white, floral mini dress.

'Fifty grand a month,' I say.

'Fifty?' she looks startled. 'Well, Aman's been really generous here!'

'Maybe he was looking for a good tenant like me,' I say gesturing at the three-seater couch. I have laid out chairs around it for everyone to sit.

'Good tenant? Or a hot woman like you,' Anna says.

I raise my eyebrows in mock disbelief. 'Oh, come on, Anna. Not all men are like that,' I say to put an end to the discussion, but Anna doesn't give up.

'Oh yeah?' Anna raises a sceptical eyebrow at me. 'Well, if you insist!'

'Water or alcohol?' I ask Ash.

He looks at his watch. 'Time for alcohol now. But let me help myself,' he says gesturing at the bar that I have set up on one of the side tables. He looks at Anna.

She nods. 'Okay, then. Let's dive into the party.'

Anna makes a rum and coke for herself; Ash is having a gin and tonic; while I pour myself a glass of red wine. I need to be careful with my drink. I have the whole party to take care of.

'Did we finish that creative on Sweetbeat?' I ask. It's an artificial sweetener brand that we handle.

'Yes, sweetie, it's done,' Anna says, standing by the window, looking at the view. 'Work does happen in the office even without you being there, you know.' She is referring to the half day I took to organize the party.

I am taken aback by her rudeness for an instant, but I don't react. 'When is Ram coming?'

'He said he is going to be at Salt Water Café, meeting one of his friends,' Ash replies.

Then Ash and I get into a discussion about Sweetbeat for a while. Anna keeps to herself, standing by the window, sipping her rum and coke and smoking a cigarette. The doorbell rings.

'Hey, you look smoking hot!' Aman says, putting his arm around me and giving me a side hug.

Shiv, carrying his bag, stands behind him.

His sudden compliment makes me blush. 'Your flight was on time?'

He nods. 'So, what's happening here, guys? This is a rare case of me being invited to my own house for a housewarming party, no?' he says as he hugs Ash and then Anna. She gives him a bear hug and seems to cling. One odd woman she is turning out to be tonight!

'Where's my drink?' Aman asks. He spots the bar on the side table and then looks at the glass of wine I am holding. He makes himself a scotch. 'So, where's your boss? Have you guys invited him?'

'He's meeting one of his friends. Should be here any time,' Ash says.

'Hope it's not a woman he is meeting. I doubt he's going to come then,' Aman says, half smiling.

'He's not as bad as he's made out to be,' Ash retorts.

'I wish a woman had said it. You're lucky to be a man at Grassroot, Ash,' Aman says, as we break into laughter.

Anna seats herself next to Aman and whispers something in his ear. Aman shakes his head vehemently. We start talking about the celebrity world, one that Aman is so familiar with. Even Ash knows a lot of them pretty well because he gets to play a lot of gigs at celebrity private parties. Both of them regale us with starry stories for a while. I notice Anna is drinking a bit too fast. She looks like she has something on her mind. *Well, she's a big girl! I say to myself.*

I look at the watch and then at my phone. No message from Dhruv yet. The doorbell rings again and when I open the door, there he is, holding a bouquet of flowers and a bottle of wine. All the memories come flooding back. Memories of him standing at my door so many times. How happy I would feel each time I saw him there! I never wanted him to go back. I wanted him to stay with me forever, in my house, in my heart. Overwhelmed, I hug him instinctively.

'What took you so long?' I ask, appreciatively inhaling his familiar scent. He hands me the gifts, glancing inside my living room.

'There was a board meeting at the head office. It got extended by a couple of hours,' he says.

Dhruv looks as good as ever. He is wearing a black, collared T-shirt under a grey linen jacket and jeans. I introduce him to everyone as my erstwhile boss at C&M. I can see Aman appraising him.

'How come we've never met before?' Aman asks him, as Dhruv sits down next to me on a chair with his glass of vodka.

Dhruv smiles. 'My Mumbai trips are limited to the office or a one-off client meeting. Work keeps me mostly in Delhi.'

'Mojo was a big win for you guys,' Anna says.

'It was. All thanks to her,' Dhruv says looking at me.

'Does she have a completely unbroken track record of doing great work?' Aman quips. Anna looks at Ash, I can see her making a face.

Dhruv takes a sip. 'Anuradha is the best creative brain I have seen during my entire sixteen-year stint at the agency.'

'Wow, that's what I call a huge endorsement,' Ash exclaims.

'Well, the truth better be told,' Dhruv says raising his glass.

Aman looks at me, locking eyes. 'Hope she recreates that magic for Café Maximum as well.'

'Inshallah. Cheers to that,' Ash raises a toast.

'Where's Ram?!' Ash exclaims. Just then the doorbell rings and Ash gets up to dutifully open it.

'Speak of the devil,' Aman exclaims.

'Hello, people!' Ram says loudly, entering the room. 'Look who is here! Mr Dhruv Saxena, I wasn't expecting you.' Then he turns towards me, 'Why do we have the competition here?' he smirks.

'C&M is no competition to Grassroot,' Dhruv says, shaking his head.

'And what makes you say that?' Ram asks, looking into his eyes dramatically.

'Because we don't consider you one,' Dhruv says with a straight face. Aman smirks as Ram fumbles for an answer.

~

It's half past nine. Everyone has had a few rounds of drinks by now and snacks are being passed around. The room is bustling with chatter, jokes and laughter. Aman and Ash have taken the lead in entertaining everyone. Dhruv has opened up a bit too, sharing anecdotes about clients in Delhi and how different they are from the ones in Mumbai. I am flanked by him and Ram. Ram is leaving no stone unturned to denigrate other agencies and their heads. Well, no one is surprised. Ram is like that, both cocky and horny. We are all having a good time when Anna, who has been quiet for a while, speaks up all of a sudden.

'Did she work very closely with you in C&M?' she asks Dhruv.

Dhruv looks at me and then shifts his gaze to her. 'Not very. Workwise she was reporting to the creative director, but we got to work together on a few projects.'

'See, I told you,' Anna says looking at Ram. 'She's a sweet-talker. She has this knack of charming the right people everywhere.'

I can't believe Anna just said that! *What's wrong with her!* 'Dhruv was not just my boss but a close friend too. I hope you know that some bosses can become good friends as well,' I say sarcastically.

Anna bobs her head. 'I know that, sweetie, more so now.'

I shake my head and go to the kitchen to get more snacks. I am heating them in the microwave when Ram walks in.

'This Anna is acting weird, no?' he says, standing close to me.

'It's fine. She can be like this sometimes,' I say nonchalantly as I don't want this female rivalry to go too far and allow the men to take advantage of it.

He wraps his arm around my waist. 'I can tell her off for you, if you want me to.'

I detest his sudden touch and try and wriggle out of it even as Aman walks into the kitchen. He looks at Ram, his face hardening all of a sudden. Ram moves away.

'Don't bother, Ram, I can handle her. Can we all go out now?' I say looking uncomfortably at both of them. Ram walks out.

'Everything all right?' Aman asks gesturing to Ram.

I nod, walking out of the kitchen. He follows me.

The doorbell rings again. I open the door to find Shiv, with Aman's father standing behind him. I greet him before inviting him inside. He hesitates at first, but then steps into the house.

Aman looks a bit upset to see his father and gives Shiv an irritated look. 'Dad, what brings you here?' he says, getting up.

Shiv shrugs. 'He insisted on seeing you.'

'Aren't you coming home now?' his father says.

Aman nods. 'I will. After some time.'

'With whom will I have dinner then?' he asks.

'Uncle, you can have dinner with us,' I respond instinctively. Aman looks at me sharply, almost as if he didn't want me to say that.

His father takes a long hard look at me and then shakes his head. 'No. I would rather go back,' he says. 'Sorry for barging in like this.'

After he has left, Aman glances at us. 'I am sorry. Dad's old and can act weird sometimes.'

'Guys, let's do something interesting,' Ram says, changing the topic.

'Like what?' Ash asks.

'Let's play "Truth or Dare". Okay everyone?' he looks around.

'You're good at playing all kinds of games, Ram. Let's do something else,' says Dhruv.

'Don't chicken out, Mr C&M. Everyone okay?' Ram asks again.

Aman nods. 'What'll the questions—'

'Wild, crazy and embarrassing,' Ram interrupts him.

'But there's a client in the party and here's Dhruv, who doesn't know most of us,' I protest.

'Well, I don't mind,' Aman says, smiling.

Ram rolls his eyes at me. 'So now, the two of you. In or out?'

'Okay,' I say, looking at Dhruv; he nods as well.

'Any repercussions if we are totally truthful?' Ash asks.

'None. Everything stays here between us in Cedar Grove. Nothing goes out,' Ram says, crossing his heart.

'No sexual or vulgar questions,' I say.

Anna retorts. 'Who defines the levels?'

'The rest of us, besides the one who is asked the question,' Aman says.

'Well then let's get the bottle,' Ram looks at me.

We sit around the table; an empty wine bottle rests on top of it. Everyone's agreed that Ram will be the first to spin it. He looks at our faces, grinning, and then flicks his fingers. I watch the bottle spinning, fast initially and then slowing down. It stops with its mouth towards Anna.

'Well then,' Ram rubs his palms together. 'Truth or dare?'

'Truth,' Anna says, sipping from her glass. She has started to slur slightly.

'Of all the people in this room, with whom would you like to make out?' Ram asks.

I throw my hands in the air. 'That's vulgar. I don't think she would like to answer that.'

'I don't mind,' Anna says looking at me, her face flushing. 'Aman.'

Aman looks totally zapped. 'Hey, where's that coming from?'

Anna shrugs carelessly and says with inebriated bravado, 'Well, now you know. My turn,' she says picking up the bottle. The bottle stops at Dhruv.

'Well, Dhruv. Truth or dare?'

'Truth,' he says.

I see Dhruv's face, and I know he's nervous.

'What's the worst thing that you've ever done?'

He clears his throat and speaks after a pause. My heartbeat races. 'I had to let go of someone I truly loved.'

Ash is all keyed up. 'What do we have here? Some kind of catharsis?'

Ram pats his shoulder. 'Wait till your turn comes.'

Dhruv spins the bottle. It stops at Ram. 'What is your biggest fear?' Dhruv asks.

'Death,' Ram says, his demeanour turning sombre almost instantly. 'I am shit scared of dying,' he says before picking up the bottle to spin it again. It stops facing me. I choose truth as well.

'Okay, Anuradha. Is anyone worth your love here?' he asks.

I wait for a second before nodding. 'Yes, there is.'

Ram looks at the group and chuckles. 'Who is going to get lucky of the four of us? I hope it's not Anna.'

'What a lame thing to say, Ram!' I remark.

I catch both Aman and Ash looking at me intently. I turn towards Dhruv, he looks away—either engrossed with his thoughts or unhappy with my answer. *With whom does he think I would want to fall in love?* Maybe he is scared to get drawn into my life again or maybe he is simply pretending to look aloof, pretending to be okay with my new life and acquaintances. Whatever it is, I will find out soon. It's my turn now to spin the bottle. It stops at Ash.

'Who do you think is the most deceptive person in this room?' I ask. He might just name me after the way I hurt him the last time.

Ash takes a deep breath. 'Aman.'

Anna reacts sharply. 'Why would you say that, Ash?'

Ash fumbles. 'Well, we said before we began the game that no one will be judged for his confession.'

I glance at Aman; his expression is enigmatic. One can't make out what is he thinking.

'It's all good,' he speaks after a few moments. 'Let's respect what Ash feels. All of us have a strong reason to feel the way we do,' he says, patting Ash's shoulder. 'No hard feelings, man.'

Ash smiles tightly, and then, loosening up a bit, he spins the bottle. It's Aman's turn to answer when the bottle stops.

'Before you ask your question, don't forget that I will be your client again tomorrow,' Aman cautions.

Ash smiles and then speaks slowly, 'Tell us that one thing you wouldn't want any of us to know?'

Aman smiles. 'Well,' he pauses, 'I like Anuradha.'

I don't know how to react. Obviously, I feel happy. Any girl would, if a guy like Aman says this to her. But. I want to steer this conversation away.

'Three more questions and then dinner, okay?' I ask. I want this game to end.

Aman nods. 'Yeah. I have an early morning meeting in town. So, let's wrap up soon.'

'Oh, come on, guys,' Ram wheedles, 'the night is still young.'

Dhruv pats his shoulder. 'You can party elsewhere, party animal. Let us mortals retire.'

Ram sniffs. 'Okay. Do we go for a drive, then?' He looks at me and Anna. She looks tipsy and doesn't react immediately.

'Let it be, Ram, let's call it a night. Maybe next time,' I say.

～

My phone rings suddenly. I look at the clock, it's close to eleven. It's a Lucknow landline number, but it's neither Mom nor Dad.

I'm a bit surprised and also a bit worried. *I hope all is okay with them.* There's a signal issue in our building so I get up and walk towards the window.

'Hello!' I say. There's a woman at the other end. I can't make out what she is saying.

'Hello,' I repeat a few times before I realize who she is. She is Sarla Mathur, Sid's mother. *Why is she calling me and why at this hour?* I am surprised and incensed. Anything to do with that bastard, any reconnection with his damn memory, pisses me off. *Calm down, it's just his mother, an old lady who has lost her only son.*

'Hello, Aunty. Can you hear me?' I say a bit more loudly. I look at the people in my living room. They're staring at me. I make a face and quickly walk into my bedroom. The signal weakens.

'Hello, hello,' I repeat a few times. She is saying something, something long and complicated. I can only hear a few random words . . . *accident . . . face . . . Siddharth . . .* The rest I am unable to hear.

'Aunty, can I call you tomorrow? The signal is weak, and I can't hear anything,' I say. The signal suddenly improves.

'Take care of yourself,' she says. I hear that.

'Thank you, Aunty. I will,' I say, wondering why she is suddenly feeling protective after two years. It's kind of weird.

'Do call me for sure. *Sid has come back, Anuradha,*' she says. I can hear her raspy voice before the call disconnects.

Sid has come back, Anuradha.

For a second my heartbeat stops. Hearing Sid's name in the present tense is one hell of a shocker. But then reality kicks in. He has been dead for almost two years. But then what was his mother saying? What did she mean by saying, 'Sid has come back?'

Dhruv! I've to tell Dhruv about this strange conversation. I peep out of the bedroom and call his name. He gets up and looks at me quizzically. I smile tightly and gesture to him to come over. I pull him into the bedroom so that his back is to the living room.

'What happened?' he asks.

'Sid's mother just called,' I say.

'So?'

'She has never called me since he died.'

There is no sign of anxiety on his face. Maybe he has stopped worrying about me. Has he moved on? Am I merely his 'friend' now?

'So what, Anuradha? Maybe she just wanted to talk to you. You guys were family friends, no?' he says casually.

'Dhruv,' I say anxiously, 'I couldn't clearly understand what she said, the signal was bad. But what I could hear was—*Sid has come back. Take care of yourself.*'

Dhruv doesn't bat an eyelid, and then, after staring at me for a minute, snorts with laughter. 'Anuradha, for heaven's sake, stop getting so paranoid whenever you hear Sid's name. He was just a bad dream. He is dead. For good. Period.'

I look at him with raised eyebrows. 'So, what was all that about? All what she said?'

Dhruv takes a deep breath. 'He was her only child. Who else will she miss or dream about? Maybe he has been appearing in her dreams more often these days. Perhaps that's why she was thinking more about him and feeling melancholic. So she called you and told you to take care of yourself. Big deal!' he shrugs his shoulders.

I purse my lips, thinking. Dhruv is right. I am being plain stupid. 'Let's go back to the party,' I say making a sorry face.

'Hope everything is fine?' Aman says.

I nod, smiling. 'A common friend's mother called.'

'Let's get back to the game,' Ram says, getting himself another drink.

I look at Aman, making a face, pointing at the clock.

'Ram, I think it's late and we've already given away too many secrets,' Aman says.

'Yeah,' I say, adding, 'and no one opted for a dare.'

Anna's eyes are closed. 'Now that we know what lies in each of our hearts,' she slurs, 'we know the truth.'

'She has had way too much to drink,' I whisper in Ash's ear. 'You had better take care of her.'

Ram gets up with a jerk. 'Okay, guys, you can stop me from playing, but not from drinking.'

After a reasonably quiet dinner, I sit chatting casually with Dhruv and Aman, while Ram, Anna and Ash are at the window, smoking. Both Anna and Ram haven't stopped drinking. Ash looks at me, shrugging his shoulders, indicating his helplessness in controlling Anna. I shake my head and smile ruefully.

Dhruv gets up after a few minutes. 'I had better get going. I have an early morning flight to catch.'

'Stay for a while, please?' I say. I wish he could stay here with me for the night.

He smiles. 'There's always a next time. I'll see you soon.'

Aman gets up and shakes hands with Dhruv. 'It was a pleasure meeting you. Let's get together soon, possibly here?' he looks at me.

'Why not? Any time,' I exclaim.

'Leaving so early, Dhruv? Don't tell me the next time we meet will be at the Ad Club Awards, where Grassroot will clinch the prize for the best campaign,' Ram scoffs.

'Stop dreaming, Ram. None of that will happen, neither that night, nor the award,' Dhruv says smiling at him and clasping his hand. Standing at the door, he waves goodbye to Ash and Anna.

'Thank you for inviting me,' he says to me, 'I had a good time.'

'Thanks for coming.'

'Take care, Anuradha. Aman is a good guy,' he says. Dhruv tries hard to hide his emotions, but he can't; not from me. He doesn't get it. I just don't feel that way for Aman. He's charming for sure and I am attracted to him, but it's way too early for me to have any serious feelings for him.

I smile. 'He is, but we're just friends. I don't even know him that well.'

He nods and gives me a tight hug. It feels so familiar and warm. I wish I could tell him that I want him to stay here forever. I wish I could tell him that he is the only one with whom I could ever fall desperately in love. That was an honest confession I had made during the game. But I stay quiet as I watch him walk away from me.

'We had better get going,' says Ash after a while. 'I'll book an Uber for Anna,' he looks at his phone. 'Do you want me to stay, help you clean up the place?'

'Thanks, Ash, I will manage. The maid will come in the morning, anyway,' I say.

'My offer for a drive is still open,' Ram says.

'You will land them in jail if you drive around with that much amount of alcohol in you,' Aman says.

'That's true,' I say.

Ram sighs dramatically. 'Okay then, I had better leave as well.'

We are at the door, saying our goodbyes. 'Thanks for the lovely evening,' Ash says, looking at Aman standing by my side.

'Hey, the elevator isn't working,' Ram shouts.

Aman laughs. 'Take the stairs, Ram. It will help you lose some weight.'

'Fuckin', ten floors!' Ram howls. 'Are you serious?'

'Goodnight, Anna, see you in the office,' I say.

She glances at Aman and me, and says mockingly, 'You guys have a goodnight too.'

Ash turns around as they are about to take the stairs. There's a flash of anger on his face.

'Anna is totally sozzled,' Aman says after they have disappeared.

'Yeah. I hope she is fine; otherwise Ash will have to drop her,' I say.

'I left my bag inside,' Aman says and goes back into my apartment. He picks up his bag and then seems to remember something.

'I had got you a bottle of really fine French wine. A glass before we say goodnight?' he says cutely. It's hard to say no to a man like him. Aman has been exceptionally sweet.

I nod and get two fresh wine glasses from the cupboard. We pour it out and stand with our glasses at the window. Fresh breeze wafts in, bringing the fragrance of the sea.

'The weather is great,' I say, sipping from my glass. Aman nods. 'It was a good party. I played this game after ages.'

'Me too. It was crazy.'

'It feels good, getting to know you,' he smiles.

'Same here. It would have been really difficult to find a house if it hadn't been for you.'

'Oh, come on. It's nothing great,' he says, putting his arm around me.

'No, really. I mean it,' I reiterate, looking at him.

'I did say a while ago that I like you, Anuradha,' he declares. His warm, reassuring eyes looking at me intently.

I feel a bit numb suddenly. For a moment, I lose my bearings. Perhaps it is the alcohol I have been having all evening. 'I like you too, Aman. You're a good man.'

Aman pulls me closer and before I realize it, his lips are pressing firmly against mine. I feel dizzy; is it his touch that is doing this to me? I feel his hand caressing my thigh and travelling upwards. I wake up suddenly, as if from a trance, moving my face aside and pushing his body away from mine.

'No, Aman, I'm sorry. I can't do this.'

He looks surprised, as if I have messed up a special moment. I step back, leaning against the wall, breathing hard and not feeling good about what just happened.

He takes a deep breath. 'No, it's I who should be sorry. It was my fault. I came on too strong, too soon.'

'I was in a relationship, and I still can't get over it. I am sorry if it sounds complicated and confusing.'

'No, it doesn't. These things take time to heal,' he pauses. 'I am sorry again. Goodnight,' he picks up his bag.

'Thanks for understanding,' I say.

'Goodnight, Anuradha. Sleep tight,' he says at the door.

~

'Are the two of you still chatting?' Ram says, walking in unannounced, panting, sweat beads running down his forehead.

'What brings you here again?' Aman asks.

'Fuck, I forgot my car keys, man. Had to climb ten fuckin' floors.'

'Is it? I didn't see any keys around,' I say, letting him walk around the furniture in the living room, peering under the tables and chairs. Aman follows us. The three of us look for the keys everywhere, but they are nowhere to be found.

'They're not here,' Aman says finally. 'Maybe you dropped them somewhere around your car. Just go and check around it once; if you still don't find them, better take a cab. You can look for them tomorrow.'

Ram nods. 'Yeah, I have no other option.'

I finish off the leftover wine in my glass after they both have left. My head spins and it's tough to keep my eyes open. It is with difficulty that I change into my nightgown. I lie in bed, thinking about the day, the way it unfolded and then the way it surprised me. Faces flash before my eyes: Aman, Dhruv, Anna, Ash, Ram, then that unexpected call from Sid's mother. And finally, that kiss. What was that? I like Aman, but this attraction of his . . . it can't be so sudden, so brazen. It is only with Dhruv that I feel a physical connection. It is stupid, I know, but this is how I feel. Even now. It is at such times that I hate Dhruv for leaving me alone, vulnerable, like I am right now. My eyelids fall shut after I think of him once, standing at my door, looking at me. I drop asleep then.

19

Ash firmly held Anna's elbow as they started to walk down the stairs from the tenth floor. Ram followed, swearing under his breath, hating this unexpected torture.

'That bitch has got him all over her,' Anna muttered, her tongue loosened by alcohol. Ash was glum, his face hardening, for what Anna said couldn't be completely discounted. That asshole Aman was laying his trap around Anuradha and despite seeing it all so clearly, he was unable to do anything. To top it all, today he declared, right in front of everyone, that he liked her. Ash liked her too, although he had been more of a silent admirer up until now. But not any more.

'Did you see how attentive Aman was towards her? And then he also admitted he liked her?' Anna said, her speech a bit incoherent.

'There's nothing to it, Anna,' Ash glanced at her. 'All of us were having a good time. It was more in fun than anything serious,' he said.

Ram scoffed from behind, 'You two got your plans jacked completely.'

Ash turned around. 'What are you saying, Ram?'

'Well you like Anuradha and Anna likes Aman. While both Anuradha and Aman like each other. Now how is that for a complicated situation?' Ram said.

'Oh, come on, boss!' Ash said, 'this is so not true. I can speak for myself at least.'

Ram patted his shoulder, snickering, 'I run the company where you work, dude. Do you think anything is hidden from me? That secret longing and desire you have for the chick upstairs? Do you think I can't see it?'

'And look at our poor Anna?' he said, patting her head. 'Her crush, Aman, likes the woman you like. Bloody fucking irony for you two,' he guffawed.

'Just shut the fuck up, Ram. As it is I am so horribly pissed and drunk,' Anna said. 'Where are we? Have we reached the fuckin' ground floor?'

'Four more floors to go. You two losers get to spend some more time in each other's company to decide who is the bigger one,' he said, cracking up again.

Ash clenched his teeth, his heart rate going up and blood rushing into his arteries at twice the speed. His head throbbed as he steadied his gait with utmost difficulty. He could hear Ram singing a self-made crappy song. His heart ached as Anna begged Ram to stop his nonsense.

Ash is a loser . . . Anna is a loser!!
Both crib and shout,
As their lovers make out!

He could have killed Ram right there, Ash thought. They reached the ground floor with Ram still humming the silly song.

'Okay guys, time to go,' Ram gestured at his car. 'Are you guys leaving, or sharing notes about your broken hearts?'

'Oh, come on, Ram, for heaven's sake, let it go! I'm waiting for my cab,' Anna said, looking at Ash, who kept his face impassive.

'Okay, okay,' Ram said, raising his hands in the air. 'You guys have a good night.'

'Pathetic asshole,' Anna muttered after he had left.

She shook her head repeatedly. 'This bastard is going to talk about this night to the entire agency. Like his zipper, he can't keep his mouth shut either.'

Ash mumbled something.

'What?' Anna asked.

'Your cab is a minute away,' he said looking at his phone.

'Fuckin' shit! I think I forgot my keys upstairs,' they heard Ram's voice and looked up to see him walking back to the building's gate, totally worked up.

'Up on the tenth floor? Seriously, are you really going to climb those stairs again?' Anna asked.

Ram wiped the sweat off his shaven head. 'Hell, yes! I have to. You two giving me company?' he glanced hopefully at them.

Anna made a face. 'This is what you get for all those malicious taunts. God is watching.'

Ram took a deep breath. 'Okay, it's only me then.'

The Uber arrived a couple of minutes after Ram had gone. Anna gave Ash a hug before getting into the taxi.

'Sleep well, Ash. Don't get too worked up,' she muttered. Ash nodded.

She looked back after a few seconds to see that Ash hadn't gone into the building. He was still standing there.

~

The old man sighed and shook his head before looking at the clock. It was almost half past eleven and Aman wasn't back yet. *Hasn't the party ended,* he wondered? *The new neighbour is a beautiful girl, as good looking and vulnerable as Vidya.* He walked over to the window and looked down from the tenth floor. He could spot two or perhaps three people standing at the apartment gate, but they looked hazy; his old eyes had lost the sharpness they once had. He went back to his room and picked up a pair of old midsized binoculars. He had bought them long ago when they had gone to Corbett National Park as a family. This was when Aman was five and his wife was still alive. The old man held the binoculars to his eyes and looked at the apartment gate. He saw a young boy and a tall girl talking animatedly. *They are the ones from the same party,* he remembered. Then, from the opposite side, a bald man, who had also been at the party, walked towards them, looking all ruffled. He stopped near them for a few seconds and then hurried back into the building. The old man placed the binoculars on the window ledge. *Where is Aman?*

～

Ram was exhausted by the time he exited the building for the second time. 'All my fucking fault!' he muttered, searching his pockets for the nth time. No sign of the keys. He jogged his memory: he had locked the car and then, with the keys and the phone in his hand, he had pressed the elevator button. After that he couldn't remember what he had done with them. Did he put them in his jacket pocket, or on the side table in Anuradha's house, next to where he was sitting? He couldn't seem to remember at all. He scanned the area around his SUV, with the torchlight on his phone. Nothing. He bent down, tucking his stomach in and pointing the torchlight's beam underneath the vehicle. No sign of his keys. He got up and yanked at the door in frustration. With a click, the door swung open. *What the fuck!* Ram wondered. He was certain he had attempted to do the same thing at least a dozen times earlier, but nothing had happened; the door had remained locked. He got into the car. The key was in the ignition. 'Am I bloody drunk?' he mumbled. The road ahead looked a bit blurry, his head was heavy with too much drinking, but something like this had never happened before.

Ram shook his head and turned the key in the ignition. He'd had more than his quota that evening, a lot more. He lived in Khar West, a fifteen-minute drive away, so he didn't have to drive far. It was okay, he would be able to manage that distance even in this state, he thought. He became conscious of a faint sound from the back seat, a rustling, as if someone had sat up. Ram blinked his eyes once and bent forward to reach for the rear-view mirror of the car. Before he could do that, he felt the jagged edge of a knife press hard against his throat. Ram froze.

Someone was sitting behind him. 'Keep driving,' the voice said.

Ram was numb with fear. He was a bully to the outside world, but a pussy inside.

'Take everything I have, but please let me go,' Ram stuttered.

'Shut up. Keep driving on the Western Express Highway, towards Dahisar Checkpoint,' the voice said.

'Sir, please let me go. You can even take this car,' Ram pleaded.

The pressure on his throat increased, the knife piercing his skin. Ram felt blood trickle down on to his collar. His heartbeat rocketed, his body, sweaty from the ten-floor climb and descent a short while ago, oozed out more sweat. He peed a little in his pants.

'One more word from your mouth and this blade goes into your neck,' he heard.

Ram bobbed his head. 'No, sir. Please, sir. Don't put any more pressure. I don't want to die,' he cried in anguish. He drove on the Western Express Highway with that knife at his throat.

The SUV had crossed the Kandivali flyover and was racing towards Dahisar Checkpoint. Ram's mind had stopped functioning, he was driving like a zombie. He couldn't think of a reason why he was being made to drive there. Who was sitting behind him? What did he want from him?

It was after midnight. The number of private vehicles on the highway had started diminishing, replaced by trucks that raced freely, travelling to Gujarat and the rest of the country. The checkpoint was fast approaching; there should be some security there . . . perhaps he could raise an alarm, Ram thought.

'Pull over to the side,' he was told, half a mile before the checkpoint. Ram parked the SUV and glanced at the highway. Trucks zoomed by at high speed, attempting to gain an edge over the others, to reach the checkpoint first. Ram glanced at the rear-view mirror and before he could utter a word, he felt a sharp, piercing sensation behind his neck. He shrieked in pain.

'It's just an injection. The pain will go in a moment.'

'Injection?' Ram howled. 'For what?'

'Morphine. It will ease your pain. Now give me your phone.'

With trembling hands, Ram handed his phone over, without turning around.

'What's the password?

'0007,' Ram said.

He heard a chuckle. Ram couldn't see it, but the unknown person opened Ram's mailbox. As he punched the letters ANU, her name appeared automatically, Anuradha Dixit. He clicked on it, then typed a few words before clicking SEND. Then he deleted the email from Ram's 'Sent' folder and tossed the phone back on the front seat, next to Ram.

In a few minutes, the injection started to take effect. Ram felt dizzy at first, his head spinning and his sight becoming blurry. He found it hard to keep his eyes open. Every time he let his head fall forward, even a bit, the sharp edge of the knife pierced his skin, making him pull his head up with a jerk.

'Please let me go,' he mumbled incoherently every now and then in his semi-unconsciousness.

'Time to go,' the stranger said, throwing a hooded black windcheater on Ram's lap.

'What do I do with it?' Ram mumbled.

'Wear it!'

~

It took Ram some time to unlock the seat belt and then wear the jacket as he swayed. Then he sat back in the car.

'Now get out!'

Ram had lost the ability to think. He unlocked the door and tried to step out, but fell down on the ground. The stranger stood behind his hunched body and pulled the windcheater's hood over Ram's shaven head. Then he waited for a few seconds, glancing at the incoming traffic. There was a bunch of trucks speeding in their direction.

'Stand up,' the man said.

Ram didn't move, he remained crouched in the same position.

'Get up or you are dead!' the stranger said. Ram got up; he couldn't stand straight.

The stranger pushed him on to the highway. 'Run to the other side and save yourself. Don't you dare look back!'

Ram looked at the divider that separated the highway lanes.

He staggered hastily, going deeper into the highway, oblivious to the honking that ensued, vehicles swerving away desperately, trying to save an invisible man on a poorly lit highway. A man dressed all in black. A man who had appeared on the highway all of a sudden out of nowhere.

Ram's body was thrown up by the impact when the truck hit him. It flew a few feet into the air, before falling down and being caught under the wheels of another truck that sped up from behind.

Sid peered inside the car, opened a half-empty bottle of scotch and placed it in the cupholder next to the driver's seat. He pulled off the plastic gloves and thrust them inside his jacket pocket. No fingerprints. Then he walked towards the crowd that had gathered around the body on the highway.

Sid glanced at Ram's dead body once, before walking away.

Aman entered his house around 3 a.m. The living room was dimly lit. He peeked into his father's bedroom, the interfering old man was fast asleep. He locked his bedroom and clicked on the camera feed on his computer screen. He couldn't see anything; the lights in the bathroom were switched off. Anuradha must be fast asleep, sedated by the wine that he had spiked. He was careful enough to take just one sip, but she had had more than half a glass before he left her house. He looked at his watch. The drug was powerful enough to knock her out for six hours, if not more. She was as good as dead. Aman had been thinking about it since she had pulled away. Why did she have to? She liked him, he liked her; and more than that, he wanted her. He had wanted her body tonight. He had played his best to get her.

But then it had all fizzled out at the last moment. He hadn't expected that to happen at all.

He switched off the computer and got up. No more watching. *I am feeling her tonight.* He took out a key from his drawer—the key to the door that connected both the apartments. He had given her both the sets, but he hadn't told her he held a third one with him. He unlocked the door and entered her apartment wrapped in semi-darkness. She had not switched off the fairy lights in the living room. The bottle of wine and the glasses were on the table. Aman looked at them and smiled tightly. He tiptoed into the bedroom, some light from the living room wafted inside. Anuradha lay curled in her bed, drugged by the wine, oblivious to him standing right next to her.

Aman poked a finger in her shoulder. No movement. She was gone. He sat down beside her, bent down and kissed her on the lips, nibbling them gently. It was uncomfortable, sitting like this. He got up and walked around to the other side of the bed. He pulled the pillow away, lay beside her and snuggled closer. He slid his hand inside her gown and felt her naked breasts. He bent over her and kissed her nipples, one after the other. He felt the smooth skin of her thighs, her shapely tight butt and then gently stroked her clit. Excitement surged inside him. What he desired was right before him. He had wanted her from the time he had laid eyes on her. But he had to be careful. Any stupid mistake could lead to disaster. He had to stop now. He couldn't take a chance. For him to be able to come unobtrusively like this whenever he felt like it, he had to make sure he left no trace behind. It was better to take precautions than raise even an iota of suspicion in her mind.

He kissed her lips once before getting up from the bed.

'Welcome to Cedar Grove,' Aman whispered in her ear before walking out of her bedroom.

20

Dhruv

The flight is late by more than an hour when I land at the T3 terminal in Delhi. It is not unusual; during the winters, the fog in north India can be as unpredictable as the rains in Bangalore and can derail all your plans. It's 11 a.m. when I get out of the airport. The weather is a frothy concoction of fog and cold winds and the sun has decided to take the day off. I switch on my cell phone and book an Uber. Even as I'm booking the cab, messages start downloading on my phone. Three missed calls from Anuradha! My heart pounds. Since we reconnected, we have only communicated through messages. We haven't spoken over the phone even once. And now suddenly, three missed calls today?

I call her back, but she doesn't take my call. As I am getting into the cab, my phone beeps. It's a message from her. I am stunned on reading the message. I read it one more time:

Anuradha: RAM MET WITH AN ACCIDENT LAST NIGHT. HE'S DEAD.

I can't believe it. The series of taunts we had aimed at each other just a few hours ago flash through my mind. He was not the best of men I had met, but he did have his own signature style. I suddenly feel awful as I think back about last night's party, and that I had been with him just a few hours ago.

Dhruv: GOD, THAT'S TERRIBLE. HOW DID THIS HAPPEN?

Anuradha: NO IDEA. HE LEFT SOON AFTER YOU BUT NO ONE HAS A SINGLE FRIKKIN' CLUE HOW HE LANDED UP IN DAHISAR.

Dhruv: DAHISAR? HOW DID HE REACH THERE?

Anuradha: YOUR GUESS IS AS GOOD AS MINE. ASH GOT A CALL FROM THE POLICE EARLY THIS MORNING. THEY GOT ASH'S NUMBER FROM HIS PHONE AS THAT WAS THE LAST CALL HE HAD MADE TO TAKE DIRECTIONS TO MY HOUSE.

Dhruv: SO?

Anuradha: I'M ON MY WAY TO THE KHAR POLICE STATION WITH AMAN AND ASH. THE COPS HAVE CALLED US FOR A STATEMENT SINCE WE WERE THE LAST ONES TO SEE HIM.

Dhruv: WHO ELSE IS THERE IN HIS FAMILY?

Anuradha: RAM WAS A BACHELOR AND LIVED ALONE. I THINK HIS PARENTS LIVE IN DELHI.

Dhruv: THAT'S VERY SAD. JUST A FEW HOURS AGO, HE WAS ALIVE AND NOW HE IS NO MORE.

Anuradha: IT IS. FOR ALL HIS QUIRKS, RAM WAS A GOOD MAN.

Dhruv: I AM SURE HE WAS. THE GUY HAD MADE A NAME FOR HIMSELF IN THE INDUSTRY. MAY HIS SOUL REST IN PEACE.

Anuradha: YOU'VE REACHED DELHI?

Dhruv: YEAH, JUST NOW. THE FLIGHT WAS DELAYED.

Anuradha: OKAY, THEN. I'LL LET YOU KNOW WHAT HAPPENS AFTER I AM THROUGH WITH THIS BIT AT THE POLICE STATION.

Dhruv: TAKE CARE AND LET ME KNOW.

Anuradha: I WILL. AMAN KNOWS PEOPLE IN THE POLICE DEPARTMENT. SO, I GUESS IT WON'T TAKE LONG.

Dhruv: THAT'S GOOD.

~

Shalini works on Saturdays, so I take the kids out to Dynasty, a Chinese restaurant in DLF Phase 4 in Gurgaon. Kabir and Siya have grown up, in age as well as in height, and even though they've become quieter, they fight brandishing forks and spoons. I have to intervene a couple of times, pleading with them to be careful lest they end up hurting each other. Kabir loves Chinese food and Siya seldom says no to what her older sibling says. It is just a matter of a few years before they begin to think independently. Hopefully, their love for each other will remain intact. We have placed the order for food and the kids have a go at dim sums as a starter, while I tuck into my bowl of soup. My phone rings, Anuradha's name flashes on it.

'Hey there, how was it?' I ask.

She doesn't reply for a moment, I know she is thinking. I can hear her sniff. 'Anuradha, are you there?' I say instinctively, forgetting who I am with. I glance at the kids. Kabir is looking at me.

'Hello, are you there?' I repeat clearing my throat.

'Where are you, Dhruv?' she asks, her voice a bit shaky. It alarms me.

'Out for lunch with the kids,' I say, putting my spoon down.

'I won't disturb you then. Call me please, as soon as you're free.'

'I can talk. Tell me?'

'No, Dhruv,' she sniffs again. 'I'll wait for your call.'

She disconnects. I'm certain that something isn't right from the way she spoke. I can't wait to get back home and talk to her.

'Who is Anuradha Aunty?' Kabir asks casually, slicing the dim sum with his fork. The kid has his mother's genes.

'Papa's colleague from office,' I say.

~

The moment we get back home and the kids have disappeared into their room, I call her. She answers after a single ring.

'Dhruv, this is crazy,' she says, the shakiness in her voice has doubled.

'What's wrong, Anuradha; what happened at the police station?'

'The police station was fine. It's not about that. I have an email,' she says.

'An email?'

'An email from Ram, sent late last night. After he left my house, the time on the email is 1.20 a.m.'

'So?' I ask.

'Don't you get it? It was sent right before he met with that accident!' Anuradha cries.

'What does it say?' I ask, my heartbeat racing. Anuradha gets worked up a little too soon and I refuse to do that. I have to remind myself that I am no more her boyfriend—just a friend. I have to behave like one.

'I'm sending you a pic of the email. Take a look.'

The image appears on my phone. I zoom in to read. '*Running away from your past is a race you will never win. Everything that you do comes back to you.*' It is sent from Ram's email ID.

I read it again. '*Running away from your past is a race you will never win. Everything that you do comes back to you.*' It's strange that Ram sent this message to her before he met with an accident. What past was he talking about? *What did he know?*

'It's weird. Why would he write this in an email and send it to you? He was drunk of course, but even then, why?' I ask.

'The cops found a bottle of scotch in the car so he was obviously quite drunk,' she says. 'But what past is he talking about, what did he know?'

'That's exactly what I was thinking,' I say. 'Maybe he wanted to send it to someone else and sent it to you by mistake. Some old fling he might have been pissed with.'

'Maybe,' she says after a pause. 'But I do have a past, Dhruv. Could he have known any of that?'

'You mean Sid?' I scoff. 'Oh, come on, no one knows about it except you and I. Sid is long dead and the case is closed. That tape I gave you, where is it?'

'I destroyed it the same day,' she says. 'You said you didn't have a copy and I am certain you never spoke about it to anyone.'

'Never. And you?' I ask.

'You've got to be kidding me!' she says. 'What on earth could his email imply?'

'I am assuming you didn't have anything to do with Ram except for work,' I say tentatively. She has lied to me once, I cannot seem to get that out of my head.

'Fuck. Not even in my dreams!' she says.

I take a deep breath. 'Then for sure this email isn't meant for you but was written for someone else. Look at the words he has used. You get this kind of intellectual insight only when you're smashed out of your wits. What was he doing in Dahisar, anyway?' I ask.

'God knows. He was itching to go for a drive last night, so he might have gone for a spin alone. It seems he walked out of the car in an inebriated state and that's when the trucks hit him. At least that's what the cops were saying,' she says.

'What else did they ask you?'

'Who all were there at the party? How long did it last? Any other important detail that we could think of?' she says.

'So, what did you say?'

'Aman was doing most of the talking. Out of the five people at my party, three of us were there in the police station. We told them about Anna and you, and that you had gone back to Delhi.'

'What else?'

'When they found his body, the cops said he was wearing a black windcheater. He wasn't wearing one at the party. Why would he wear one and walk out on the highway, making it almost impossible for anyone to spot him?' she says.

'People do strange things when they are drunk. They even commit suicide. Wearing a windcheater is just a minor thing. Alcohol is known to bring to the fore your hidden quirks, your worst behaviour and your deepest fears.'

'Wearing a windcheater and stepping out on the highway in the dead of the night can't possibly be either,' she says.

'Who knows, Anuradha? Remember what Ram had said was his worst fear last night during that game? Death was what he feared most.'

'Yes, I do. He had no clue it was coming to him so soon.'

We go silent, taking in the irony behind Ram's statement. 'Okay. So, what do the cops intend to do next?' I ask.

'They have sent his body for post-mortem; his cell phone was found in the car, so they will be checking the records. They will also be looking at the CCTV footage of my building,' she says.

'What's the need to check the CCTV footage?' I ask.

'They just want to make sure, I guess, although they haven't found traces of anybody other than him in his car,' she says.

'Dhruv,' her pitch rises suddenly, in panic, 'that email he sent to me would be there in his outbox too. What if the cops question me about it?'

'If they do, you feign complete ignorance as to what it means,' I say. 'You don't have anything to do with him except for being an employee in his company. Say that you were surprised to get it from him and that perhaps he sent it to you in his state of drunkenness.'

'Yeah, you're right. That would be the right thing to say if they ask me about it. I have been so worked up from the moment I saw that email. Also Sid's mom's call last night; do you think Sid's back?'

'What? No! he was cremated, remember?'

'But . . . his mother said . . .'

'What about it? Arré, she's a woman who's lost her son; she's still in denial and depression. Remember she asked you to be in touch? Maybe she wants to connect with people who knew Sid, to find some solace.'

'Yes, that's what it must've been; and I shouldn't mix up the two issues. Phew, much relieved, Dhruv!'

'I'm glad you're relieved,' I say.

'Thank you and sorry to have pulled you into my paranoia,' she apologizes.

'No problem. You know I'm there.'

'Yes, I do,' she says and then hangs up after saying goodbye.

It is strange, yet heart-warming, the way she confided her innermost fears in me once again, the way she used to do, earlier. What I don't realize then is how much murkier this mess is going to get.

21

Anuradha

I put my cell phone aside after disconnecting Dhruv's call. I feel relieved; so much better than how I had felt after seeing that email in my inbox. I sigh deeply. Despite being something of a pervert, Ram was a solid professional. He was responsible for all the success that had come Grassroot's way in such a limited time. I don't know what will happen now, after his sudden demise. Perhaps the other co-founder, Jay Agnihotri, will start taking an active interest in running the agency. Jay has always been on the sidelines because Ram liked to take centre stage; always keen to run the show. My head is heavy, partly due to last night's drinking and partly because of the overwhelming start to the day. Ash said I had not picked up my phone despite him having called many times in the morning when he heard from the police about Ram's death. He had rung the bell thrice before I got up to answer the door. I glance at the other side of the bed: the pillow isn't where it's supposed to be, adjacent to mine. Strange, I never keep it there. I pick it up and put it back in its place.

Ash calls. He wants to know if he can come over for a coffee. I tell him it would be nice if he came after an hour. More than half the Saturday is already gone, and I haven't even had a shower. It's been a terrible day. First, there was the disastrous news of Ram's accident and then that disturbing email. I am glad to have Dhruv back in my life, albeit merely as a friend. His presence has made all the difference to my mental state. I hope the rest of the day and tomorrow, which is a Sunday, alleviates my anxiety. Monday is going to be a different ball game altogether with Ram not being there any more. I am certain everyone will be pretty anxious about the stance of the management. Anna calls, sounding very apologetic. She admits she had too much to drink last night and is in a state of shock about what happened to Ram. Being my boss, she has worked more closely with him and hence has reason to be more upset. She says she is grateful to Aman, Ash and me for taking the lead and meeting the cops in the morning. I give her a complete lowdown of what happened in the police station, about the post-mortem and tell her that the cops will be looking into Ram's cell phone details and the Cedar Grove CCTV footage. She wants to know why they would want to do that since it was an accident. For closure, I guess, I reply. Anna and Ash were the last ones with Ram at the gate of my apartment. They were the last people to bid him goodbye. Anna says she will call up Ash and Aman as well. We go on to discuss our apprehensions about how Grassroot will run its operations starting Monday and then end our conversation. She has been with the agency since its inception, hence she is more worried about whether the clients will continue to support it with Ram no longer there to run it. His sudden passing away has left everyone stupefied. There is also a shroud of uncertainty that will take a while to clear up.

An hour later, Ash rings my apartment bell, looking sullen and unwashed.

'I hope I am not bothering you,' he says.

'Don't be stupid, Ash, and stop being formal all the time,' I say, grabbing his hand and drawing him into the house.

We are quiet for a while. Ash takes a deep breath and shakes his head. 'It's so frikkin' unreal. Just a few hours ago, Ram was here, sitting with us, confessing that he feared death the most,' he says, gesturing at the chair where Ram had sat. 'And now, he's dead.'

'Yeah, Dhruv said exactly the same thing,' I say instinctively.

Ash glances at me. 'You told him?'

'Of course. He was rattled too, just like all of us. He had reached Delhi.'

'You like him, no?' he asks all of a sudden.

For a moment I don't know what to say. I love him, I want to say but I can't.

'He was my super boss at C&M. He supported me a lot all through my stint there.'

Ash nods slowly, his eyes scanning my face. 'Why did you leave C&M?'

Because the man you are talking about left me with no other option. 'I wanted to be in Mumbai; I had worked long enough in Delhi.'

Ash moves his gaze away; I breathe easy. It's the one relationship I cherish the most and yet I haven't ever been able to talk about it.

'I still can't get over the fact that when I waved at Ram last night it was actually going to be the last time I would see him,' Ash says.

'Yeah. He thought he had forgotten his keys here. He climbed up ten floors to look for them, but couldn't find them.'

Ash nods. 'He must have dropped them around the car and would have found them later when he went back after searching for them in your apartment.'

'He must have. How else could he have gone to Dahisar?' I say.

Ash takes a deep breath. 'We had met him at the gate, then Anna's cab arrived after a few minutes and she left. I came back to my apartment after that.'

I am a bit surprised to hear this. 'I know, Anna told me over the phone. Didn't you meet him again on your way up to the eighth floor? The lifts weren't working yesterday, and Ram was here for just a few minutes, looking for the keys, before heading back down.'

Ash fumbles for words. 'Perhaps I had already reached my apartment by then.'

I am not quite convinced with his reply. 'Some coffee?' I ask, getting up.

'That would be good. I'll give you company while you make it,' he says, following me into the kitchen.

'Let's see what management changes happen on Monday,' Ash says, as I boil the milk and warm up the coffee pot.

'Jay will have to take over, there isn't any other option,' I say.

'Yeah,' Ash nods. 'There isn't. I wonder what's happening with Ram's family. They must be devastated.'

'Hmm . . . the cops told us this morning, didn't they? His parents have been informed and should've reached Mumbai by now,' I say looking at my watch. 'It's almost five in the evening.'

The coffee is ready and we carry the mugs back to the living room and sink into the sofas.

Ash looks around the room. 'Your house is more or less settled.'

'Yeah. The housewarming party made me hurry up and sort my stuff.'

He nods and sips. 'None of us will be able to forget this party for the rest of our lives.'

'That's true.'

'How's Aman doing?' he asks, looking closely at my face.

'I wouldn't know. He went back to his house after we returned from the police station. He said he was cancelling his meetings for the day.'

Ash nods slowly. 'There used be a single girl like you who stayed here earlier.'

'Oh, is that so?'

'Vidya Apte. She was a Miss India runner-up.'

'Wow. I am staying in a celebrity abode then,' I say teasingly.

'She left this house in a huff one day. Something had happened,' he says, his face hardening.

'She must have had her reasons. Why should we be concerned?' I shrug.

'I'm going to find her and ask her what happened,' Ash says.

I raise a quizzical eyebrow. 'And why would you do that?'

'Because I want to know,' he replies, getting up. As he prepares to leave, he looks at me seriously. 'It's important. It's time I did.'

'C'mon, Ash, don't scare me!' I say, as tiredness suddenly washes over me.

'I won't. Ignore me. Forget I said that,' he says, smiling.

I smile too as we say goodbye.

I take a deep breath after he leaves. I know what's bothering him—my growing closeness with Aman. He confessed yesterday that he doesn't like Aman and I know why. Despite my telling him that Aman and I are just friends, he doesn't seem to believe it. Now he's on this ridiculous quest to find out some earth-shattering secrets about Aman's ex-tenant, just to prove that Aman is not quite the man he is made out to be. Happens.

It's 8 p.m., and I am watching the new season of *Narcos* on Netflix, when the doorbell rings. I find Aman at the door with a bottle of wine.

I look at him for a few moments with a serious expression on my face before breaking into a smile. 'You're going to spoil me like this,' I say, inviting him in.

'You got me worried with that look there,' he says stepping inside, smiling warmly at me. 'I will have a scotch though.'

'Sure. The bottle you brought last night is still here. Why did you bring this one?'

'That's fine. I was worried about you and thought, with the kind of day we've had, a glass of wine would be a good idea.'

'You bet,' I say, handing him the bottle of scotch.

I pour myself the wine. 'What a day, huh?' I say. Aman notices the gloom in my voice.

'What had to happen has happened. There's no point revisiting it again and talking about it,' he says, taking a sip.

'You're right,' I say, appreciating his maturity after witnessing the kid in Ash a while ago. 'Let's not talk about it any more.'

'I hope you guys are giving us the new campaign this week,' he says.

'Yeah, we should be able to do that, although I will need to check once with Anna on Monday,' I say.

'Anna called in the afternoon. I couldn't take her call,' he says.

'She told me she'd be calling you,' I say.

'Did you tell Dhruv?' he asks.

I nod. 'Thankfully he had reached Delhi when I told him.'

Aman narrows his eyes at me. 'He's a smart man. You guys are pretty thick, eh?'

'Yes, we are. Dhruv was my super boss at C&M,' I say, wishing he wouldn't ask me any more questions about Dhruv.

He nods slowly, taking a sip. 'Does he have a family?'

'Yeah,' I say, as casually as I can. 'A wife and two kids.'

The living room becomes silent for a while. 'I want to apologize again for getting carried away last night,' he says.

'I've forgotten about it. It would be wise if you do too,' I say.

'Thanks. What happened last night, by the way?' he jokes. We laugh.

'Who was staying here before me?' I ask. I glance at Aman and find him staring back at me, his face expressionless.

'A charming woman, but not as charming as you,' he replies.

'Oh, come on, Aman. I believe she was a Miss India runner-up,' I say.

'Who told you that?' he smiles, pursing his lips. If he's shocked, he doesn't show it.

'Ash was mentioning it,' I reply casually.

'Oh, Ash. Okay,' Aman says and looks away.

~

Aman leaves after a while. I drain my second glass of wine and place it on the table. Aman's glass of scotch also lies on the table, half full, he only took a couple of sips from it. He was trying to lighten things for me because of Ram's death, I know, and then we veered towards the kiss. Perhaps he also wanted to come over and make sure that I was not offended after what happened last night. I am not. Who could get upset with a guy like Aman? He could make any woman go weak in the knees. It's just that I'm not ready for another relationship. If I look at it rationally, a future with Dhruv seems like a bleak possibility because he intends to stick with his wife for the children's sake and, at the moment, we are 'just friends'. Getting into a new relationship seems like a better option, especially if it's with someone like Aman. But I am scared too.

My head feels heavy and I feel dizzy again. Perhaps it's not the wine this time but fatigue and anxiety that seem to have taken a toll. I almost drag my feet to the bed and fall on the mattress. I think about my mom; she always said that I was very naïve as far as my relationships were concerned. 'You need to settle down now,' she tells me every time she calls. As if I don't want to settle down. But I always seem to end up with the wrong kind of men. I wish I was rational in the matters of the heart. So far that hasn't happened. I sigh and drift off.

22

Sid

Look what you did! Turned me into a murderer. Yet again. Just like you. Though, technically speaking, it wasn't I who committed it. It was someone else. My new face arrived, and I couldn't stop myself from wearing it and creating chaos in your life.

I will be watching you all the time. I will make sure that I keep this game of hide-and-seek going. I want to keep switching identities whenever I want to. The first murder was a warm-up. I'm working hard on trading places with this person whose face I now have. Full-time.

It was my first signal: the email that I sent you. To let you know that I'm back. The murder of your boss was just to set the ball rolling. If you thought that I was gone, you were wrong. Now that the first signal has been sent, there will be more, so that you begin to believe that I am not dead. So that you know that the dead can come back. To make you fear every moment that you live.

I want you to start hating yourself. Your life. I want you to live in your own fuckin' hell. I've lived in one, so I know how it feels. You were responsible for sending me there, so you should get a taste of your own bitter medicine as well. No?

That idiot lecherous boss of yours was insignificant to me. I killed him so that you know what I am capable of. I've started taking a keen interest in others around you. Knowing them, little by little. I am decoding each one of them, taking my time, putting my plan in place through them. I am especially curious about that man, Dhruv. You guys seem to have a different connection. I am yet to figure it out fully, but it's different. I will be watching you two very closely. I have made technical arrangements for that already, to know what the bond is that is binding you two.

The end of your story has to be spectacular. I want you to hate yourself for what you did to me. You will.

But by then it will all be too late.

23

Aman called up Anna after entering his house. He looked at his watch. It was half past nine, but he was certain Anna wouldn't mind him calling her at this hour.

'Hey, Aman,' she said.

'Hi, Anna. I hope I'm not disturbing you.'

'Not at all. In fact, I was wondering why you didn't return my call.'

'Sorry, I was tied up. It's been a crazy day. You know . . .'

'I can understand. Ram's accident shocked me out of my wits. I've been feeling terrible since I heard about it,' she sighed.

'It was destined. It can't be undone.'

'I know. Thank you for helping out with the cops today. If one is not familiar with their ways, it can be quite a bother.'

'I know the people who matter in that department. Not to worry, Anna, it's been taken care of. What's happening, otherwise?' he asked.

'Nothing much. I'm alone at home,' she said, dragging out her words.

'Why? No boyfriend to pamper you?'

'Hardly. You don't get my type that easily,' she said.

'Your "type"? Where are they found?' he asked, leading her right where he wanted her.

Anna laughed. 'I confessed yesterday, didn't I?'

'You embarrassed me, although I won't deny I was flattered. I liked it,' he said.

'Did you? Really?' she said, sounding a bit surprised. 'I thought last evening you were gushing all over Anuradha.'

'Oh, come on, Anna. I think you've known me long enough. I was just trying to be nice to her at her housewarming party. You know how I am.'

Anna quipped. 'I know: "AB the charmer". That's what they call you on the page-three circuit, no?'

'Yeah, they do, but I am still looking for my kind of girl.'

'Like me? I am also looking for my kind of guy.'

Aman laughed, he had practised it long enough to make it sound sexy. 'Maybe we should get together one of these days.'

The line worked; Anna was tongue-tied. 'Is that for real? Are you asking me out?'

'Only if you don't mind going out on a date with your client,' he said. He could imagine Anna fist-pumping the air.

'Of course. I would love to,' Anna said, not believing this was happening for real.

'Okay. Let me confirm a date,' he said and then paused, 'one more thing, Anna . . .'

'What?'

'This has to remain our little secret. Not to be leaked outside, not even to Anuradha or Ash.'

'Why would I tell them? No way,' she said firmly. Last night, by this time, she was feeling shitty and miserable and now, within twenty-four hours, she felt right on top of the world.

'Good. I'm not sure about Ash after the way he behaved last night and Anuradha is someone I've got to know only recently,' he said.

'I know. Ash behaved like a total jackass when he said he thought you were deceptive,' she said.

'Yeah,' Aman said. 'I respect his feelings, but why say so for no rhyme or reason?'

'I know why he said that. It's because he thinks Anuradha and you have a thing going on.'

'You've got to be kidding me. Does Ash have a thing for Anuradha?'

'Yes, he likes her, but Ash can be a real kid sometimes. That's why he is hell-bent on getting info about your ex-tenant.'

Good. It had started going his way. Aman had foreseen this. Ash would share more details with someone like Anna than with Anuradha.

'Vidya Apte. Why would he do that?' he asked.

'I don't know. He feels there's a story behind her leaving your apartment.'

'I don't believe this,' Aman said. 'She left because she wanted to. And even if there were a story, how would it help him?'

'He befriended a watchman from your building who gave him some story that she left in a huff because of something that happened between the two of you,' she said hastily.

Aman scoffed. 'Fuckin' cock and bull story! But how does this help him?'

'He thinks by telling this story, he'll be able to prove that you're not what people think you are.'

Aman laughed mildly. 'And what do people think of me? What am I?'

Anna spoke slowly, adding drama to her voice, 'Successful, charming and gracious. The complete package that any woman would desire,' she paused. 'He wants to show you in a bad light, so that Anuradha looks through your façade, and the two of you cease to be an item.'

'Wow,' Aman sniffed. 'Ash's really got time on his hands. Don't you guys give him work at Grassroot?'

'He's a kid, Aman. He'll tire of it soon enough.'

'You bet he will. But such kids mess up things sometimes. I don't want him doing something stupid that may end up spoiling my reputation,' Aman said sombrely.

'Don't you worry,' Anna said. 'I'll be the first one to know about whatever he is doing. I'll keep you informed so you can intervene whenever you want to.'

Aman smiled and looked up at the ceiling. 'Yes, that's a good idea. We need to know what this little kid is up to,' he paused. 'See you soon, Anna. Let me call you tomorrow and fix up a time and place.'

'I'll be waiting!' Anna said in an excited, sing-song voice, before disconnecting the call.

~

The old man listened in on the entire conversation that his son had had with Anna and shook his head. What had caught his attention was the mention of the name of their earlier tenant, Vidya Apte. He had heard Aman say that the girl had vacated of her own will. It wasn't true; something had happened, although the old man had never figured out exactly what it was. Aman was up to something again, he knew that for sure. His thoughts were disturbed by a sudden knock on his bedroom door.

'Sahib, can I leave now?' It was Shiv entering his bedroom.

The old man turned around, glancing at him. 'You haven't gone to your room as yet?'

'No, sahib,' Shiv replied. 'I was waiting for you to retire.' Shiv lived in the servant's room attached to their apartment.

The old man nodded. 'Go to your room and get some rest.'

~

Aman entered his room and switched on the computer. He had some emails to attend to: investor queries, vendor invoices, daily business reports from his cafés and general administrative emails. He spent more than an hour going through each one of them and responding to some of them. After his office work was done, he opened his Facebook account and typed Anuradha's name, whom he had befriended a few days ago. He clicked on her friends list and searched for Dhruv Saxena. He clicked on Dhruv's profile. He looked at the posts Dhruv had put up. Luckily, he had not applied any specific privacy settings to his profile, so all his posts were visible. Aman scanned through them: Dhruv, who used to be pretty active on Facebook earlier, had hardly posted anything over the last one year. He looked at his posts from the previous year, all of them had a common thread. Anuradha had liked most of them, but none after that. What had happened in that one year? It was strange, he thought, and then he remembered what Anuradha had said in that moment when she had resisted his advances: *I was in a relationship that I still can't get over.* Had she been in a relationship with Dhruv? Were they still together? Aman pursed his lips, clicking on Dhruv's photo album. He looked at a few pictures of him with his family. He zoomed in on one of them that had his wife and two kids.

'Pretty wife,' he nodded. Now he knew exactly what to do if he managed to confirm that Dhruv was having an extramarital affair with Anuradha.

Aman looked at his watch, it was past midnight. He switched on the camera in Anuradha's bathroom. The bathroom was pitch dark, she would have conked out by now, courtesy the spiked bottle of wine that she was drinking from. He pulled out the set of keys from his drawer and unlocked the common door in his bedroom that opened into her house. The house was draped in darkness, his prey was sound asleep. He tiptoed across the living room and stopped as he glanced at the table. The half-filled glass of scotch that he had left behind lay there. Aman smiled, picked it up and, in a quick couple of swigs, polished it off.

The alcohol warmed his body instantly and aroused him. Let's get some action, he muttered, rubbing his crotch and entering Anuradha's bedroom.

24

Anuradha

I wake up unusually late on Monday morning. My head feels heavy and I have a throbbing headache. I look at my watch, it's already 9 a.m. What the fuck! I get up with a jerk and look around. Bright yellow sunshine is seeping into the room through the sheer curtains on my window. I get out of my bed and quickly walk to the bathroom. *Horribly fuckin' late*! I exclaim. The day when major management changes are expected, I'm bloody horsing around here. I get out of my clothes in a jiffy and as I am getting under the shower, I catch a whiff of perfume on my body that is not mine. I step away from the shower, smell my bare hands, it's the same faint unfamiliar scent. I lower my face and smell my chest; the same aroma wafts out. I am a bit alarmed now and rub my hands all over my stomach and on my thighs, after which I bring them close to my face and smell them. They smell of the same fragrance. I get under the shower and shut my eyes. It's not even close to any of the perfumes I wear. It smells more like a man's cologne! I wonder how that's possible. The last three days have been rather strange. First, there was Ram's death in that accident; then, I have not been feeling my best: headaches in the morning, waking up much later than my usual time; and now, this odd scent on my body. *Is this for real or is my mind playing tricks on me?* Another really peculiar incident happened yesterday. I woke up in the morning with that irritating headache and went out to the living room to find the glass of scotch that Aman had been drinking from empty. Not a drop in it! I clearly remember the night before, when I had seen it on the table. The glass was half full. Something doesn't feel right here. But whom should I talk to? Dhruv? I shouldn't be doing that because pulling him time and again into my affairs seems very selfish. I hope it is just a useless misgiving and it will soon be proved wrong.

~

We are in the office cafeteria during lunch—Anna, Ash and I. There was a small prayer meeting in office in the morning for Ram. The mood was sombre. The entire agency's top brass was present along with the co-founder, Jay Agnihotri. Jay addressed the team after the prayer meeting, highlighting Ram's achievements and making a solemn promise to the entire team that the company would continue to run at the same pace and with the same vigour as it had under Ram's leadership. I think the entire team was much relieved after listening to Jay. It will take a while to get over Ram's absence, but things should soon fall in line.

Ash takes a deep breath and, looking towards Anna and me, says, 'Jay spoke well. He was forthright in his views and seemed absolutely committed to the Grassroot vision.'

Anna purses her lips tightly, nodding at him. 'I have never seen him give a talk like this. He is usually quite reserved, preferring to be in the background.'

I give a sniff of approval. 'Adversity has the power to bring out the best in people.'

Anna glances at me. 'Well said, sweetie.' She looks relaxed today, more than she has been over the last couple of weeks. The insecurity welling inside her has vanished and she looks much more in control of her emotions. In fact, there is a certain cockiness to her behaviour. We have been gelling together rather well since morning, like the good old days.

'Why don't you guys come for our gig tomorrow?' Ash asks.

Anna smiles. 'Tomorrow? No, honey, I have a date.'

I glance at her. 'That's news, Anna, I thought you were single until last week.'

She laughs animatedly. 'The weekend changed my status, honey. This hot guy came out of nowhere and swept me off my feet.'

'Wow. Lucky you!' I exclaim

'Does this guy have a name?' Ash asks.

'It's a little too early for that. We went out for the first time only yesterday,' she prevaricates.

'Oh, so you've already been on the first date?' I say.

Anna nods. 'Yes, sweetie, and it was awesome.'

Ash looks at her. 'Good that you are off Aman at least.'

Anna smirks. 'Why do you hate him so much?'

'Because he's a sham and I will prove it,' Ash says heatedly.

Anna looks at me and winks. 'He's doing all of this because of you, sweetie.'

'Oh, come on, Ash,' I say laughingly, 'You don't have to go to all that trouble for me!'

Ash looks embarrassed. 'Who says I am doing it for you?'

Anna slaps his shoulder. 'Then for whom? For ACP Pradyuman of CID?'

Both Anna and I break into laughter while a nervous Ash looks on at us. He waits for our mirth to subside before speaking. 'Anuradha, will you come?'

'Okay, I will,' I agree looking at his expectant face.

He looks elated. 'Great. We are performing at Trilogy in Juhu.'

'Cool,' I say. 'We can go to the gig together.'

Ash comes closer. 'There's another reason that excites me about playing there tomorrow.' His eyes jump from my curious face to Anna's like a ping pong ball.

'Vidya Apte also stays in Juhu,' he says.

'What the fuck, Ash!' I groan, shaking my head. 'Get over it, dude!'

Anna looks at him fixedly. 'How the hell do you know this?'

'Simple,' Ash smiles, snapping his fingers. 'I googled her picture, went to Facebook, filtered the search for all Vidya Aptes to get the right one and finally matched her profile pic with the picture I had googled.'

'You're crazy, dude,' I say.

'When we play tomorrow, a number of our followers from Juhu will be there. It will become much easier for me to look for her. I am sure there will be someone we know from Juhu, who would know her, given that she is an ex-Miss India runner-up, no?'

Anna looks at him as if he were a lunatic. 'Are you sure you want to go with him?'

I throw my hands up in the air. 'What do I do now? I've already committed myself.'

Anna's phone rings. She smiles before picking it up. 'Hey there. How have you been?' she coos getting up. Anna walks to a corner in the cafeteria, carrying on an animated conversation.

'It's Anna's mystery man, I think,' Ash quips.

25

Anna's heart jumped when she saw Aman's name flash on the screen of her phone. She took the call and excused herself. 'I couldn't stop thinking about last evening. It was just wonderful,' she gushed. They had gone out to Zodiac Grill at the Taj, followed by a long drive home. Anna had wanted him to come up to her flat and stay for some more time, but Aman had excused himself. His dad gets restless, he had said. She always believed that Aman was the complete package. He was everything that a woman would want her ideal man to be. After yesterday's date, Anna wanted this relationship to work so badly that she decided she wouldn't leave any stone unturned to keep her man by her side. She glanced at Anuradha sitting at a table some distance away: *and this bitch thought she could take Aman away from moi!*

'Well I had a great time, too. Let's do it more often,' Aman said. 'Now, can we talk work?'

She snorted with laughter. 'Well of course, boss. Tell me.'

'How's our campaign going?'

'I was just talking to Ash and Anuradha about it at lunch. I think we will deliver it to you by Thursday, okay?'

There was silence at the other end of the line. 'Where are they? Are they near you?'

'Not at all. They are some distance away,' she reassured him.

'Good. Hope you remember our secret?' he said.

'Of course, I do,' she replied.

'Everything back to normal in office?' he asked.

'Yeah, life is getting back on track for most of us. I went out with you yesterday, Ash is playing a gig tomorrow and Anuradha is going along with him,' she said.

'That's good. Ash must be thrilled to bits that Anuradha is going out with him.'

'Of course. You should have seen his face. Do you know what else he is expecting there?'

'No, I don't.'

'Really, he's such a child! He thinks one of his friends from Juhu will give him a clue about your Vidya Apte,' she said. 'Can you beat that? He actually spent a whole lot of time on the Internet trying to find out where she lived.'

'Man, this guy is really stupid,' Aman said. 'Where is his show in Juhu?'

'Why?' Anna quipped. 'Do you want to go there?'

'You've got to be crazy!'

'Trilogy,' she said.

'I have been to that club,' he said. Aman's mind sped on overdrive. Ash was acting too fast, and Aman didn't want him to reach his destination so soon. He had to be one step ahead of Ash.

'Are we meeting tomorrow? You said you would confirm today, but I've already cancelled my plans for tomorrow, in anticipation,' she said teasingly.

Aman nodded. 'Yes, we will. Where do you want to go?'

'You can come home for a drink and then we can figure it out,' she said.

Aman looked out of his car window. 'Yes, I will. But I'll be a little late, 10–10.30,' he said.

Anna smiled. 'That's cool. I'll wait for you.'

~

Anuradha and Ash were waiting for the elevator in Cedar Grove when Aman called out from behind. Ash had come up from the eighth floor to escort Anuradha along.

'Hey, guys, where are you headed?'

Anuradha turned to him. 'Hi, Aman,' she smiled. 'Ash has a gig and I'm his cheerleader today.'

Aman shook hands with Ash. 'That's awesome. I hope you have a great show.'

Ash pursed his lips tightly. 'Thanks, Aman,' he said pressing the elevator button.

'Where are you playing?' Aman asked.

'Trilogy, Sea Princess in Juhu,' Ash said.

'Wow! That's a hot club!' said Aman.

'Do you want to join us?' Anuradha asked instinctively and glanced at Ash who looked annoyed at her invite.

'No, I'll pass tonight. I have something else to catch up with.'

He turned around to his man Friday, Shiv, who was holding his bag. 'Give it to me, Shiv, I'll take this myself. You had better stay with Dad.'

The elevator arrived and the three of them got in.

'Where are you going at this time, work or pleasure?' Anuradha asked. It was 8.30 p.m.

Aman half-smiled. 'A bit of both actually. You guys have fun.'

~

Trilogy was located in one of the oldest five-star heritage hotels of Mumbai, Sea Princess. Ash and Anuradha took the elevator to the club spread over 5000 square feet overlooking the vast Arabian Sea. The club was dimly lit and being a Tuesday, there weren't many people around. Ash had told Anuradha on their way to the club that their band had a huge following, so crowds were bound to get thicker post 9 p.m. Ash introduced her to his other EDM band members, one of them played the bass guitar while the other, a synthesizer. Ash did vocals and percussion.

Trilogy, the club, looked uber chic. It was dotted with LED pixel cubes that ran across the length and breadth of the floor. The band started playing. The music was pulsating and Ash, along with his band, soon got into the groove. Seeing Ash immersed in music, Anuradha wondered where that petulant and possessive little boy had disappeared. Ash knew the people at the club so, at his behest, she was being looked after rather well; the waiter brought her an exotic vodka-based cocktail and came back twice after to check on her, but she was going slow, lest the next morning a headache came to haunt her again. Ash was right—the crowd had swelled up to more than twice its size within the last forty minutes. She stood at some distance from the stage, leaning against a wall, taking in the vibe and energy. She spotted Ash talking to strangers during breaks, both men and women. She guessed that they were either groupies or people whom Ash knew. He looked at her from time to time, gesturing to ask if everything was okay. She gave him a thumbs-up each time to say that she was fine. She noticed a very attractive girl leaning over the DAW (digital audio workstation) on the stage, talking to Ash animatedly. She watched as one of the other band members stepped forward and nudged Ash to start the performance. Ash ignored him and continued talking to the girl. Anuradha thought this was a little odd, Ash taking so much interest in that girl. Then she remembered Ash's determination to search for Vidya Apte: maybe he was trying to extract information about her from people he knew. Ash took out his phone and started fiddling with its keys, while the girl looked on attentively. They smiled and gave each other a little hug before she disappeared back into the crowd. Ash signalled to his band to start playing. He then climbed down from the stage and almost sprinted towards Anuradha.

'Did you see that girl?' he had to almost shout to be heard above the noise in the club.

She nodded, then reached across to say loudly in his ear, 'Pretty as hell. Your fan?'

'No,' he said. 'Guess who that was?'

She pursed her lips tightly shaking her head. 'Your ex?'

He made an exasperated face. 'Oh, come on! One last guess.'

'Someone who knew that ex-tenant of Aman?' she asked, glancing at the entrance of the club. She spotted the girl, surrounded by her friends, walking out.

'You step out of your door to look for someone and the first person you meet is the very person you were looking for,' Ash said, with a winning smile.

'What does that mean?' Anuradha asked, raising her eyebrows.

Ash flashed his phone screen before Anuradha's eyes, his face flushed with excitement. The screen displayed a number. 'That girl was Vidya Apte. I have her number.'

~

Sid glanced at the frenzied crowd that had been put into a musical trance. He looked at Ash with hatred. How could so many idiots fall for Anuradha? What kind of a pull did she have on them? He had to take action . . . now.

~

Aman bent her over the dining table and looked at her smooth ass. Anna made a tempting figure; her ass thrust upwards, she moaned, pleading Aman to fuck her. He teased her by rubbing her entrance before she begged again. She cried out as he entered deep into her: he felt like an animal, primal and completely wild, and firmly in control of her. He thrust rapidly, as deep as he could, his pace quickening with each movement. He would thrust deep each time and then pull out until just his tip touched her opening and then ram his entire length into her again. Her buttocks quivered and as she moaned, Aman could feel her orgasm building. After she had come, Anna breathed heavily into his chest as they lay in bed together.

'My God, what was that?' she said, clutching her head. Her phone beeped. She looked at the screen once and flung it away.

'Ash! Why the fuck is he calling at this time?' she groaned, looking at the wall clock. It was 1 a.m.

Aman turned to her. 'Maybe it's something important. Answer it.'

She kissed him on the lips. 'Only if you insist.'

Aman could partly overhear Anna's conversation on the phone. Ash sounded terribly excited, however she wanted to wrap up the conversation quickly.

'Ash's show just ended. He and Anuradha are in the car on their way back,' she said curling up next to Aman again.

Aman nodded. 'Why did he call?'

'You won't believe it!' she said, shaking her head. 'Ash bumped into that girl in the club. Your ex-tenant, Vidya Apte,' Anna said looking at him.

'Good for him. Finally, his search ended. Could he talk to her?'

'No, he couldn't,' she said. 'Their meeting happened purely by chance, he said. Vidya happened to be in the club with a group that knew Ash well. When he asked them about her, they got her to meet him.'

Aman took a deep breath. 'Is he satisfied now?'

'Far from it. They've exchanged numbers and he said he'll be meeting up with her shortly.'

Aman stared at the ceiling. He felt his brain cells come alive. What a fucking asshole this guy was proving to be. He had to be dealt with utmost urgency.

Anna got on top of him, biting his lips. 'I don't think you are done as yet. You can finish your unfinished business if you want to,' she said teasingly.

Aman took a deep breath and got up. 'I have to leave. Dad's alone in the house.'

'Okay,' Anna smiled, she didn't protest. It had been a wild evening and she hadn't been able to resist Aman even though it was only their second date. It's better this way, the sooner you bind your man to your bed, the harder it becomes for him to stray, she thought to herself. 'When do I see you next?'

'Very soon. Let me know what Ash is up to. I know Vidya well. I will call her up and tell her not to fall prey to a psycho like him,' he said.

Anna laughed, naked under the sheet. 'I agree, he has lost it completely.'

26

Dhruv

Anuradha calls on Friday, almost a week after we last talked. It's late afternoon and the agency is already in weekend mode with everyone scurrying about in the office to finish off last-minute client deadlines. I'm finishing my last set of emails for the week to be sent to department heads and a couple of clients. In the evening, Shalini and I have to attend her first cousin's wedding in west Delhi. It's quite a distance from Gurgaon and the drive is intimidating.

'How have you been?' she asks.

'Good, and you?'

'You don't call or message unless I initiate a conversation,' she grumbles. 'If that's how it's going to be, why did we reconnect in the first place?' She sounds like she is complaining. I can make out that all is not well with her. I have known her long enough to sense that by the tone of her voice.

'Anuradha, that's so not true. It's just that I don't want to bother you unnecessarily. Both of us had agreed to follow a certain protocol and I don't want to break it.' How do I tell her that not a day goes by when I don't think of her countless times?

'I know, Dhruv. Can't we just talk to each other like friends do? What's the big deal?' she shoots back.

'I am sorry. I'll call you more often. What's wrong . . . you don't sound good?'

I can hear her take a deep breath. 'I'm fine; it's just that our second visit to the Khar police station has left me wondering.'

'Police station? Again?' I ask.

'Yeah, the cops called up Aman and asked him to bring us along. The post-mortem reports have come in.'

'And?'

'According to the reports, besides an awful lot of alcohol in his blood stream, traces of morphine were also found.'

'Morphine? Isn't that used as a recreational drug and for relieving pain?' I say.

'Yeah,' she says.

'So, what did the cops say?' I ask.

'They asked if Ram had a history of drug abuse. So we told them that, even if he did, none of us knew about it. We had never seen him doing drugs even though we had been to a lot of parties with him.'

'It's quite possible that he hid it from everyone or that he consumed them only in private.'

'Possible,' she says. 'The cops also thought so. They said the problem was that his body was so badly mutilated that it made it almost impossible to see any marks.'

'Marks of what?' I ask.

'Marks that would show if someone had injected morphine into his body or something like that. They said thieves use such techniques to rob people.'

'But you said that he wasn't robbed and all his belongings were found intact. Why would someone inject him with morphine and leave him on the highway to die?' I ask.

'Yeah, they had the same question, because Ram was not some random guy who died. That's why they have to look at all possibilities,' she says.

I nod slowly. 'You are probably right. What else?'

'They ran a check on his phone and didn't find anything suspicious,' she says, sounding a little relieved.

'Didn't they ask you about that email?' I ask immediately.

'No, and I am so glad they didn't,' she says. 'They went through the CCTV feed too.'

'What will that have?' I say, shaking my head.

'Cedar Grove has cameras inside both the elevators and one on the ground floor. It can tell who went in or out of the building, and at what time.'

'Did they find anything odd there?'

'Nothing odd; it all happened just the way we had narrated to them in our first visit. They had a couple of questions though,' she paused.

'What questions?'

'Ash had come back a couple of hours later, around 2 a.m., after dropping Anna to the cab, while Aman, who had also ventured out, came back at 3 a.m.'

'Did you know this?'

'No. In fact, I clearly remember Ash telling me the next day that he returned to his apartment right after dropping Anna.'

'Why would he lie to you? Did you ask him after you came out of the police station?' I ask.

'I did. He said he was a bit rattled that day, so he didn't remember.'

'Where did he say he was?' I say.

'Café Coffee Day, Bandstand. He said he was sitting there till 1 a.m., and after that he went for a long walk.'

'Why would one do that after a party?' I am surprised.

'Ram had been really nasty to him after the party and Ash said that he was terribly hurt. Ash is like that. He can be a real kid sometimes; he sulks.'

'And Aman, what about him?'

'He said he went to meet up with one of his investors who was travelling to the US. Aman had agreed to meet him late because he knew he would be attending my party that evening. The meeting lasted for about an hour.'

'Did he mention this to anyone at the party?' I ask.

'No, he didn't; but why would he mention an investor meeting?'

I pause for a moment. 'You are right, why would he? Just because the shit hit the fan next morning, an innocuous thing like this is seeming odd to us.'

'Yes. He offered to get the investor to vouch for the meeting if it helped the investigation. But given his stature and the kind of circumstances Ram's body was found in, the cops didn't deem it necessary.'

'So, what next?' I say.

'I don't know,' she says. 'The cops said they would look further into the reports and call us if required.'

'I hope they get done with the investigation soon,' I say.

'Yeah, I hope the same. As it is, the last few days have been quite odd for me.'

'Why?' I ask.

'I have a persistent headache every morning; I am getting up late almost every day; things are not in their usual place. I really don't know what's going on,' she says, sounding unsure and frustrated.

'Have you consulted a doctor? These look like signs of stress,' I say.

'No, I haven't. I don't think these are signs of stress. They're perhaps an indication that the one who is experiencing them is lonely.'

'Lonely? You have people around you,' I say.

'Dhruv, haven't you heard the phrase, "lonely in a crowd"?'

I keep quiet. What can I say?

She senses my discomfort and continues, 'Anyway, when are you here next?'

'Next week.'

'Are you going to meet me?' she asks.

'Let me see once I am there,' I say.

I wish I could meet you right now, I say to myself, before disconnecting the call.

27

Anuradha

The damn headache is back again. I open my eyes to a bright morning and glance at the wall clock. Late once again! An hour later than my usual wake-up time. Anna had pulled me up a couple of days back. She had said I was taking it a bit too easy and reporting late frequently these days. I get up and look at the other side of the bed. The sheet is dishevelled. Now why would it be like that? I sleep in one position and don't move around in bed. My eyes notice something more and a frisson of fear runs down my spine. I bend down and look at it closely. It is distinct, the other side of the bed clearly shows a depression. My eyes crawl up to the pillow, which has a slight dent in it too. I blink once and look at it closely, feeling it with my hand. It appears as if someone had been lying there, on my bed, right next to me. I stop breathing for a moment.

I can't get it out of my head even at work. Is my mind playing tricks again? How could there be a dent when no one visited me during the weekend except Aman, who was in the house last night only for an hour? We had some wine and then he left. And I clearly remember locking the door behind him. Since the day when he had tried to get intimate with me, he has been extra cautious, staying in the living room the entire time and not moving around in the house at all. I know that the last few days have taken a toll on me and unless I prove to myself that it was a figment of my imagination, I am going to remain jittery. Who should I tell? Or should I see a doctor first as Dhruv had suggested? Anna calls on my extension and asks me to meet her for coffee in the cafeteria.

'Why do you look upset?' she asks, swirling the stirrer in her cup.

I shake my head. 'Nothing much. It's just that the last few days have been a bit weird.'

'Meaning?' she frowns.

'I have not been feeling too well since I moved into the new house,' I say.

She peers at me. 'Isn't Aman taking care of his tenant these days?'

I look at her shaking my head. 'I don't believe you, Anna! Why would he? He's not my boyfriend.'

Anna snorts and smiles smugly. 'I was just joking, honey. Of course, you aren't his girlfriend.'

'Anyway, how is your love life?' I ask, taking a sip.

'Rocking. Loads of fun and sex,' she says like she's bursting with secrets.

We are laughing when Ash comes from behind and pulls up a chair. 'What's happening, ladies?'

'We were discussing Anna's love life,' I say.

'Oh!' Ash nods slowly. 'That sounds quite profound.' We break into laughter again.

'You haven't told us anything yet about the man in your life,' Ash says.

'There is a time for everything, dude. Let the right time come,' Anna says.

'We will wait for your announcement; however, my time to meet Vidya has arrived,' Ash says.

Anna looks at him with raised eyebrows. 'You spoke to her?'

Ash nods. 'Yes, I did. Although I haven't told her why I want to meet her as yet.'

'And she agreed?' I ask.

'I didn't give her an option. I made myself sound desperate, plus her friends are my friends too.'

'You are taking this a bit too far,' Anna says.

'Let me be proved wrong,' Ash considers her. 'Then we'll see who took it far. AB or I.'

'What if none of it is true?' Anna asks. 'And what if Vidya tells Aman about this guy who came to her asking weird questions about him?'

'Ash,' I say cupping his hand. 'This can have serious repercussions at work as well. Just because Aman has been friendly doesn't mean that we can encroach upon his private life.'

Ash raises his hands. 'Girls, no need to get paranoid, please. I will make sure that if I am proven wrong, Vidya doesn't do any such thing. For God's sake, I also need a job and a salary to run my life,' he pauses. 'That said, I am pretty sure I am not wrong. I have done enough of a background check to know that there has been some hanky-panky,' he says, his face sanguine.

Before I can say anything, Anna asks, nodding. 'When are you meeting her?'

'Thursday evening at Infiniti Mall, Andheri. She has a work meeting somewhere around there. She'll meet me after,' he says with a sigh.

'Okay, best wishes with your detective work,' Anna says getting up. 'You guys carry on. I need to make a couple of quick calls.'

'You don't need to do this to prove anything,' I react sharply after Anna has left.

'I don't want to prove anything,' he says.

'Oh really?' I say irately. 'Then why this, Ash? Even if Aman is hiding something, let it be. Why are you concerned?'

'Because that's what he has been doing all his life. Conning girls like . . .' he says heatedly and then checks himself at the last moment.

'I know what you were going to say,' I look at him. Though I am upset with his childish insecurities and obstinate behaviour, I let it pass. 'I don't have any feelings for Aman, haven't I told you that already?'

'Then why does he keep dropping in at your apartment every second day?' he retorts.

'Ash, are you spying on me? What's wrong with you?' I say, then look around quickly. Luckily the cafeteria is almost empty.

He looks chagrined. 'I am not, Anuradha. I came over to ask if you would like to go out for a bite last night, and I saw this man outside your door.'

'So? Can't he come and visit me?' I say.

'If he is just a client and a landlord, he shouldn't be behaving this way.'

'Oh, come on, Ash!' I say throwing my hands in the air. 'He's a good, fun-loving guy. So what if he wants to drop by and have a little chat?'

'I don't think he's a good guy. Like I've been saying, I have a feeling Aman is not what he appears to be,' he says.

'Ash,' I say sternly. He looks up but doesn't meet my eyes. 'I hope you know that I consider you a very special friend. Nothing more than that.'

He nods slowly. 'I know, Anuradha, and I will never stop being one.'

I take a deep breath. 'I am relieved. Now I want your help with something.'

I tell him about my fear and apprehension; things that have been happening to me over the last few days: my headaches, waking up late, the nausea I have been feeling. I also tell him about what I found on the bed this morning. Ash may have a thousand faults, but he has that one thing which is so rare—he can never stop caring for his friends.

'You shouldn't take it lightly. Get a medical check-up done,' he says. He has a look on his face which says he wants to say something, but he is unsure about speaking his mind.

'What? You seem to have something on your mind?' I ask.

He shakes his head. 'Nothing. To clear the other apprehension of yours we can a put a hidden camera in your room for a few days so you can be a hundred per cent sure it is just your delusion.'

Hidden camera? The mere mention of it drags me into my past, a past I detest. Sid comes streaming into my mind along with that strange call from his mother.

'Camera? Wouldn't that be taking things too far?' I say.

'It would help in putting your mind at ease once and for all,' he shrugs.

I think for a few moments before nodding. 'Okay. Will you help me with it?'

'I will. Let's fix it up tomorrow morning. I have a guy who helps me with all my music gizmos. He'll get this done.'

'Thanks, Ash. And promise me, if you don't find anything fishy after meeting Vidya, you will drop this damn thing.'

Ash nods. 'I will. I promise you, Anuradha.'

28

Dhruv

Wednesday, 27 December 2017
Mumbai

It's 8.30 p.m. when I reach Cedar Grove. Despite having made up my mind that this one time I was going to make an excuse and not meet Anuradha, it just took one call from her to break my resolve. The day we had met again and reconnected, I had promised myself that Anuradha and I would just be friends. Nothing more. But from that very day, all my feelings had come gushing back with force. Our emotions and our relationship, both seemed as strong as they ever were—perhaps they never went away but lived on, deep inside us, suppressed, waiting for each of us to set aside the baggage of our individual issues. It scares me sometimes, this resurgence of our feelings, because it can lead us to the point of no return. But I can't resist it either.

I reach the tenth floor and come out of the elevator. I am trying to place her apartment when I see Aman stepping out of his house. He scrutinizes my face for a second before waving out.

'Hey, there. How are you, Dhruv?' he says.

'I am good, Aman. How have you been? Sorry to hear about Ram.'

'Yeah, man,' he says, throwing up his hands in the air. 'It's all destiny, one can't undo it. Meeting Anuradha?' he asks.

I nod. 'I was close by. Just thought of dropping in and saying hi.'

Aman smiles. 'Of course. One should always stay in touch with friends, however busy one might be. By the way, aren't you a family man?' he asks out of the blue.

Why is he suddenly interested in my family? I wonder.

'Yes, I'm married and have two kids. Why?' I say.

'Oh, nothing,' he says, waving his hand casually. 'I thought if they were here, you may want to bring them to our café.'

'They aren't here, but I will remember your invitation.' Inviting me and my family is definitely not his intent; I can make that out from the fake smile plastered on his face.

'Oh, let me ring the bell for you,' he says. 'Is she back from office?' he asks looking at me.

'She probably is,' I say. I want to get rid of him as soon as possible.

The door opens and Anuradha appears. She looks flabbergasted to see me standing behind Aman.

'Hey, Anuradha, don't look so surprised. I am not planning on gate crashing. I just met Dhruv at your door and rang the bell for him,' Aman says.

'That's okay. You can join us if you want,' I cut in.

Anuradha looks at me sharply—I don't think she likes what I just said. Aman glances at her. Perhaps he caught her annoyed look. He purses his lips and smiles.

'Thanks, Dhruv, but I have a meeting to attend.'

He disappears into the elevator.

Anuradha almost pulls me into her house after he has left. 'What if he had actually accepted your offer and stayed?' she says.

'Oh, I thought you liked the guy,' I say cheekily.

What I don't know then is that Aman, instead of going away, has returned to his apartment.

'He is a good guy, but I see enough of him already,' she says, locking the door.

'I said that out of courtesy. He was asking me some weird questions today.'

'Like what?' Anuradha says, gesturing to the couch.

'Nothing,' I say.

'What will you have?' she asks, pointing at the bar, after we have had a light conversation.

'Vodka will be fine. Don't bother, I'll fix it myself,' I say getting up. 'What about you?'

'I would have liked some wine, but it seems to be messing with my head these days.'

'Vodka, then?' I say picking up the bottle.

She nods. 'Okay, I will have a vodka.'

'How was your day? Busy?' she asks, glancing at me, sitting some distance away on a chair. I think about the days when we used to watch TV in her house, sitting close together, her head on my shoulder. I pull away from the thought instantly.

'Don't even ask! After an early morning flight, I've spent the entire day in meetings with Vikas. I am already sleepy,' I say.

'You can take a short nap here if you want,' she offers instinctively.

'No, that's okay. I will survive,' I say.

She smiles. 'How's everything at home?'

I nod. 'All is well. The children are growing up.'

'Good,' she says looking away. I spot a tinge of melancholy in her eyes. 'Does Shalini know that we've met?'

'Yes, she does. She saw a picture from the awards night.'

'What did she say about it?'

'She wasn't very happy, but I told her the truth.'

'And what is that?'

I pause, taking a sip of my drink, 'That we're just friends.'

She sniffs. 'Is she okay with that?'

Come on, Anuradha, is that all you want to talk about? And make me feel even more guilty. Of course, Shalini wouldn't be okay with us being friends, but then why are we discussing this now?

She takes a deep breath before glancing at me. 'I'm sorry for bringing up all this. I've been feeling lonely over the last few days and it's you who gets the brunt of it.'

'It's okay, I understand. How are things at work?'

'We're getting back to normal, but I have been a little unsettled since I moved into this apartment.'

'Unsettled? After coming into this apartment?'

She nods. 'You know how I have been feeling health-wise for the last few days.'

'Have you consulted a doctor?'

'No, I haven't, but something happened beyond that,' she says, eyeing me.

'Like what?'

'I feel I'm not alone here,' she says slowly.

'What is that supposed to mean?' I exclaim.

She tells me how she smelt a man's cologne on her body and the depression on the mattress she discovered one morning.

'It can't be. Who can come here in your absence? As for the smell of a man's cologne, sometimes a mix of perfumes sprayed on the body can leave behind a completely different aroma.'

She looks unconvinced and starts shaking her head even before I've finished talking. 'Dhruv, I know the smell of my perfume, and I never use two different ones.'

I shrug. 'You may have picked it up from outside then.'

'That goddamn smell was on my chest, my stomach and on my thighs. Can you explain how that is possible?' she demands, looking at me.

We fall silent for a while. 'I don't know then,' I say. 'Perhaps it's to do with the body lotion you use?'

She looks at me as if I were stupid. 'Don't you think I'd have checked?'

'So, what do you want to do?' I say.

'I've already done it. It's something I hated doing, but it seemed like the only way to get rid of my doubts.'

'What have you done?'

'Installed a hidden camera behind the mirror of my dressing table in my room,' she says slowly. Hidden camera: the mere mention of it brings back dreadful memories from the past.

A hidden camera created havoc in our lives once.

I shake my head slowly. 'I don't think it will help, except to wipe away the cobwebs of misconception from your mind.'

'I hope that's true because that's all I want. Ash helped me fix it a couple of days ago.'

I glance at her. 'Okay. How is he doing? He looked really pissed with Aman that day.'

'Ash is fine. I went with him to one of his shows the other night,' she says. She is about to say something else, but then stops.

'What? You can tell me if you want to,' I say.

'Ash likes me, but he thinks I like Aman,' she says.

'That was pretty apparent the other day in your party. But is there any truth in it? Aman is an attractive man.'

She punches me lightly on the shoulder. 'You will feel like shit the day it happens.' She is right, I know that deep within.

'Why will I? Aren't we "just friends" now?' I say calmly. 'You have every right to have your own love life if you want to.'

'Dhruv,' she says sharply. 'Leave it, will you? I will have one when I want to but not with Aman and not now at least.'

I stop. 'Okay fine, so what were you saying?'

She sniffs once and looks at me with mock anger. 'You talk about my love life one more time and I will kill you.' She looks so sweet and adorable in that moment that it's a struggle to stop myself from kissing her.

She tells me how much Ash dislikes Aman and all about his attempts to dig out Aman's secrets. At the end of it I find all that Ash is doing quite unbelievable. I mean, it's stupid, the lengths some people can go to simply to prove a point.

'It's incredible that this guy is meeting Aman's ex-tenant just to dig out skeletons from his closet,' I say, after Anuradha is done with her story.

'It really is. And he's doing it despite being aware of the consequences if his search falls flat,' she says. 'He will be meeting that girl, Vidya Apte, tomorrow.'

'It's your charm, can't you see? He can't help himself,' I quip instinctively, realizing that it was a stupid thing to say.

She glances at me with deadpan eyes. 'I wish my charm had worked on someone else. Someone I had really wanted it to work on.' Silence fills the room for a few minutes before she gets up. 'I had better get dinner going.'

I rest my head on the couch, her words resonating in my mind as I drift off to sleep.

'Dhruv,' I hear her voice wafting into my ears, but I don't stir. She calls my name again; I feel her touch on my shoulder. I open my eyes, she is sitting beside me and leaning over me, her face close to mine. I quiver having her that close, her eyes looking into mine, just as they used to. I am pulled back into reality and I unlock my gaze from hers.

'I had dozed off,' I say.

She straightens up. 'I had to call out your name thrice. You were deep asleep.'

'I'll go and wash my face.' I point towards her bedroom, 'the bathroom's that way, right?'

She nods and leads me there, switching on the lights of her bedroom. Only the room has changed, most of the things inside are exactly the same as they were in her flat in Gurgaon.

'The camera is here?' I ask, indicating her dressing table with the full-length mirror. 'Yes. It gets connected via Wi-Fi to my laptop.'

I know how such devices work; I had unearthed one such camera in Lal Tibba myself. I turn on the tap in the bathroom, splash cold water on my face and look into the mirror. Little do I know that Aman watches me at that moment, his face glued to his computer screen. He narrows his eyes at Anuradha's bra and her towel hanging on the bathroom hook, right behind me on the door.

'That will make for a pretty picture,' Aman mutters.

We eat dinner quietly, making small talk. Both of us are still getting used to the ways of handling this new relationship. Her phone beeps.

'It's a Lucknow landline number, his mother's. Should I take the call?' she asks.

'Sid's mother? You must. Hear her out at least,' I say.

She nods. 'How are you, Aunty?' she says, answering the call. They exchange pleasantries briefly. It is the old woman who does most of the talking, with Anuradha answering in monosyllables, initially. Soon, I see her face change colour; she gets up from the chair and walks towards the window, glancing at me intermittently and muttering a few words incoherently, words that I can't make any sense of. After talking for a few more minutes, she begins to panic.

'No, Aunty. This is rubbish,' she says shaking her head. Agitated, I walk up to her. 'I don't believe this. I don't have to come to Lucknow and meet you for this,' she says.

I can hear the old woman saying something.

'You may have seen it with your own eyes, but I'm sorry, I refuse to believe it. I am not falling for this shit,' she says.

I can hear the old woman pleading.

'I am sorry, Aunty. How can someone who is long dead, come back after two years? His body was found, he was proclaimed dead. How is that even possible? You are mistaken,' she says forcefully.

The woman pleads again.

'I hate to refuse again and again, so either we stop talking about it or I will have to end this call.'

Anuradha pauses for a few seconds listening to Sid's mother and speaks after she has finished. 'I haven't heard anything from Sid. He is long gone, Aunty, stop thinking about him and cooking up weird stories of him coming back,' she says.

Sid coming back? What the hell!

The old woman is imploring again. Anuradha shakes her head, glancing at me before taking a deep breath.

'Okay, I will think about it with a clear head,' she says. 'I've to go now; I have guests at home. I'll call you later,' she says before hanging up. 'God! How ridiculous was that?' she says holding her head.

'What was it?' I say.

'I was trying to hear her out initially, but then it was just so much mumbo jumbo that I had to be a little rude. You were right that day when she had called for the first time; the more you give weightage to ridiculous things, the shittier you feel,' she pauses.

'Do you know what she was saying?' she glances at me. 'That Sid is alive. He wasn't dead all this time but hiding out with a ruined face.'

I can feel my heart shudder. 'What the fuck? How can he be alive when his dead body was found?'

'That explanation his mother didn't have. Just said that he turned up a few months ago with a fucked-up face, asking for money.'

'A dead man coming back, asking for money from his mother? And money for what?' I ask.

'It was ridiculous. You know, the first time she called, I was taken aback to hear her say that Sid has come back. I assumed that it was her depression talking and that she wanted to be in touch. But now, it sounds even more like a cock and bull story. She said that he needed money for some kind of a mask. He wanted to get a new face to look like someone else.'

'What does that mean? How could someone fake his death? His body was found, it went to the funeral pyre, and I had found his goddamn phone as well last year. And what is this mask thing? I mean why would one want to change one's identity?' I say.

Anuradha snorts with derision. 'She didn't know why he wanted to look like someone else and said that he is a different person now. She implied that he has turned evil. She feels that he has come here.'

'You mean Mumbai? Why on earth would he do that?' I say instinctively and then glance at her. We are uncomfortable for a moment thinking about what happened in Lal Tibba. Anuradha has a connection with Sid's death that no one knows about, except the two of us. And the dead Sid.

'She herself doesn't know the reason. But she feels that Sid has come here for me. She kept asking me if I knew something that she didn't. I said I didn't,' Anuradha says. She lied to the whole world about Sid's death, but she did it for a reason. Very few assholes in this world can match what Sid did to her.

'This is all bullshit,' I say. 'He is dead. I am sure his mother is making up stories. Maybe due to the shock and prolonged grief, she is losing her mind.'

'She asked if Sid had tried to get in touch with me. Whether I had received a message from him?'

'What message? You haven't received any—' I am halfway through my sentence when she shrieks.

'Dhruv . . . that message from Ram, remember?'

'For heaven's sake, Anuradha, that was sent from Ram's phone and it was not meant for you.'

She calms down a little. 'You're right. It's just that it was eerie. His mother wanted me to come to Lucknow and meet her. She said I could only be convinced in person.'

'Why the fuck would she want that?' I say. This asshole boyfriend of Anuradha's has brought her so much misery, and he still isn't ready to let her go.

'She said that her gut says that Sid wants to harm me. He has come here to do that.'

'Oh, come on, Anuradha. I am sorry but the old lady has lost it completely. Let's for once assume that he is not dead, and that he came here several months ago. Right? So, what was this "man-without-a-face" doing here until now? If he had to harm you, he would have done so already like it happens in those revenge films. He wouldn't be sitting here in Mumbai, twiddling his thumbs all this while. And why the hell would he need some mask to do that?'

'Why are you getting upset with me?' she says, her voice turning raspy. 'I am just repeating whatever his mother told me on the phone.'

'I'm sorry,' I pause. 'It's just that you started the conversation with complete disbelief in whatever his mother was saying, but then started panicking for no rhyme or reason.'

'But there is something we're hiding that no one else in the world knows except the two of us. Besides Sid, who died. And we know it's not a good secret to hide,' she says.

I wrap my arm around her. 'I strongly advise you to ignore her calls now. She is a troubled lady, and her son's death has scrambled her brain. I am certain that she hasn't sought medical help and that's the reason she has perhaps started hallucinating.'

She nods. 'You are right. It's got to do with my head. I'm just not thinking right either these days. I am looking at things in a way that's not meant to be. How can Sid, whom I saw was dead, come back . . . really?'

'You need rest. You should take a vacation,' I say.

'Will you come with me?' she asks instantly. I can't find the right words for an answer.

'Don't worry, I meant as friends. So many people go out these days,' she says.

I stay silent. I glance sideways, the door catches my eye. 'Where does that open?' I ask, gesturing at it.

'Aman's house, I have both the keys to it.'

I nod, not feeling very reassured by her reply, but I let it go. Today is not the day to worry her any more.

'I should be leaving now. I have meetings starting early in the morning and then a dinner with the board of directors in the evening. I take the early morning flight the day after to Delhi.'

'Any plans for New Year's Eve?' she asks.

'Oh, yes. It's this Sunday, no? No, none as yet, and you?'

'I don't know,' she says pursing her lips. 'Where are you staying?'

'Taj, at the airport.'

She nods slowly. 'Thank you for coming over. Meeting you today was the best thing that has happened over the last few days,' she says at the door.

My heart warms instantly. 'You take care and I will see you soon.'

'Yes. I will give you a call on New Year's Day.'

29

Thursday, 28 December 2017
Mumbai

Aman unlocked the door and entered Anuradha's apartment at 2 a.m. He had kept an eye on her flat and knew exactly when Dhruv left her apartment. It had been a little after 11.30 p.m. when he eventually did. He was sure by now that Dhruv and Anuradha were more than friends. They had left many obvious traces on social media. All Aman had to do was connect the dots. He was now certain that they had had an affair, but then something had happened and they had broken off. Their split was perhaps the reason why Anuradha had moved to Mumbai. Aman had no interest in the reason behind the split. All that mattered to him was Anuradha.

How could a girl like her fall for a family man like Dhruv? What did she see in him? She could have the best of men. She could have chosen him, *Aman*, had she wanted to. Then he wouldn't have had to work this hard to follow his obsession. Who does that? Who puts all he has at stake: his goddamn reputation? Who goes through all the trouble of putting a hidden camera to spy on her in the shower? Spikes her wine to drug her so that he could grope her alluring unconscious body to relieve him of his immense sexual stress? It would have been far easier if she had given in and fallen for his charm. He could have then had her without so much planning and struggle. Like Vidya, who ultimately succumbed to his charm. Unfortunately, she stumbled upon his other side. He had to pull all his strings to keep trouble at bay.

Aman tiptoed into the living room. Two glasses stood on the table along with a bottle of vodka and lime juice. The zero-watt bulb on the wall emitted a faint light that barely travelled a few feet. He stood at her bedroom door and glanced at Anuradha lying on the bed with her eyes closed, asleep. Her bare legs shone under a long T-shirt. Good, he leered, things would be easier tonight. He took a couple of steps towards her bedroom, when a thought flashed through his mind. *There were two glasses on the table and a bottle of vodka.* He turned back and walked quietly to the living room again. He picked up the glasses from the table and smelt them one after the other. Fuck, both of them had been drinking vodka last evening, which meant that she was not knocked unconscious with his spiked wine, but was merely sleeping. A tremor of anxiety ran through his body. If he would have touched her it would have meant hara-kiri. What a colossal fucking waste of time, he thought walking back into his house, locking the door behind him.

~

That day in the evening, Aman's car had just entered Cedar Grove, when Anna called. Aman looked at his watch, it was 6 p.m.

'Hey, there. What's happening?'

'I am done with work. Are we meeting up this evening?' Anna asked.

'Yes, we are. I might be a bit late though.'

'That's all right. By the way, Ash has just left the office,' she said.

'He has gone to Infinity Mall, no?' Aman asked.

'Yeah, just as I told you the other day. Vidya's office is somewhere close by,' Anna said.

Aman smiled tightly, his face hardening. 'So, finally, Ash gets to meet his Vidya Apte.'

'I don't think she will have a lot to tell him,' said Anna.

'A guy like Ash is capable of misconstruing even a straightforward narrative,' Aman paused. 'He will spice it up to present a different story to everyone.'

'You mean his own version?'

'Yes, and his version can be diametrically opposite to the truth,' Aman said, getting out of the elevator.

'Why don't you talk to Vidya yourself? You could do that, no?' Anna said.

'Yes, I can, but let's hear his version first,' Aman said, walking into the house. 'What time did you say he was meeting her?'

'7–7.30 p.m. When will you be coming over?'

'After 10 p.m. But give me a call as soon as you know what happened at Ash's meeting.'

'I will be the first one to know for sure. I know you're worried about your reputation. Don't worry; things will fall in place,' Anna said.

'They have to,' Aman said before disconnecting the call. He glanced at Shiv who had kept his bag on the rack.

'I'm going out. You stay here,' he told Shiv and walked out.

~

Ash was ecstatic. He fist-pumped the air after Vidya Apte exited the gates of Infinity Mall. She was indeed one of the most gorgeous, yet grounded, girls he had ever met. You can't become a Miss India runner-up just like that; you've got to have something special. A spark. Vidya surely had that. Ash had met her at Waffle House, a dessert parlour on the second floor of the mall. After a light conversation, Ash had broached the topic that he was there for. She looked shocked when Ash told her that he knew her erstwhile landlord, Aman, had something to do with her leaving his apartment so abruptly. Ash had to spend a lot of time with Ghanshyam, the Cedar Grove guard, to extract this information. He even had to hand him some dough for his favours. Ash knew that they had grown close, Aman and Vidya, and spent a lot of time together. They had been open about their relationship and the guards at Cedar Grove were observant enough to notice that. But then, one fine day, Vidya had just walked out.

Vidya was reluctant to give any information. She bluntly refused at first, unwilling to share anything with the stranger who happened to know some of her friends. But then Ash persisted. He told her that one of his closest friends had moved into the very same apartment where she had lived earlier and that she had fallen for Aman. Ash told Vidya that he did not believe Aman was a clean guy and that she was his only hope to help his friend. Ash promised her that everything she told him would remain confidential and that the only purpose that the information would serve would be to help his friend get away from Aman, if he sought to prey on her. Vidya had relented finally and had poured her heart out to Ash. *How could she not help another woman who was being set up to be wronged by the same man who had once wronged her?* Ash had asked, and the former Miss India runner-up had no option other than to answer.

'"He is a first-rate bastard." That's the first thing Vidya said as she began spilling her secrets,' Ash said, laughing over the phone.

'You met her?' Anna asked.

'Yeah, our meeting only just ended. I told you he is a wolf in sheep's clothing, and I've been proven right.'

'What did she say?'

'I'll give you the gist. The details will be shared later in one of our sessions. You and Anuradha owe me a big one for this,' he said.

'Okay, Ash, get on with your story and stop bragging,' Anna said.

'The day she moved in, she felt AB had a thing for her. He went out of the way to charm her, giving her gifts, inviting her out for dinners and all of that. We all know how charming AB can be.'

'Then?' Anna asked.

'She said it took time for her to warm up to him initially. She felt he was coming on too strong, too soon,' Ash paused. 'But then, soon, his charm started working, like it does on every other girl. A successful, charismatic man and an eligible bachelor like him, I mean, let's face it, he's a dream catch for any woman, isn't he?'

'Yeah, I get that.'

'So, their mutual affection soon turned into a relationship, and they started dating each other. Vidya said that AB came across as generous, fun-loving and mature. She saw a future with him.'

'Then what happened?' Anna asked hastily.

Ash took a deep breath. 'I more or less knew the story till here, but what happened after that was bizarre beyond imagination. It's mighty weird for any sane guy to even think about such a thing.

'One day, when she was in Aman's room, while he was taking a shower, she logged into his computer to check her

Facebook account and while she was doing that she noticed a folder named after her. She clicked on it, thinking it would have her photos clicked by Aman. However, what she found there totally freaked her out.'

'What did it have?' Anna said circumspectly.

'You won't believe it. The folder had naked pictures and videos of her,' Ash said slowly, his voice quivering.

'What? This is bullshit, Ash. How could Aman have naked pictures of her unless she had allowed him to take them? This is absurd!' Anna said.

'It gets even more absurd—the pictures were clicked inside her bathroom. AB had put a hidden camera there.'

Anna flew off the handle. 'That's fuckin' enough, Ash. Even if, for a moment, we assume this to be true, tell me why he would film her in the bathroom given that she was already his girlfriend?'

'Why are you freaking out on me? I am simply telling you what Vidya told me. Take it or leave it,' Ash said. 'She confronted him after he came out of the shower and asked him the same question. She said Aman was shocked to know that Vidya had stumbled upon the truth.'

'What happened next?' Anna asked.

'He didn't have any excuse. He had to admit to what he had done. He said that he had done it before they had started dating, that he was obsessed with her, in love with her and all of that crap. He literally begged her to forgive him. She said she wanted to go to the cops, but AB pleaded with her. He said that dragging in the police would create a mess not only for him, but for her as well.'

'And she let it be then? That doesn't make sense,' Anna scoffed.

'She was smart enough to delete that folder from his hard drive after emailing it to herself so that she had proof. She also took pictures of that folder sitting on his computer and kept them with her along with pictures of that camera hidden in her bathroom.'

'This sounds over the top and unbelievable. It doesn't match up at all with the kind of person Aman is,' Anna said.

'You guys just sit tight. Wait till I get proof from her. That will make you believe me.'

'And what is that proof?'

'The emails that Aman wrote to her pleading forgiveness along with pictures of the hidden camera in her bathroom.'

'Why would someone like Aman, who can get any girl he sets his eyes on, endanger his reputation by putting a hidden camera in a woman's bathroom? It sounds preposterous to me,' Anna said.

Ash shook his head in desperation. 'Why don't you get it? It's got nothing to do with name and fame. The guy is a freak, he has issues. He needs to go and see a shrink.'

'Aman seems like a total gentleman to me. He has been our client for a couple of years, and I have had countless interactions with him. I never felt anything weird. It would have been apparent if he were a pervert,' Anna said.

'Anna, serial killers don't kill everyone they see on the road. Obsessive behaviour is a state of mind that gets triggered by a certain kind of woman, not any goddamn woman.'

'Ha! So, you are comparing Aman to a serial killer now? Well done,' Anna said.

'Who said that? It was just an example,' Ash exclaimed. 'It's just that you're not listening to me. You're behaving as if I'm making it all up.'

'You could be,' Anna paused. 'You like Anuradha, and for her, you just might be making this all up.'

'Fuck it then,' Ash said. 'Let Vidya send me those emails, then we'll talk.'

'Yeah, let's,' Anna said hotly. 'Maybe they will be more convincing than your story.'

'Well, okay, she won't take long. She said she'll send me the emails by tomorrow and then I can show them to my friend.'

'Why are you doing all this, Ash?'

'To unmask the guy. To make my friends believe what I've been saying right from the start.'

Ash disconnected the call and shook his head in frustration before putting his phone in the back pocket of his jeans. Goddammit, why the hell was she not willing to believe his story? Guys like Aman were experts in disguising their dark side. They showed one face to the world outside and kept the other, their real face, hidden: Dr Jekyll and Mr Hyde, same person with a split personality. But he had cracked it finally. After receiving the emails tomorrow, which would prove what he had been saying so far was true, he'd let Anna and Anuradha decide what they thought about Aman. They were his best friends, especially Anuradha, who was more than just a friend to him. He needed to show her the emails to expose Aman's dark side. He didn't want to alarm her now especially because she was already freaking out about the goings-on in her apartment.

~

Anna called Aman as soon as she disconnected Ash's call. She could hear faint sounds of traffic in the background when Aman picked up the phone.

'Hey, are you somewhere outside?'

'Yeah, I'm meeting someone in a short while. Tell me?'

Anna took a deep breath. 'This guy has a serious problem with you, Aman. The kind of stories he is making up are so far-fetched that they can become serious fodder for Bollywood.'

Aman snickered, but his heartbeat quickened and his face hardened. 'What did he have to say?'

He didn't interrupt Anna once or try to put another point of view across, as she repeated her entire conversation with Ash.

'So, what do you have to say?' she said at the end of it.

'What do you think? Would I put a hidden camera in your bathroom?'

Anna laughed softly. 'I would actually allow you to do that kind of kinky stuff. But were you and Vidya really an item?'

Aman cleared his throat. 'We went out a few times like friends do, in groups, nothing more than that. But then I figured she wanted something more than friendship. You know how it works, right?'

'Yeah, with an eligible bachelor like you, I can imagine.'

'Exactly. So, I started avoiding her and that increased her desperation. She ended up hurt and that's why she vacated the apartment.'

'Why didn't you tell me earlier?' Anna asked.

'Vidya is a respectable girl. I didn't want the world to know about what happened between us. I thought, after moving out, she would grow out of her infatuation and the story would end there. However, with all of this now, I think I was wrong. She hasn't moved on as yet, and to compound matters, she has an ally like Ash.'

'What about those emails that Ash claims she is in possession of?' Anna asked.

'I haven't sent any emails to her. Ash must have made up a story about her having them. God forbid, even if she sends any such emails to Ash, they would all be forged.'

'Why don't you call Vidya and tell her to stop behaving like a child and to get on with her life?' Anna said.

'I think I'll have to do that now. I was really hoping that common sense would prevail and she would not meet Ash, but it didn't happen that way.'

'Anyway, let's talk about it when you are here. Around 10 p.m., no?' Anna asked.

'Yes,' he said and disconnected the call.

Bloody. Motherfucking. Asshole. Aman muttered to himself disgustedly. He never thought Vidya would agree to meet Ash. Even if she did, he had thought she wouldn't spill the beans. *The bitch hasn't kept her promise!* he fumed. Every other shred of evidence that she had could be challenged, all the emails, et cetera, but not her nude pictures and the other pictures that she took: the picture of her folder on his computer and the picture of the hidden camera. She had to be stopped before she did anything stupid. He would have to deal with her, but he had someone else to handle before he did that.

30

Sid

I've been waiting for a while now: behind the electric pole, body concealed, gaze fixed, scanning the entry of Infinity Mall. I straighten up the moment Ash steps out of the mall. I watch Ash slip his phone into his back pocket. He crosses the road and walks towards me. I immediately turn away and face the opposite direction, waiting until Ash walks past me. Then I follow him, keeping some distance between us, but not losing sight of him even for a moment. It has to be done today. I can't wait any longer. By the time Ash reaches the crossing, the traffic lights have turned green. This intersection in Andheri West is always extremely busy, even at this hour. They don't call Mumbai the 'city that never sleeps' for nothing.

As Ash waits, a small crowd of pedestrians gathers around him, everyone eager to cross the road as soon as the lights turn red again. Impassive, weary faces, their shoulders slouched under the weight of office bags and purses. I look up at the green flashing signal; forty-four seconds remaining for it to turn red again. I unobtrusively sidle close to Ash who is now within arm's reach. The vehicles zip past on the road, picking up speed as they approach the crossing lest the signal turn red again and they have to halt with idling engines through another interminable wait.

I spot two red BEST buses some distance away, heading to the intersection at high speed. They seem to be racing each other, trying to get to the bus stop on the other side of the junction.

This has to be the moment. I pull out the darning needle from my pocket with one hand, while my other hand creeps into Ash's back pocket and closes around his cell phone. Ash feels something and twists around instantly but, by then, the sharp end of the needle has already penetrated his shirt and pierced his skin. Ash shrieks and lunges forward. At the same instant, the speeding bus comes rushing down the road. Ash's body is flung into the air upon impact with the massive vehicle. By the time it lands on the ground with a huge thud, it has already gone lifeless. The bus driver applies the emergency brakes and the vehicles behind follow suit. Complete pandemonium reigns for a while at that busy crossing in Andheri West with damaged vehicles, incessant honking and a chattering crowd that has gathered around the corpse.

I stand alone on the kerb, at the same spot where Ash had been standing a few moments ago, typing a small message on Ash's phone. I wait for a few moments after sending it, then delete the email from Ash's 'Sent' folder.

I shoulder my way through the crowd and squat near Ash's body, covertly sliding his cell phone under his crumpled leg. I stand up.

'The man is dead,' I say, before making my way out of the large crowd.

31

Friday, 29 December 2017

Dhruv reached the Taj Hotel at the airport a little before 1 a.m. The dinner with the board of directors had gone on way too long and the only thing that Dhruv wanted to do now was to get into bed and catch a few hours of sleep before his flight the next morning. Luckily, he had checked into a hotel that was within the airport premises. A short walk from the reception through a customized passage would take him straight to the airport departure gate. He signed the roster of the cab driver and walked through the well-guarded gates of the hotel after a security check. He had the room key card in his pocket, so he made his way directly towards the elevators through the lobby.

'Dhruv,' he heard someone call out to him. It was her, Anuradha. Dhruv turned around to find her standing there, staring at him unblinkingly, looking distraught. He walked a couple of steps towards her, but by then she was already running towards him. She hugged him hard, crying inconsolably. The duty manager and a couple of hotel executives looked up and moved towards them to help, but Dhruv gestured to them to let it be. They nodded, smiling, and moved back to their desks.

Dhruv led her to a corner table in the coffee shop.

'Ash is dead. Sid has killed him, just like he killed Ram.'

'Ash is dead? What are you fucking saying!' Dhruv was aghast.

'Yes, in an accident. Just like Ram. It can't be a fuckin' coincidence. It's all to get at me Dhruv . . . it's all to get at me . . .' She was shaking badly.

'I don't think so, Anuradha. Calm down, will you!'

'Calm down? Look at this!' She took out her phone from her purse and opened a window, 'Here,' she handed over her phone to him.

Dhruv took her phone in his hands and brought it closer to his face. It was a short email, shocking enough to instil a crippling anxiety inside him.

'If you thought you killed me at Lal Tibba, you were wrong. I am back, Anuradha. And I am coming for you.' Dhruv scrolled up to see the sender's name. It was sent from Ash's email ID.

'It's impossible! How could he get to Ash; and why send these messages? Why not come straight at you?' Dhruv exclaimed, his voice shaky.

'That sadist fucking asshole wants to torture me; that's why.'

'But what about his death? All of that. What was it?' Dhruv said instinctively and paused. 'It's not real, Anuradha. Maybe someone knows about the past and is using him for revenge?'

'Then what should we do? Wait . . . and watch me die in an accident too?'

'Shut up, will you? Okay, what do you want?'

'I want us to believe, for once, that he is not dead. And that he is back for revenge,' she said locking eyes with him.

'Okay. Fine, Anuradha. Let's talk.'

She looked at him, her eyes filling with tears. 'Dhruv, I only came to you for a friendly shoulder to cry on. You don't have to get into this. It's my shit and I can handle it.'

'You know I won't let you handle this alone,' Dhruv replied.

32

Friday, 29 December 2017

They sat in silence at the hotel coffee shop assimilating their thoughts. They couldn't run away from the impending danger any more. Neither knew what to do or what would unfold next. They were not dealing with a challenge thrown at them by a normal man. This was an unbelievably evil man. He had come to haunt their lives. They were pitched against an unseen enemy with little clue as to how to deal with him.

'Out of the six people from my housewarming party the other night, two are already gone.'

It struck Dhruv that she was right. Why hadn't he seen it that way?

'Yeah, you're right. But then, besides me, the other four are the only people you are close to in Mumbai, no?'

'I have only just got to know Aman. There are a couple of other office colleagues whom I am close to.'

'But just think, Anuradha, for the last few days, they were the only people you had been spending time with, isn't it?'

'Yes. That's true. For the last few days . . . so?'

'So that leaves us with two probable scenarios: scenario one is that out of the remaining four, which is you, Anna, Aman and I, any one could get harmed next.'

She gripped his hand instantly. 'What makes you say that?'

'It's the way things have been unfolding. What we are facing here is a hidden enemy. He looks difficult to stop, and we should accept that. And he is targeting people who are close to you. But what if there is a scenario number two?'

Anuradha looked at him questioningly. Dhruv looked up at the hotel ceiling once. 'After your call last night with Sid's mother, I read up about the hyperrealistic silicone masks on the Internet.'

'Meaning?' she said.

Dhruv sniffed. 'His mother had mentioned that Sid had wanted money for a mask. Having searched the Internet, I now know such masks do exist. Perhaps you can't get them locally. But they can be procured from other countries. They look almost real and can even be used to switch identities. Once you put that mask on, it turns you into a different person. Remember those *Mission Impossible* flicks? How often does Tom Cruise use them to change his identity?'

'You mean that shit is real?' Anuradha asked.

'Of course, it is. From realistic Halloween and celebrity masks to the ones these film stars use. Recall that big Bollywood film in which Shahrukh Khan turns into Hrithik Roshan by wearing one?'

'*Don 2*.'

'Yeah. That film. These masks can be any face that you want. It's possible.'

Anuradha sighed. 'This complements Sid's mind: manipulative, hidden, disguised. He can be trusted with indulging in crap like this. So, if he has this mask, what's he been doing with it? Killing people to scare me?'

Dhruv shook his head slowly. 'No. It doesn't seem that random. The way he is sending those emails to you means he is carefully *choosing* these people. To do that he has to be around you. Know these people and the connection they have with you.'

'Stop talking in riddles, Dhruv. As it is my mind is fucked and it can't think.'

'Sid may be hiding behind someone you know. He may be wearing his face to become that person when he wants. He is inside your world, but your eyes can't see him, because he is concealed behind a mask.'

Anuradha fell silent for a while. 'Two of them are dead. They were close to me in a sense. Who is left? Anna, Aman and you.'

Dhruv smiled feebly. 'If I rule myself out, what if Sid is using either Anna or Aman's face?'

'Anna's face? It is highly unlikely that Sid is disguised as a woman. But Aman. I wouldn't be able to tell, but then, that night when Ram was killed, the CCTV footage showed him leaving the house after the party and coming back around 3 a.m. He told the cops that he had gone to the airport to meet a client, remember?'

Dhruv nodded. 'What if it's his face that Sid is using? He could be switching his identity to become Aman whenever he wants. Is there any way we can ensure he isn't Sid in a mask?'

'I can get the CCTV footage from the building . . . I've made some friends.'

'That'll be good; we can look at it when I am in Mumbai next,' Dhruv said. Anuradha looked forlorn. 'With you gone, Dhruv, I feel scared.'

'Don't worry, it's just a matter of a few days before I am back in Mumbai again.'

'I understand. I can't keep dragging you into my shit time and again.'

'After Ash yesterday, I don't think anything will happen soon,' replied Dhruv.

She glanced at Dhruv. 'Either we discover Sid's true identity and stop him,' she paused, 'or, if there is no other alternative, we send him back to hell ourselves. And this time we make sure that he is finally done with.'

Dhruv was pulled out of his maze of thoughts instantly. 'We commit a murder? Is that what you're saying?' Anuradha looked at him; her eyes went blank before her face hardened. 'If it means killing him again so that he can do you no harm, I would do it a million times over.'

33

Dhruv

Friday, 29 December 2017
Gurgaon

By the time I reach my apartment in Gurgaon after being in office the whole day, it is already after 9 p.m. The maid opens the door and greets me. I respond with a tired half-smile. It has been taxing since the *Sid horror* was unleashed on us, and I haven't slept a wink. I wanted to stay on and investigate further but I had a flight to catch. Anuradha was scared to let me go and I don't blame her. But had I not come home, things would have gone out of control here.

I spot Shalini's laptop and her bag on the table. She must be inside the bedroom, I think. I drop my travel bag by the shoe rack, walk into the living room and sink into the couch. I lean back on the headrest. I can hear Shalini's footsteps with my eyes shut.

'How was your trip?' she asks. I open my eyes. She has changed into her nightgown; her face is expressionless and her hair is drawn back into a tight bun.

'It was good. Got back this morning and was in the office all day,' I reply. 'Why don't you sit down?' I gesture towards the couch. Her expressions and demeanour are making me uncomfortable. I know her well enough to sense something is wrong.

'Can you explain this?' she demands. I notice that she is carrying her phone, which she shoves in front of my face. All the sleep from my eyes vanishes in an instant as I see the picture on display. It's of me in Anuradha's house, during my last visit, when she had just awoken me from my slumber. She is sitting next to me, her face close to mine as we laugh together. It's a brain fade moment for me. I am unable to react for a few seconds.

'What were you doing in her house?' I can hear Shalini's words punching my eardrums.

I try to speak, but it's as if words refuse to bail me out. I fumble for them. 'It's not the way it looks at all, Shalini.' At the same time my mind is whirring. *Who the hell sent this?*

'Then tell me what it is, Goddammit?' she says sharply.

'You need to calm down and listen to me.'

'No, Dhruv, I've listened to you enough. Now you need to listen to me.'

'Shalini, please,' I get up and reach for her shoulder. She takes a step back.

'Don't you dare touch me,' she says, her voice shaky.

'You've got to believe me, Shalini. She is only a friend now.'

'This picture, taken inside her house, tells me what kind of a "friend" she is?'

Who sent her this picture? My mind is ticking. It seems to have been taken by a hidden camera in her living room. Who has put it there? It has to be Aman. Or Sid with Aman's face. I remember how annoyed Aman had looked when he saw me at Anuradha's house the other day. Also, that connecting door that opens into her house had made me uncomfortable the moment I saw it. That asshole likes Anuradha! He had said as much at her housewarming party. But how did he reach Shalini? He had asked me that day about her. He could have looked up my social-media profile and got all the information he wanted. Shalini runs a goddamn psychiatric clinic. It's all in the public eye. If Aman has sent her this picture, then there isn't a shadow of doubt that he is a slimy, manipulative bastard. Just like that dead guy who has come alive suddenly. Fucking out of the blue. Fucking Sid. Is Aman the guy we are looking for?

'Where did you get this picture from?' I ask tentatively.

'A well-wisher, with no name, sent an email. Perhaps someone wanted me to know that I am married to a creep, who is a compulsive liar!'

I know I've lied, but this time around I have maintained my distance from Anuradha. I have been trying hard, but Shalini just doesn't seem to believe anything I say when it concerns her. I know I'm wholly to blame for that, but I wish she would believe me just this one time, for heaven's sake!

'Can I see that email?'

'I don't believe this, Dhruv! You only want to know where that email came from? You have nothing to say about what you were doing in her house?' she says shaking her head.

'Anuradha is in deep shit. And for all we know, the guy who has sent you these pictures is behind all of it,' I say hastily.

'Don't keep bullshitting me with your stories, Dhruv. I've heard enough of them.'

I clear my throat. 'You have to believe me, Shalini. For once, please do,' I plead.

She glances at me; her eyes filled with tears. 'I don't know what's going on with you, but I need some time away.'

'Away from what?'

'From you!!' she screams.

'Why Shalini?'

She looks at me, her eyes glistening with tears. 'Whatever it is that's happening with you, it doesn't belong here, in this house.'

I take a step forward, fumbling for words, 'Look I . . . I think if we—'

'There's no more "we", Dhruv. It's you,' she pauses. 'I need you to leave, Dhruv. I want you to go,' Shalini turns around and walks into the bedroom.

I stand transfixed for a while, staring in her direction and wondering at the emptiness she has left behind in the room and inside my being. I pick up my bag from under the table and walk out of my apartment.

I check into a guest house nearby and don't telephone Anuradha purposely. I don't want to tell her that there is a hidden camera in her living room. I want to find out myself and shove it up that bastard's ass.

34

Friday, 29 December 2017
Mumbai

Anuradha was exhausted, both physically as well as emotionally, when she reached her apartment from the hotel. She was in no mood to cook for herself or to order out either. She took a quick shower, for some relief from the accumulated fatigue, and lay down on the bed thinking about all the happenings. What a day it had been! It could have been much worse had Dhruv not been with her. She wasn't sure if he would continue to be with her in this horrendous journey that she had been forced to undertake. But he was never one to shirk what he thought was his responsibility. He chose to walk by her side, like he always had. That's why she loved him and missed him.

She hadn't even found time to mourn Ash's death. Ash, who had been a true friend, ready to do anything for people he cared about. And now he was no more, just like that, in a matter of twenty-four hours. How could fate be so cruel? Ash didn't deserve to die just because he was her friend. What kind of an evil unconscionable psycho was she dealing with? A frisson of fear ran down her spine. But now, what was important was the present and the future, which she had to safeguard. They had to find out where that worthless evil soul was hiding. Behind whose face. She sighed and dozed off for a few hours.

She opened the door when the doorbell rang, thinking it could only be Aman at this hour and she was right. He stood there at the door with a bottle of wine. She smiled tightly.

'Destiny is a cruel bitch,' Aman said.

'Yeah. It was unbelievable hearing about Ash,' she said moving away from the door. He handed over the bottle to her.

'Why do you keep me getting so many gifts? There is no need really.'

'I like doing that for people I care about.'

She glanced at him. Could it be him behind all this? Does Sid *hide* behind his face sometimes? She thought about their conversation at the hotel as she poured the wine into a glass.

'I'll have a vodka today,' he said picking up the bottle. 'What was Ash doing in Andheri, do you know?'

'No, I don't,' she said. It was better to lie than to tell Aman that Ash had been spying on him. 'He was a very good friend; always there for people when they needed him.'

'I am sure he was. He always came across as a good guy. Way too young to die,' Aman said.

Ash hated him and Aman wasn't too fond of him either. Who could have killed Ash? Could Aman have killed him? But would Aman even have the balls to kill Ash even if he detested him? Was he really a killer? Her mind worked in a frenzy. Wait. Vidya was supposed to meet Ash yesterday. Did she tell him something about Aman? Who would know what transpired in their meeting—Anna? Ash was closer to her, maybe he told her what happened in his meeting with Vidya. Anuradha had been so stuck in her own paranoia since yesterday that she'd had no time to think about anything else. Not even Ash's death. How selfish was that? She would check with Anna first thing in the morning, she thought.

'Where have you been since yesterday?' Aman asked. 'I tried your number.'

'I was away at a friend's place. I have been extremely upset since the time I got the news about Ash,' Anuradha said.

Aman nodded. 'I wanted to know if you were all right.'

'Isn't all this goddamn strange, Aman?' Anuradha said, looking at him closely. 'All the people in my circle are dying one after the other. I find it hard to believe that this is a coincidence.'

She could see his jaw muscles tightening. He seemed to have become a bit uncomfortable. Could it be him behind all of this? Then where did that leave Sid? And those emails to her from both their phones? How could Aman know the secret she has been hiding if he were the killer? About Sid. About Lal Tibba. About her murdering Sid. So, mind-fucking it was. All of this. Nevertheless, she decided to stretch the conversation further.

'What else could it be, if not a harrowing coincidence?' Aman said, taking a sip.

Anuradha glanced at him. 'What if someone wanted to make a murder look like an accident?'

'Oh, come on! Why would someone want to kill a harmless musician like Ash?'

'I don't know . . .' Anuradha pursed her lips, shaking her head. 'Maybe he was hiding a secret that could cause problems for someone.'

What the bloody hell! How does she know that? Aman thought. *I hope that asshole didn't blab to her besides Anna before his death.* Aman gave her a sidelong glance, the rim of his glass between his lips, his face partially hidden behind the glass.

Anuradha knew that what she had said had made him deeply uncomfortable.

'What secret could be so deadly that he had to trade his life for it? And what about Ram's accident?' Aman sniffed. 'Both of them couldn't have been carrying the same secret, I guess.'

'Yeah,' Anuradha nodded slowly. 'You may be right.'

Why would Aman murder Ram? No reason. But then where is Sid? Where is he hiding? Does he come out whenever it's convenient? Whenever he spots the right opportunity? How does he commit them? The murders?

Aman bent and gripped her hand tightly. The smell of his cologne was distinct, she had encountered this fragrance earlier somewhere, but where? She was unable to place it. But she knew this smell.

'Listen, I know this sounds really inappropriate at this time, but I suggest you let the police do their job. In the meantime, I suggest you don't stay alone. What are your New Year plans?' Aman asked.

'None, as yet. But I'm sure you have many parties to go to,' Anuradha said.

Aman smiled warmly. 'We can do something together, if you want.'

Anuradha felt dizzy after a glass of wine. She was finding it difficult to keep her eyes open, barely half an hour after Aman left. *Fuck, I had just got up after having slept for several hours straight. Sleepy again? Why?* She picked up the bottle of wine and sniffed it. It seemed okay, nothing odd about the smell; but then, spiked drinks were not supposed to smell any different from the innocuous ones. She couldn't trust anything or anyone now, the situation had turned very grim all of a sudden. She would get a blood test done first thing in the morning tomorrow she thought, before switching off the lights and falling on to the bed. In a matter of seconds, she was as good as dead.

~

Saturday, 30 December 2017
Mumbai/Gurgaon

Aman entered her house at 2 a.m. It had been a few days since he had fondled her body. If just caressing her unconscious stunning body could give him so much sensual pleasure, how wonderful would it be to have her alive and kicking? It would be mesmerizing to go all the way with her. It was getting tougher by the day for him to wait. This New Year's Eve, when the world celebrated, he might find the perfect opportunity. He wouldn't screw it up like last time. Now, with Ash gone, all traces of his obsessive behaviour were gone as well. He smirked to himself before entering Anuradha's bedroom.

~

Dhruv woke up late the next morning in the guest house. It was all quiet at 10 a.m. Guest houses, such as this one, were often chock-a-block over weekdays. As soon as the weekend came around, however, most guests deserted them as they returned to their respective hometowns. Last night, Dhruv had decided to go back to Mumbai for the weekend. He saw no point in remaining cooped up in the guest house and dampening his spirits even further. It was better to be back in Mumbai where his presence was far more valued. Also, he had to solve the mystery behind that picture that had been sent to Shalini and make sure that no more trouble ensued in Anuradha's life. He booked himself on a 3 p.m. flight to Mumbai and decided not to tell Anuradha. He planned to just land up at Cedar Grove. It would be a good surprise and would raise her spirits, he thought. Maybe they could go out for a nice quiet dinner as well.

~

Anuradha had woken up with a splitting headache again, similar to the ones that she had had in the past. The first thing she did was to look for one of those SMSs from pathology labs that flooded her message box. She called up one of them and asked them to collect her blood sample before noon. It was Saturday, but she had some pending work in the office. She looked at her watch, it was past 10 a.m. She thought about telephoning Dhruv and telling him that things were all right. But then he would be with his family now. She resisted her urge to call him and postponed it to a later hour.

~

Sid entered Anuradha's apartment long after she had left for office. He looked at the light bulb on the wall in the living room; the light bulb hid a camera. Sid extracted it from the socket, replacing it with a normal bulb, and then walked into the inner rooms. Sid glanced at the mirror inside her bathroom. Sid knew what had to be done.

35

Dhruv

Saturday, 30 December 2017
Mumbai

By the time I ring the bell at Anuradha's apartment, it's already dark, the evening passing the baton to the penultimate night of the year. Bandra has kicked off celebrations in advance. Most of the houses and bungalows at Bandstand are lit up, ready to welcome the new year with open arms. I take a deep breath and wait for her at the door in anticipation. She would love this little surprise. Shalini hasn't checked on me. I guess being caught out as the culprit once has turned me into a habitual offender in her mind. To her I am someone who lies endlessly, and she isn't prepared to listen to any of my pleas.

For a moment Anuradha is dazed to find me at the door, but then she hugs me instantly. 'Dhruv, I can't believe you're here. Why didn't you tell me you were coming over?' she says, delightedly, before pulling me inside. I wonder at the irony of my situation. While I have been thrown out of one door, another is thrilled to welcome me in.

'Don't ask. It's a long story, but let me get over with something else first,' I say glancing around her living room.

I look at the couch where we were sitting in the picture, and then I visualize the angle from which the picture must have been taken. My gaze travels upwards, above the window in her living room that overlooks the road, and I spot it, sitting discreetly on the wall under a decorative lampshade. Light bulbs have a habit of revealing their innermost secrets to me. I have done this earlier, in Lal Tibba. And what I found in that bulb had shaken the core of my relationship with Anuradha. I ask her for a stepladder. She looks puzzled but then goes inside to get one. I climb up and take the bulb carefully out of its socket. I get off the ladder and examine it closely, there isn't anything odd about it. Unlike the white one in Lal Tibba, this one looks like an ordinary bulb. I shake it once, nothing. I scrutinize the wall, there's nothing there except a socket for the bulb that I am holding in my hand.

'I can't believe this,' I say, shaking my head.

'Are you going to tell me something?' Anuradha asks.

I nod. 'Give me a spare cloth please,' I say. I wrap the bulb carefully in the cloth and smash it on the kitchen counter. I carefully unfold the fabric and find nothing but pieces of glass. I walk out of the kitchen with Anuradha trailing behind me and plonk myself on the couch.

'It's fucking unbelievable, you know?'

She puts her hand gently on my shoulder. 'Dhruv, will you tell me what happened?'

I don't stop until I've poured out the whole story. Her eyes are brimming with tears when I finish. 'It can only be Aman who is behind all of this,' I say.

'Dhruv, he is not some random guy we can accuse just like that. The picture which was sent to Shalini doesn't prove anything.'

I nod. She is right. We can't do anything unless we have some solid proof in our hands. She rubs her temples twice. 'It's terrifying, the way these things are happening around us.'

'We've got to be very careful about everything,' I say.

She looks at me closely, scanning my face. 'You had the option of not being a part of all of this. You had no obligation towards me and yet you risked your marriage for a second time?' she says, the glint of tears still in her eyes.

'I couldn't have left you alone; it was impossible for me to do that. It was unfortunate that Shalini didn't believe me when I told her that you were facing a crisis.'

She looks away, out of the window, into the void. 'No one can understand our relationship but us, Dhruv. Our relationship, in the eyes of others, will always be "a moment of weakness".'

'But it's not that and we know it. My heart beats for you just as it does for Shalini and my kids.'

'The society around us doesn't allow a person to be in love with two people at the same time,' she says. 'And in today's times, loyalty is deemed a greater virtue than love. Your wife will always have to be your first choice.' She smiles tightly, and I can feel her pain. 'You made the wrong choice yesterday.'

Silence returns to fill the room. Both of us struggle with the countless emotions that play inside our minds and weigh down our hearts. She sighs as she rises.

'Why don't you have a drink, Dhruv, while I go and take a shower,' she says.

After Anuradha has disappeared inside her room, I go over to her bar cupboard and fix myself a scotch.

36

Saturday, 30 December 2017
Mumbai

Deep in thought, Anuradha took a long warm shower. She came out and put on a sleeveless V-neck T-shirt over a pair of pyjama shorts. She applied moisturizer until she felt smooth all over and tied her hair back with a hairgrip, before returning to the living room. Dhruv sat on the couch, his head on the headrest, his arms outstretched along the back. His drink sat on the table. Did she walk? Did she run? Perhaps she moved on air. Neither of them knew how she got there, but there she was, sitting in his lap, her legs encircling his hips. Dhruv opened his eyes with a jerk. He looked at her beautiful face, inches away, her lips so close.

'Anuradha, we made a promise,' his lips quivered, longing to break that promise. He thought of Shalini, the promise he had made to her. He had kept his promise, but his wife had refused to believe him.

'Don't say a word, Dhruv. Just forget everything,' she said, touching his lips with her trembling index finger. She inhaled his scent. Her face was burning when she parted her lips to possess his. Dhruv was motionless. He felt her tongue dancing in his mouth, taunting and teasing, laying claim with utmost passion. His heart begun to hammer, his mind turned numb as he twirled his tongue in her mouth. How much had he missed her! Her smell, her lips, her neck. All of her.

His hands claimed her soft rump, then skimmed over her arms, her back and her neck. Her breasts ached; she grabbed his hand and rubbed his palm over her nipples, till moans rose from her throat. When Dhruv attempted to raise her T-shirt, she jerked it over her head and threw it across the room. She wasn't wearing a bra so when his warm mouth opened over her nipples, ripples of unbearable tension shot inside her and she let out a cry of surrender.

'Please take me to bed, Dhruv,' she pleaded, as he suckled her. His head snapped up and he gazed at her, but she pressed her face to his chest. His hands stroked her back tenderly as they walked into her bedroom. He took her hand and stopped by the bed.

'Are you sure you want to do this?' he whispered.

'I don't want you to stop, Dhruv,' she said. She threw herself on the bed. He hunched over her and kissed her naked skin. With every touch of his lips on her skin, arrows of desire struck right between her entrance. He peeled away her shorts slowly and her nerves rioted inside her. Dhruv stopped and looked at her beautiful naked body, even as desire roared inside him with an overwhelming force.

He stripped as she watched him impatiently. He knelt beside her, kissing her from head to toe. As he trailed gentle kisses on her stomach, her hips swayed involuntarily. 'I have missed your touch, Dhruv,' she moaned.

He didn't want to rush it. He kissed her thighs, moving to the inside of them, then slowly upwards till he reached it. He kissed her till she couldn't bear it any more and pulled him up.

'Dhruv,' she moaned. 'I can't . . .'

He nodded and gathered her in his arms and let her feel him all over. She gasped once as she lifted her hips to receive him. He rose above her and stared down into her eyes after he had entered her. 'I love you, Anuradha. I have missed you so much.'

She smiled, pulling him down. He levered himself on his forearms and kissed her eyes, her cheeks, her nose and her neck. She tried to find his lips, but they were busy caressing her chin. Heat seared her body and spasms of electricity ran through her veins as Dhruv began to move slowly and carefully. He thrust slowly at first, then went faster and faster, till they had synchronized their rhythm, his power becoming hers finally.

He increased his pace until her whole being erupted with ecstasy like molten lava, and she let out a cry of pleasure. Then, when their rhythmic movements eventually ceased, he held her close as if he would never let her go. With a powerful shudder, he collapsed in her arms. They lay locked together, his body within hers, entwined. Speechless. Still undone from the sheer magnitude of force that they had just experienced.

After a few minutes, he separated. 'Why did you let it happen?'

'It was the last time, Dhruv. I promise. Never again,' she said.

He rolled over and lay next to her. 'I really hope it is. It will be good if we can keep our friendship intact.'

'After this is over, we can't be friends, Dhruv . . .'

He glanced at her. 'Why would you say that?'

'What's the point of being in a relationship that doesn't make anyone happy?'

'Being friends makes us happy at least. Doesn't it?' Dhruv said.

'It makes us happy only for the few moments that we are together.'

'Isn't that a good enough reason to be friends?' he said.

'No, it isn't. Because neither of us is able to move forward in our life because of this one relationship.'

'I've never stopped you from moving on, Anuradha.'

'I have tried, Dhruv, but as long as I have you in my life—as a friend, or whatever—I just can't seem to do that. You have a family and two wonderful children. I am beginning to have a feeling of tremendous guilt. I feel like I am the one keeping you away from them.'

'Are you suggesting I choose between you and them?' he asked. It was something he had never said, or even thought about, earlier. He never wanted to have to choose, but now that he was backed into a corner, he knew he needed a helping hand. As things stood today, it didn't seem likely that it was going to be Shalini's hand.

'If you had asked me earlier, I would have said that all I ever wanted was you. But not any more. I have created enough bad karma for myself by the choices I have made. No more of it now,' she said. They let the silence talk again for a while.

'Why were you in such a hurry to get married, anyway? Couldn't you have waited for a few years?' she looked up at him.

He smiled. 'It would have been a rather long wait considering the difference in our ages,' he said spontaneously.

She chuckled, slapping his shoulder gently. 'Oh, come on. The difference isn't that much.'

He turned around on the bed to face her. 'But seriously, Anuradha, if you leave me, you will be leaving behind a man who will never be happy.'

She cupped his chin in her hands before drawing him close and kissing him on the lips. 'I can leave you, Dhruv, but I can never stop loving you. We are connected from here,' she said, touching her chest after touching his. 'Aren't we?'

He nodded before they embraced and hugged each other eagerly. Dhruv shut his eyes, a world without her in it was hard to imagine. He fervently hoped, before drifting off to sleep, that what she had just said was in the heat of the moment and would be forgotten by morning.

37

Sunday, 31 December 2017
Mumbai

Dhruv woke up early. Anuradha lay in his arms fast asleep. He gently stroked her forehead, kissed it, and climbed out of the bed quickly, lest he got aroused again at the sight of her naked body. His clothes were strewn all around. He picked them up and put them on before walking into her living room. It was the last day of the year. They could go out for dinner in the evening, he thought, picking up his phone. There were a few WhatsApp messages, one from Shalini, with an attached picture. *Not at this time of the day, please*, he muttered before clicking on it. Like before, this new picture shocked him: it was of him standing in Anuradha's bathroom, staring into the mirror, her clothes hanging behind him from the door hook—her bra and a towel. Shalini had written a message: Busy sorting out your girlfriend's crisis inside her bathroom? Best of luck. He cringed. What a bitch, Shalini! And then it struck him—where had the picture come from? He thought of Aman first.

'I am not going to spare that son of a bitch now!' he muttered angrily, rushing into her bathroom. Dhruv looked at the mirror in fury. He held it and yanked it out with force from the wooden cabinet. The mirror came out with a loud crack and exposed the empty cabinet behind it. Dhruv scanned the empty cabinet: *What the fuck? Where did that picture come from then?*

Anuradha walked into the bathroom wearing a sports bra and a pair of shorts. 'What are you doing here? What happened to the mirror?' she yelped.

'Take a look,' he said handing her his phone.

'Fuck. That's my bathroom,' she exclaimed. She stared at the hollow cabinet and then at the mirror in his hands. 'There was a camera here?'

Dhruv nodded. 'There had to be one here, but now it's gone.'

'Oh my God. This means that someone was watching me whenever I was in the bathroom,' she said, her face panicky.

'Yes, he would have your pictures as well, just like this one. This *someone* can be none other than that bastard, Aman. Who else could have put this here in the tenant's bathroom except the psychotic landlord?' Dhruv said.

Anuradha was shaking her head. 'That asshole Sid loved hidden cameras. But why would he want to look at me naked? And why take your pictures and send them to your wife?'

'I don't know, Anuradha. You may be right. Maybe there are two of them. Aman and this Sid or whoever is posing as him. And neither knows what the other is doing. The pervert next door, Aman, is watching you through this hidden camera, while that Sid is killing off the people you know. Both of them are fucking around with our lives, without our knowledge. But we have to find out the truth now. No more wasting time.'

Suddenly it struck him. 'You have a camera in your room, no?'

She nodded.

'I haven't had the time to look at it though.'

'If someone took this camera away after these pictures were clicked, then he would have been caught on your camera for sure.'

'Yes, he would. There is no way he can get into the bathroom without getting captured on the camera installed by poor Ash.'

Only the Good Die Young

If someone took this camera away after these pictures
were clicked, then he would have been caught on your camera
the same.

Yes, he would. There is no way he can get into the bedroom
without getting captured on the camera installed by poor Ash.

38

They connected the camera in Anuradha's bedroom to her
laptop via Wi-Fi. She glanced nervously at him. Dhruv nodded
and she clicked the button. She played it from the start, the day
Ash had installed it in her room. She thought back to that day
when Ash had come over with a friend to do the installation. He
had been a good friend, and she missed him. They watched the
screen for a few minutes but found nothing except Anuradha
walking in and out of the room a few times. Then the view
of her bedroom turned still, there was no movement for a
few minutes.

'I went to office after that. Nobody was at home,' she said.

Dhruv took a deep breath. 'Yeah, this is from a day
earlier, when I had come over the last time, no?' She nodded.
'Let's fast forward this a little bit. I want to see the footage
of the evening that I had come over,' he said. She pressed the
fast-forward button. 'Let's skip all of this,' Dhruv said, his
eyes firmly on the screen. 'Does the camera have enough
memory?'

'Yes, enough to last a week—at least, that's what Ash said.
It was installed on Tuesday; you had come over on Wednesday.
So, it should have everything till today.'

'Look . . . here I am walking into the room,' Dhruv said looking at the recording from Wednesday evening. The camera showed him entering the room, trailing Anuradha. She gestured at the mirror once, then the bathroom and walked out of the bedroom, after which Dhruv entered the bathroom.

Dhruv took out his phone and enlarged the picture that came from Shalini. 'Do you see it? This was clicked when I was inside.'

She nodded. 'Let's see what happens after this.' A minute later they see Dhruv coming out of the bathroom and walking back to the living room. The screen goes still again.

'Do you remember, Sid's mother had called up that night?' she said.

He nodded. 'Yes, I left after that. What did you do then?' She shook her head slowly, trying to remember.

'Nothing. I went to sleep after a while,' she said pressing the fast-forward button. They could see her coming back inside the bedroom, stifling a yawn before lying down on the bed. Although the lights in the room were switched off, the camera worked on the night-vision mode. It turned motionless again. She pressed the fast-forward button. The images on the screen flickered as they transposed at a much higher speed.

'Wait,' Dhruv said. Anuradha removed her finger from the button. 'Go back, go back.'

She pressed the rewind button for a couple of seconds and then pressed PLAY. Dhruv looked at the screen with rapt attention.

'Stop,' he said. 'Can you see it?'

She pressed the PAUSE button and looked at it closely; she could see a silhouette inside her room. It was the shadow of a man. Her fingers trembled as she pressed PLAY again. The man walked a couple of steps towards her bed, and then suddenly turned to walk out of the bedroom. Those couple of seconds were enough for them to know who that bastard was.

Aman Bhalla.

She was too shocked to say anything for the next few seconds. 'Aman could walk into my house unnoticed? Fuckin', why?' she cried. 'And how could he do that?'

'Through that goddamn door, Anuradha, and you thought you had all the keys to it? But why did he enter the room and then leave suddenly?' Dhruv said.

'I don't give a fig, Dhruv. I want to go to his house right now and break his goddamn face,' she said, trying to get up. Dhruv held her hand.

'We shouldn't be in a hurry. We need to find out what he was here for. Maybe it's Sid wearing Aman's face,' Dhruv said.

'It can't be. How could Sid come through the door that opens from Aman's house without his knowledge?'

Dhruv pursed his lips and nodded. She took a deep breath and pressed the PLAY button again. They looked at the recording for an hour, but nothing happened except her sleeping blissfully on the bed.

'I don't think he came back again,' Dhruv said, gesturing at the fast-forward button. They looked at the next day's recording, going through it in fast-forward mode and finding nothing unusual.

'This was the day Ash died, and I had come to your hotel in the night,' she said, looking at the screen.

Suddenly something struck her, 'The next day, when I had returned from the hotel, this creep had come over with a bottle of wine.'

'Did he? What did you do then?' he asked.

Anuradha inhaled deeply, clasping her hands together. 'I had a glass of wine and, like every time I have had wine over the last few days, I felt very dizzy.' She nodded. 'It's strange, but every time I have had wine from one of the bottles that he has gifted me, I have had this odd woozy feeling.'

Dhruv was alarmed. 'We have to get a test done to confirm if there is anything amiss.'

'I've already done that. I should get the reports this afternoon.'

Dhruv shifted his attention back to the screen. 'Let's see if he does come back again,' he said pressing the fast-forward button. They saw Anuradha entering her bedroom at night, looking tired and a bit tipsy. He pressed the PLAY button, to bring the recording to normal mode.

'Can you see how wobbly I seem?' she said pointing at the screen. Dhruv nodded. Barely a few seconds later, she dropped on to the bed and was fast asleep.

'You're sleeping like a log. Are you sure you only had a glass?' Dhruv said after half an hour.

She nodded before pressing the fast-forward button. But almost immediately she had to switch to normal mode, when they saw Aman entering her bedroom again, in the dead of night. Their hearts pounded out of their chests. What they saw next was something that made their stomachs churn as well. Aman entered the bedroom and sat down beside her, gazing at her unconscious body for a few minutes, before his hands began caressing her stomach, breasts and her thighs.

'Oh my God, Dhruv,' she gripped his hand, her face ashen. 'The motherfucker molested me while I was unconscious!'

Aman bent over her face, kissing her on the lips, sucking on them. Anuradha's nails were tearing Dhruv's skin but he withstood the pain. He wanted to see how low this man could stoop. His entire being singed with fury to see Aman disrobing her, suckling her nipples, one hand travelling down inside her panties, his dirty fingers inside her. Anuradha couldn't watch it any more. She looked away and hugged Dhruv, crying inconsolably, burying her face in his chest. Dhruv was numb. He felt as if someone had sucked the life out of him. The brazenness and ferocity of Aman's sexual assault on the woman he loved was tearing him apart. The only reason that held back that devil from having sex with her unconscious body was perhaps fear. Dhruv paused the recording when Aman left her bedroom after satiating his sexual desires.

He gazed at Anuradha's face, which was wet with tears. 'I am sorry, Anuradha, I really am. I wish I had listened to you when you repeatedly said that you suspected there was something wrong around here,' he said, tears rolling down his own cheeks as well. 'But I am not leaving until I make sure that this bastard is stripped of all he has. I want to see the fucker rot in jail.'

Her tears had stopped, she sniffed. 'He raped an unconscious body, a body as good as dead. Only mentally disturbed people can do such a thing. This freak should be in a mental asylum.'

'Should we call the police now that we have this proof,' he asked, looking at his watch. It was almost ten in the morning.

She shook her head. 'Not yet. Let's first find out how Sid is connected to all of this, if he is. I am not sure this guy who molested me is Sid. The only thing that Sid would want from me is revenge. It isn't any of this.'

'But Sid *is* connected to Aman. I am dead sure about that. Even if the guy we saw in the video is not him. Nevertheless, Aman is also a criminal. Let's stop wasting any more fuckin' time here and go and catch him by his balls for heaven's sake? We should nail one guy at least out of the two,' Dhruv threw his hands up in the air. 'A fuckin' sex maniac who assaults a woman after drugging her; sends emails to someone's wife to set him up; and who knows, perhaps he's the one behind both the murders.'

Anuradha looked at him with deadpan eyes before holding his hand. 'Okay. Even though I feel we are dealing with different people here, let's go to Aman's house.'

39

Sunday, 31 December 2017
Mumbai

Shiv, Aman's flunky, opened the door as Dhruv barged into the house, Anuradha in tow. He scanned the living room, then asked Shiv to fetch his boss. Shiv told them that Aman was out of town and would be back in the evening.

'Give me his number, I want to talk to him right away,' said Dhruv.

'Let's call his father first,' Anuradha said. 'He should know what bastard of a son he has.'

Shiv glanced at them impassively, then disappeared to call Aman's father. Anuradha paced the giant living room. Bright morning sunlight shone in through the ceiling-to-floor windows, yet it did not carry enough cheer to light up their glum hearts. Aman's father walked into the living room after a few minutes. He looked surprised to see them at this hour.

'Didn't Shiv tell you that Aman will be back only in the evening?' he asked.

Anuradha walked up to him, her hands folded at her chest. 'I wanted to tell you something that you should know before I go to the cops.'

His face fell; it was almost as if he were anticipating this. 'Has Aman done something again?'

She nodded and spoke sternly. 'I wish you hadn't fathered such a perverted son of a bitch.'

Grief enveloped the old man's face instantly. Anuradha narrated the entire sordid tale of what Aman had been up to, with Dhruv adding his bit intermittently. Finally, his father spoke, 'He wasn't like this as a child. This side of him emerged only when he was older. He couldn't keep any relationship going. Aman has sinned, and he will have to pay for it,' he looked at them sombrely, with tear-filled eyes. 'I can't give you back what he has taken from you, your dignity and your pride, but I promise you that you will find me by your side when Aman faces the law.'

'We have enough proof. He can't escape public humiliation and punishment now,' Dhruv said.

The old man looked up, tears running down his withered cheeks. 'I warned him so many times after what happened with the last tenant. But he paid me no heed at all.'

'Vidya Apte?' Anuradha asked. 'So what Ash had been saying all along was true. It is sad to see him stand vindicated after he is dead.'

'What?' the old man looked at them, aghast. 'Ash is dead?'

Anuradha nodded.

'Yes, and so is Ram. Both of them.'

'How?' he asked.

'In separate "road accidents" supposedly. However, we think they were premeditated murders,' Dhruv said.

'Ram was that bald gentleman at your get-together the other night?' the old man coughed.

Anuradha nodded. Aman's father looked perplexed; it appeared as if he wanted to say something but was holding back.

'But why would someone kill them?' he asked.

'It's a long story; we'll save it for another day,' Dhruv said coldly. 'The person behind the murders could be your son as well.'

The old man shook his head. 'I don't think so. I know him. He can be an obsessive, lecherous man, but he doesn't have the balls to commit murder. It is only his status and name in the society that makes him come across as a strong, confident man.'

Dhruv glanced at Anuradha. 'Perhaps someone else is behind these murders then.'

'Is someone else also involved in this?' the old man asked.

Dhruv didn't have the patience to talk to Aman's father or to explain Sid's story. He just wanted to take his son head-on and for that Aman had to be there before him. 'How do you want to deal with this? Should we call the cops now?'

The old man took a deep breath. 'It's your wish, you may proceed however you want to. I suggest we wait for a few hours until he comes back from Delhi. I can persuade him to confess to the police and surrender rather than making things even uglier.'

Anuradha glanced at him sharply. 'We are going to be back soon. You had better get your son ready to go and confess to the cops. Otherwise, he will have hell to pay for the kind of evidence we've got.'

~

'Why don't we call the police now?' Dhruv asked, entering her apartment. 'Why do we have to wait until he comes back?'

She locked the door, held both his hands and made him sit down on the couch. 'Dhruv, I was unconscious when he did all of that to my body. I have been treated worse than this by my boyfriend of that time, Sid. You know everything about it, so stop being so insanely mad. I hated it when I saw it for the first time, but what we are dealing with here is something far more sinister. Aman will pay for what he has done, I promise you that. Even if the world conspires to protect him, I will not let him live in peace.'

Dhruv glanced at her determined face, wondering where she drew this strength from. From a vulnerable woman crying on his shoulders, she had turned into a fierce fighter in a matter of minutes because the situation demanded it. She had proved her mettle once in the past, Dhruv knew, and today she wouldn't hesitate, once more, in showing what she was capable of.

Dhruv nodded. 'How do we know where that goddamn Sid is? What is he up to now?'

'He is not someone who will remain in hiding for long before he makes his next move. If he is somewhere around, he will strike again—pretty soon.' Her cell phone beeped. 'It's Anna,' she said before taking the call. Dhruv waited till she finished.

'She wants to meet me,' Anuradha said. 'She wants to talk about something, but she didn't say what it was on the phone.'

Dhruv shrugged his shoulders. 'No point in meeting her right now. Let's nail this bastard first.'

'She wants to talk about Aman; she knows some things about him that we don't. She sounded disturbed, Dhruv, let me go and meet her. I will keep the visit short,' she said.

'Okay. Maybe she knows something we don't know yet. When are you meeting her?'

'In a couple of hours.'

He nodded. 'Where are the keys to this door?' he asked, gesturing to the connecting door to Aman's house.

'In my cupboard, top drawer,' she replied. 'Remember you had asked for the CCTV footage of the building from the night of my party? I got it from the building security, in case you still want to see it,' she said, indicating her laptop.

'Well, okay. I might as well take a look.'

'I'll go and take a shower. We seem to have a long day ahead,' she said.

'A good way to spend New Year's Eve when the entire world is celebrating,' he said.

'I am sorry, Dhruv. You didn't have to do this.'

Dhruv pulled her close and pressed his lips to her forehead. 'In a few hours, after we get Aman, maybe we can also get Sid. Perhaps the two of them are together, working in tandem. Or even if they aren't, we may get some clue that leads to him, I'm pretty sure about that.'

~

Dhruv shut the laptop after watching the CCTV recording and sat staring at the ceiling. 'Did you find anything?' she asked, emerging from the shower.

He inhaled deeply. 'Just what you said, both Aman and Ash went out after your party, and did not return until early the next morning. But I noticed something when I watched it longer, even after they had come back.'

'Longer?'

He nodded. 'From 6 p.m. that evening to 6 a.m. the next morning.'

'So . . . what did you find?'

'Where does this guy live? Aman's flunky?'

'Shiv? He stays in one of the rooms in their house. Why do you ask?'

'He left Cedar Grove around 10 p.m. and came back only in the morning around 6 a.m. Where could he have been all night?'

She shook her head. 'He could have gone anywhere. He has a separate entrance to his room; he could have gone to visit relatives or friends.'

'Did the cops question him?'

'No, why would they? According to them, Ram's death was an accident. So they thought it was enough to focus on all of us who were at the party. There would have been hundreds of people who would have gone in and out of Cedar Grove within that time period. He is a harmless guy, Dhruv, he hardly opens his mouth,' she said as her phone beeped.

The two-minute call left her uneasy. 'It was a call from the laboratory. That bastard drugged me every time he made me drink that spiked wine.'

40

Sid

Sunday, 31 December 2017
Mumbai

Your time has come. No more hiding and no more emails to haunt you any further. Aman's secret is out in the open. And with that, it's time for both of you to make an exit from this story, Dhruv and Anuradha.

The day I saw this man, Dhruv, with you, I knew there was a deeper connection between the two of you. You think you two are fuckin' soulmates, but in my dictionary there's just one word for you: cheaters. He cheated on his family for you, while you cheated on me by throwing me out of that window in Lal Tibba. And then, bitch, you forgot all about me and found solace in this married man's arms. How disgusting is that?

But you see, life has a way of coming full circle. If you thought for a moment that your world had turned all pink and rosy after I was gone, you thought wrong. I survived. I came back to make your life miserable. But, by the time I got here, I already had company. Because by then you had already chosen this lecherous rat, Aman Bhalla, as your landlord. So, besides me, there was another asshole plaguing your life. I didn't mind that. It's only

242

fair that you get what you deserve. You always tend to make the wrong choices. Me, Dhruv and then this playboy son of a bitch. I knew all along what Aman was up to. Because I was always right beside him. At first, I had to manipulate that lowly flunky of his to get all the right information. Shiv was my eyes and ears in Cedar Grove till the time I got my customized face and entered your plush condominium. Just as I had done before, I manipulated Shiv with money and alcohol until then. He was an easy prey and could not withhold his master's secrets. I struck up a conversation with him in a nearby cheap bar and our friendship just soared from that dingy joint. He bared Aman to me; the dark side that he had kept hidden from the world. Free alcohol and money made Shiv forget all the virtues that he had learnt till then—honesty, integrity and all of that shit. I got lucky once again. Shiv and I had a few things in common. We were almost the same height, similar body structure, so replacing him didn't seem very tough. With some keen observation and practice it was possible. I could turn into Shiv. In fact, after spending many hours with him in the bar over the next few days, I was also able to copy his mannerisms and the way he spoke. He was a man of very few words and preferred answering in gestures. So that became easier.

Shiv told me about the hidden cameras that he, along with his boss, had been planting in their ignorant tenants' bathroom. First Vidya Apte and then you. I don't know about the other woman, but you deserved a pervert like Aman. Shiv introduced me to Aman's world. His house, his family, relationships, habits and quirks. He also fed me with all the relevant information about the other characters in my story—Ram, Ash and Anna— to the best possible extent that he could. Rest I decoded, when I received the mask from Italy with Shiv's face on it. And then I became Shiv. This is what I wanted. To be around you, watching you and keeping an eye on all the other characters from the story. That camera in your living room? It was installed by me. Those pictures sent to Dhruv's wife. All my doing. But you were not as stupid as I had thought. You trumped me by putting a camera in your bedroom. I had no fucking clue about that. And that's how you guys trapped Aman and blew his cover. Now with Aman gone, I am left stranded. What will I do without him? Who will I hide behind? This guy, Shiv, is useless alone. I can't be Shiv any more now that Aman Bhalla stands exposed.

I did not want to kill Shiv. But there was no other way of trading places with him. So I had to poison him and dump his body in the forest area of Aarey Colony. A jungle in the middle of a bustling metropolis. Golu Da's cab helped me transport Shiv's body. It didn't worry me, his murder. Because even if the police were to discover Shiv's mutilated body and get my footage from the CCTV cameras in the neighbourhood, who would they see? A Bengali doctor who had long been dead in Lal Tibba. Bankim Da's face had come in handy. It had served its purpose. After getting rid of Shiv, I left the taxi at Golu Da's house and along with it my old identity. Bankim Da's. Then I entered the gates of Cedar Grove as Shiv. It was just a couple of days before your housewarming party. It took me no time at all to replace Shiv in Aman's household. Who cares to scrutinize their household help? The face was the same, and I was smart enough to learn the rest.

And after that those two murders. To scare you and make you suffer. The murders were orchestrated in such a manner that the needle of suspicion pointed towards Aman. But then you put that hidden camera in your bedroom and fucked it all up. Aman's acts are captured on it and this has put an end to my game. It can't go on any further. He will ultimately confess to being a pervert, but never a murderer. He might go behind bars for a while. So where does that leave me? Nowhere. If he hadn't been caught, the next in line was Anna. And then the two of you. But now this story has to be fast-forwarded. Everything has to be done before Aman confesses to his crimes and disappears from the story.

I want to make sure that it ends the way I want it to.

41

Sunday, 31 December 2017
Mumbai

The old man paced the living room in restless circles. His chest was contracted with fear, tears flowed down his cheeks and his head throbbed. His blood pressure was rising by the minute, he felt as if he was having a heart attack. He walked to the giant windows in the room and opened all of them, one after the other. A pleasant afternoon breeze wafted in and comforted him a little. Aman had done it again! Now there wouldn't be any respite: their name, fame and their respect, built over the years, would all go in a matter of a few hours. What a repulsive, perverted, evil creature his son had turned out to be! That girl was right, what he had done to her was unforgivable and he deserved the severest of punishments for it. The old man was helpless for he had seen this coming. He couldn't help his son any longer.

He had telephoned Aman twice; both times he had not answered. He lay on his bed, his body almost shivering by now. *This is what a horrible, unanticipated turn of events can do to your old withered body*, he thought, lying down on the bed. He had seen something through his binoculars the night of the party in their tenant's house.

He had seen Shiv entering the bald man's car. Today, after hearing that Ram was no more, he wanted to ask him what was he doing there that night. Just then Shiv entered his room.

'Where have you been? I have been calling you.'

'Sahib's car had gone for servicing. I had gone along with the driver to pick it up,' he said.

The old man nodded, scanning Shiv's face. 'What were you doing that night in the bald man's car? What was his name?' the old man asked jogging his memory.

'Ram,' Shiv said emotionlessly. 'Aman sahib had sent me to pick up some stuff from the car that his friend had forgotten.'

'But I didn't see you coming out of the car,' the old man said.

Shiv smiled tightly. 'You can ask Aman sahib as soon as he returns. I came up and gave him what he had wanted from the car.'

The old man nodded and closed his eyes.

Sid turned around and came out of the old man's room. He went into Shiv's room and pulled out an injection from among his crumpled stuff in his old suitcase. Morphine. It had to be put to use again. Sid put it in his pocket and entered the old man's room once more.

The sound of footsteps made him open his eyes and he saw Shiv standing by his bed.

'I don't need anything. My whole body is aching. I need to rest,' the old man said.

Sid took out the injection from his pocket. 'This is what you need to get rid of your pain,' Sid said, jabbing the injection into his neck. The old man shrieked. Sid picked up the spare pillow from the bed and held it over the old man's face, pressing down hard. The dose of morphine was strong enough to start working within two to three minutes, then it would become easy for both of them. Aman's father resisted, but Sid knew he wouldn't be able to take it for long: his old limbs and his frail body reeling from the sudden shock of the lethal injection; the pillow over his face cutting off his oxygen supply. It was all too much for the old man. His body turned lifeless soon, and when Sid uncovered his face, his open eyes stared at him blankly.

'Good. You didn't have to live to watch your son die,' Sid said, covering the old man's body with a blanket.

~

Aman Bhalla had to ring the doorbell thrice before Shiv opened the door. 'Where are the maids today?' he said angrily, handing over his bag to Shiv.

'They're on leave, sahib. It's the last day of the year today,' Shiv said, walking behind him.

'Damn, since when have these maids started celebrating New Year?' he muttered. 'Have you had the other car serviced?'

'Yes, sahib.'

'What's Dad doing?'

'He has just gone off to sleep, sahib,' he paused. 'One more thing, sahib. Anuradha madam had come with her friend, Dhruv; she wanted to meet you.'

'So, did you tell her that I would be back this evening?' Aman asked. The news of Dhruv's arrival only irritated him further. *Why the fuck has this man landed here today? He can't seem to keep his hands off my woman.*

'Yes, sahib, I told them. But they wouldn't leave until they had spoken with Bade sahib.'

Why would she insist on seeing his father when he wasn't there? Aman's mind worked at a frantic pace. 'Would you know what they talked about?'

Shiv shook his head. Aman walked into his father's bedroom and looked inside; the old man was asleep, wrapped in his blanket.

'I hope it had nothing to do with the camera in her bathroom?' Aman whispered.

'No, sahib. She won't be able to find it. Ever,' Shiv said.

Aman smiled tightly and walked into his bedroom. He switched on his computer and clicked on the camera button. Nothing happened. He couldn't see Anuradha's bathroom as he usually did. ADD CAMERA—the notification appeared on the screen. He clicked once more; the same notification appeared. What the hell? Maybe there was a problem with the connections. He would have to get the camera connection checked when no one was in her house. Perhaps he could tell Shiv to take care of it tonight after he took Anuradha out. He hoped that Dhruv hadn't decided to stay back to celebrate New Year's Eve.

Aman typed 'gmail' into the search bar. He wanted to send a few personal emails to his friends, wishing them a happy new year. The gmail account opened, but it was not his. Someone else had used his computer and had not signed out before logging off, which was why the account opened automatically. It was a new account. There were only a handful of emails in the inbox, all spam. Aman clicked on the 'Sent' folder and what he saw blew his mind. There were two emails sent to the same person: Shalini Saxena. Aman knew who she was. He clicked on the first one— it had nothing but an attachment, a picture of Anuradha and Dhruv in her living room. What the fuck? What was that picture doing there? He had never seen it before. With a trembling

hand he clicked on the next email. Another picture, but he knew
this one. He had saved it in his folder, it was Dhruv's picture in
Anuradha's bathroom. But who the hell had sent these emails
from his computer? Fuck. He cupped his forehead and checked
the email ID: letmeentertainyou123@gmail.com. No one else
had ever used his computer. His father wouldn't dare to, while
Shiv wasn't literate enough to handle it. He picked up his phone
and telephoned Shiv.

'Did anybody touch my computer while I wasn't here?'
he snarled.

'No one, sahib. Why?'

'Come to my room right now,' Aman said.

Sid took a deep breath. *Your time is up Aman Bhalla*, he said.

~

Aman clicked on the folder titled AD. It had all her pictures,
most of them naked. When he couldn't see her without her
clothes on the camera hidden in her bathroom, these pictures
and videos came to his aid and satisfied his unnatural carnality.
Calmed his mind. He had saved Dhruv's picture in the same
folder; it was there, as he had left it. With his back towards the
door, he heard the sound of Shiv's soft footsteps.

'Yes, sahib,' Shiv said.

'Who the fuck has been fiddling with my computer?' Aman
said, closing his files quickly.

'I did,' Aman heard Shiv's voice, cold as ice, and not from
near the door but right behind him. Before he could turn around,
Aman felt the jagged edge of a knife at his throat and before he
could utter another word his throat had been slit open. Aman fell
to the ground with a thud, along with the chair, blood spurting
from the deep gash on his throat. His bearded bloodied face

looked in horror at his assistant, Shiv; the flunky who had served him for so many years.

'Why did you do this?' he garbled, covered in blood, gasping for breath.

Sid hunkered down and sniggered. 'Me? I didn't do anything. *It was Dhruv who killed you.*'

Sid picked up Aman's phone and left the bedroom, leaving Aman behind to bleed to death.

42

Sunday, 31 December 2017
Mumbai

It had been an hour since Anuradha left to meet Anna in
Santacruz. It was madness out on the streets—she had called
to tell Dhruv this about half an hour ago. She was still on the
way and hadn't reached Santacruz yet. This was no surprise
considering it was New Year's Eve. Dhruv switched on the
television and stared at the flat screen mindlessly, not really
absorbing anything, questions running amok in the maze of his
mind. In a bid to divert his attention, he tried to focus on what
was playing on the television. It was a science fiction show on the
History Channel: *Look beyond what the eyes can see*—the voice-
over said, as the image of the universe unfolded on the screen.

'Look beyond what the eyes can see. Look beyond . . .' he
muttered to himself. A sudden thought flashed in his mind
and he sat up with a jerk. They were going to find out who had
taken away the hidden cameras from her living room and her
bathroom. That was why they had started looking at the footage
from the hidden camera in her bedroom. But then, after seeing
Aman and what he had done, they had forgotten all about their

original intent. It had completely slipped their minds. Fury had taken over their senses and they had rushed to Aman's house.

He switched on Anuradha's laptop. He connected it to the camera in her room and fast-forwarded till they had watched: Aman leaving her bedroom after molesting her. Dhruv started watching from there again: *Look beyond what the eyes can see*, the words resonated in his ears. He kept pressing the fast-forward button until he reached the following morning. It was yesterday's recording. Once again it showed nothing untoward. As long as Anuradha was in the house, it showed images of her entering and exiting the room. The house went still for a while after she left for office. Dhruv looked on until he saw him—unfurling one more possibility of the face behind which Sid was hiding.

Shiv entered her bedroom, a camera dangling from his hand and walked into the bathroom. Dhruv watched the screen unblinkingly until Shiv came out. He had one more camera with him. The mystery behind the two missing cameras that had captured those two pictures was solved finally.

It was Shiv who took the cameras away: the one in her living room and the other in her bathroom. It was he who was Aman's ally in the crime. He or Aman was hiding Sid, or Sid was masquerading as one of them. Dhruv picked up the phone and called Anuradha right away. She didn't answer his call.

I AM WITH ANNA. I'LL CALL YOU BACK ASAP, she messaged.

Dhruv removed the memory card. There was no need for it to be there any more. Everything seemed crystal clear. It had to be either Aman or Shiv.

There was a beep on his phone and he looked at the screen to see Aman's name flash on it. He had taken Aman's number from Anuradha and had stored it on his phone in the morning, because he had wanted to call that sex predator as soon as Shiv told them that he was not in town. He watched the flashing screen. Should he answer the call? Should he go alone or wait for Anuradha so that the entire exercise could be concluded in one shot? Aman disconnected by the time he decided. He must have called because his father would have given him the worst news of his life. He was a sick asshole; he might try to ask for forgiveness or even offer them some obscene amount of money to hide his nefarious deeds from the public glare. Little did he know that whatever he might try to do to prevent the consequences, his life was screwed, Dhruv thought. His phone beeped: it was Aman calling again. Dhruv shook his head, he couldn't go to Aman's house without Anuradha; she had to accompany him. But then what if Aman panics and runs away? Dhruv remembered what his father had said about him, about him being a coward at heart. He had to go and confront him now, even if it meant he had to do it without Anuradha. At least he would keep Aman busy until she arrived. He could force him to accept what a lowly bastard he really was.

Dhruv took a deep breath, stood outside Aman's house and pressed the doorbell. He waited for a response, for the sound of hurried footsteps rushing towards the door, a panicked Aman appearing before him. Nothing happened. He heard nothing. There was complete silence. He pressed the doorbell again and then one more time. It went unheard. He pushed the door tentatively. It was unlocked and creaked open on its own. This was damn strange, Dhruv thought. Had all of them decided to flee? Then why did Aman call him? Dhruv walked through the passage into the living room. It was after 6 p.m. and it had started to turn dark. Dhruv called out Aman's name. Pin drop silence. He called out his name again but got no response. The living room was dimly lit, its large windows left open. The curtains flapped and fluttered in the evening breeze, producing an eerie whistling sound. Dhruv scanned his surroundings; the house looked deserted. *Where the hell is everyone?*

Suddenly he heard the click of a lock—a door being locked. It came from the direction of the main door. He ran back through the passage and reached it swiftly. He tried to yank the door open. It had been locked from the outside. What the fuck was going on? Why would Aman do that? He came back into the living room and walked into another room on his right; the room was dark. Dhruv tried to find a light switch on the wall; but couldn't find one. He walked a couple of steps in the dark, trying to find his way, when his foot caught on something and he stumbled. Dhruv lost his balance. He put out his hands to break his fall, but the floor was slippery and he fell. His hands came away wet. Shit, he muttered, gingerly reaching for the cell phone in his pocket with his wet hands. He switched on its torchlight and pointed its beam towards the ground. He froze! Aman lay dead on the floor, his throat slit open, his head lolling to a side, blood all over his body and on the floor. Dhruv looked at himself. He had fallen into the pool of blood and it was all over him, on his shirt, his hands. He sat frozen for a few moments trying to calm down, then got up slowly.

He walked out and headed towards Aman's father's room. He remembered from where the old man had emerged that morning. There was a big kitchen on his left, he pointed the torchlight's beam at it. Empty. There was another bedroom right opposite the kitchen. He shone the torch's light there. Empty again. He walked a couple of steps ahead; there seemed to be another bedroom on the right. He shone his light into the room. Someone seemed to be sleeping under a blanket. It must be Aman's father, he thought, walking towards him. He shouldn't be bloody sleeping when someone had just killed his son in the other room. Dhruv shook him, trying to wake him. His body felt cold. A frisson of fear ran through his own body as he shook him again, this time with some force. The old man's body turned to face Dhruv, his eyes wide open, lifeless. The old man was dead. Dhruv's phone rang. It was Anuradha. The murderer could be somewhere around. Dhruv's heart missed a beat.

'Hello, Anuradha. Where are you?' he whispered.

He could hear sounds of traffic around her. 'I've just come out after meeting Anna. I'm stuck in traffic. Ash had confided in her after his meeting with Vidya. Aman is a fuckin' psychopath; he had put a camera in Vidya's bathroom too.'

Dhruv interrupted her. 'Listen, Anuradha, stop. We don't have much time. I'm trapped in Aman's house.'

'Trapped? What do you mean, Dhruv?' she shouted. 'Has Aman harmed you? I'll fuckin' kill him.'

'No, no, Anuradha, listen. Calm down,' Dhruv hushed her.

Anuradha wouldn't stop. 'Anna has been sleeping with Aman, she gave him all the information about Ash. Now it's certain that either Aman killed Ash or that maniac, Sid, is wearing Aman's face.'

'No, it can't be. We've been missing something,' he said. 'It was not Aman who committed those murders. It was his flunky, Shiv.'

'How can you say that?' she almost shouted.

'Because Aman is dead. It can only be Shiv who is Sid,' Dhruv whispered. Before he could utter another word, a syringe was thrust into his neck and his head was struck with a baseball bat. Dhruv's cell phone dropped from his hand as his unconscious body fell on to the ground.

43

Sunday, 31 December 2017
Mumbai

Sid sat on the window ledge. The dim light over his head crackled and the breeze that hit the curtains on the windows emitted a low humming sound. When Dhruv opened his eyes, he was crouched on the floor of Aman's living room, his back resting against the couch. He had no clue how he had got there. The last thing he remembered was discovering the corpses of Aman and his father. He remembered receiving a call from Anuradha. *Where was she?* His head hurt like it had been put under the giant wheels of a steamroller; the blow to his head had completely knocked him out; but for how long, he didn't have a clue. Dhruv's neck still burned where the syringe had pierced him. If he could still feel it, it meant that he hadn't blacked out for too long. He felt deadened, his senses struggling to get a handle on the surroundings. He was finding it difficult to keep his eyes open. He looked at his blood smeared body and then it all came flooding back. He remembered slipping and falling into the pool of Aman's blood. He remembered Aman's lifeless body lying there with a gash in the neck. He realized he was holding something. His gaze travelled down to his fingers. It was a knife. Its sharp blade dripping with blood. *What the fuck was that?*

'It's fuckin' ironical, isn't it?' said Sid.

Dhruv looked up in the direction of the voice. That flunky of Aman sat on the window ledge. Shiv.

'What?' Dhruv said with some difficulty.

'After all this time, we get to meet here, like this. Finally,' Sid said.

'What do you mean?' Dhruv said.

'I mean you and I. We get to meet under such circumstances. With all these dead bodies around to give us company. Who do you think I did all this for?' Sid said, spreading his arms, grinning.

'We know that it's you behind that mask, Sid,' Dhruv muttered. 'There's no need to wear someone else's face any more.'

'Ah, you got that? Who told you about this mask thing? You're a smart man, Dhruv, just like that bitch, Anuradha. *My ex,*' Sid sneered.

'Your mother told her. But why did you do this for me? We never knew each other,' Dhruv said.

Sid smirked. 'My mother? She is one stupid woman! Anyway. What makes you think I don't know you? I do, Dhruv. Right from the time that I saw you; first at that hotel and then here at Cedar Grove. I've been studying you. I've watched you every time you stepped inside this building or her house. I thought you were one of her friends. But very soon I figured out it wasn't so. Both of you were connected in a whole different way. I too had my little secret camera inside her living room, no?'

'Yes, I know,' Dhruv nodded slowly. 'You removed it later.'

'Yes, I did. And look at you! You guys had installed a fucking camera too. In her room. I found out about that only when you came over today and told Aman's father about filming Aman when he visited her at nights. I knew if you watched the recording closely you would find me in it, and look . . . that's what you did. That's why I've been waiting here, to welcome you.'

'Is this what you call a welcome?' Dhruv asked.

Sid nodded slowly. 'It's nothing compared to the suffering I've been through, thanks to your fuckin' girlfriend.'

'What else could she have done? You manipulated and tortured her. You left her with no choice.'

'Ah, there you go. No choice, eh? Trying to take my life and kick-starting my endless misery? I have come back to return the favour.'

'What purpose will it serve by making her suffer more? Haven't you done enough already?'

'Enough?' Sid scowled. 'Is killing a few people enough? Do you know what she did to me? Do you want to see it?' He lowered his head, slid both his thumbs under the neck and peeled off the mask. 'What if you were left with a face like this? A face that makes you shudder every time you looked in the mirror,' he said and flung the mask at Dhruv.

Dhruv glanced at him. He looked terrible. Like one of those zombies from a cheap horror movie. 'You've taken your revenge. Haven't you done enough, Sid? Killing innocent people. Why did you kill them? They had nothing to do with any of this!'

Sid sniggered. 'As if I cared a fuck about their lives. I wanted that bitch to live in fear, every single moment of her life. Her life to become a fucking hell. A replica of my life. That's what I wanted it to be. I had to kill all those sons of bitches, who were close to her, to make her suffer. Ram and Ash, their lives served me no purpose; but their deaths did. I instilled fear in her heart by killing them. Didn't I do well?' he asked, grinning maniacally.

'I didn't want to kill the old man, though. His death was of no use to me. But then he saw me that night, getting into Ram's car. That night, I flicked his car keys when I dropped in at the party for a few minutes along with the old man. He might have told his son or the police, and that would have meant disaster. I couldn't afford to change another identity. You don't get meek idiots like Shiv so easily,' Sid said.

'And Aman?' Dhruv said.

'You of all people shouldn't be worried about that asshole after what he did to your girlfriend. As far as I'm concerned, I had no other option. Where would I go if Aman was caught? What would I do next? Nothing. Aman was my window into her world. I couldn't have done shit if that window was shut. So that's the reason I had to fast-track all of it. That's why you're here tonight.'

Dhruv struggled to get up but fell down, slumping against the couch, his legs weak.

Sid's smile broadened. 'I've put plenty of morphine inside you. It won't let you do anything more than stay conscious for the next fifteen or twenty minutes. So it will be good if you stay put and don't try any more stunts.'

Dhruv nodded. 'And that's why you killed Ash as well. Same reason. Right?'

'In a way yes. That silly little boy had also come in the way of executing my plan. He had discovered the truth about Aman Bhalla, and I knew what Ash knew about Aman. I was always with him—when his girlfriend, Anna, would call him: in the car, in the house, in the elevator. Everywhere. Aman had this useful habit of repeating important things during his conversations. Besides, I am smart. I am able to anticipate things, so I knew exactly what Ash was up to. He was determined to expose

Aman, and I couldn't let him do that. I had to stop Ash for two reasons: first, to scare the shit out of that bitch; and second, to make sure that Aman's reality was not exposed until I was done with my plan. Aman was my shield. But you guys blew it away by planting that camera in her bedroom. You discovered his dark side. But it's okay. It has panned out pretty well even then. My plan.'

'What plan are you talking about?' Dhruv slurred, the morphine seemed to be working in overdrive.

There was some noise to his right. He could hear the creaking sound of a door opening. It was the same goddamn door that connected both the apartments.

'It seems that the lady both of us have been waiting for is finally here,' Sid sniggered, picking up the baseball bat in his hand.

'Don't hurt her. Seriously, don't,' Dhruv pleaded. From the corner of his eye he saw Anuradha entering the room. She glanced at Dhruv. Her face paled with horror at the sight of him covered in blood, holding a knife in his hand. Then Sid, hiding behind the door, hit her on her right foot with the bat, and before she could take another step, she slumped to the ground, crying with pain.

'Shut up, will you? It's all thanks to you that I look like this. So no need to panic.' Sid held the wooden bat over her head as she lay on the ground. Before she knew what was happening, he pierced her right thigh with an injection held in his other hand. She screamed again, in pain. Sid kept the bat poised in the same position, over her head.

'I didn't intend to meet you like this, sweetheart, but what to do, you left me with no choice. Stay right where you are. Two minutes and the morphine will start to work,' Sid said, grinding his teeth, keeping the bat over her head.

Two minutes passed. He looked at his watch and waving his bat walked back a couple of steps to perch on the windowsill again.

'I hope you don't make me swing this bat once again. Yes, what was your question again, the plan, eh? Well my plan is simple, you need to make a choice, Dhruv. And you have two options to choose from.'

'Why would he do that, asshole?' Anuradha muttered, still in pain.

Sid clapped sarcastically. 'Just look at you! Not one bit excited to see your ex-boyfriend again. No warm welcome for me, huh? You stand at the door of death, yet all you can think about is him? I wish you had shown such concern when you pushed me out of that window. You wouldn't be facing all of this, bitch!'

'You're a slimy bastard, Sid, and that's why I had to do that. I had no option,' she said, crouching down; balancing her body on the floor with her left hand, she held her right injured leg with the other.

Sid pursed his lips, clasping his hands together. 'Oh, my dear! My innocent little girl. So, you have a licence to kill slime-balls, right? Now without wasting any more time, let us come to the options.'

'What are they?' Dhruv asked.

'Make a choice,' Sid said, glaring at him. 'It won't be hard. That knife you are holding is the one with which I slit Aman's throat. It has your fingerprints all over it; his blood is on your clothes. So, for the world out there it's you who killed Aman.'

'What motive does he have to kill him?' Anuradha howled.

Sid smiled menacingly. 'He has every goddamn reason to kill him. Aman was secretly filming his girlfriend, he was drugging and molesting her. He was also sending emails to

Dhruv's wife, sharing pictures of you two lovebirds. There cán't be a better motive than this. Don't you see? However, I do have a confession to make: the emails from his computer were sent by yours truly.'

'Fuckin' asshole,' Anuradha muttered.

'But that's not true, I didn't kill him,' Dhruv exclaimed.

'Yes, you didn't. But you will have to take the blame. Say that you did it,' Sid said.

'But, why should I? My life would be destroyed if I do so,' Dhruv said, struggling with the words.

'That's exactly what I want,' Sid chuckled, clapping his hands. 'I want it to be hell, like hers. A punishment for loving her. That's the whole fuckin' plan!'

'Dhruv won't do it,' Anuradha said.

Sid raised the baseball bat again. 'Then let me do the simplest thing. The one I could have always done. I will kill her right here, right now.'

'No, wait,' Dhruv said. 'Sid, don't do anything to her. What is the other option that I have?'

Sid shrugged his shoulders. 'Yes, that's much easier. Walk up to this window, take a deep breath and jump out. The morphine inside your body will numb your pain when you hit the ground below.'

'You mean, kill myself?' Dhruv asked. His mind was disoriented and he couldn't fully decipher what Sid was saying.

'Exactly. You have a clear motive to do that as well. In the heat of the moment, you kill the guy who has been filming your lover and doing all those nasty things to her. You kill him as well as his father, but then you're not a murderer; you're a family man, leading a snazzy corporate life. So, what do you feel after committing this gruesome crime? Nothing but a shitload of guilt. Well, that's it. It's a vulnerable moment. You don't see any other route of escape. You jump out the window. And bam, you're gone. You fuckin' die!'

Anuradha held back her tears. 'He is not going to do it, dammit, he won't. Are you listening to me, Dhruv?' she shouted.

'Well, well,' Sid paused, eyeing her in a way that made her sick.

'If he doesn't, then you die,' he said, tightening his grip on the wooden bat. 'But just consider this once. Wouldn't it be ironic, both your ex-lovers committing suicide, which were actually planned murders?' Sid sniggered.

'Wait. Give me a moment,' Dhruv said. Finally, it had come to this. The only way he could save her was by giving up his own life. It was strange, but Dhruv felt nothing inside him other than a feeling of emptiness and a burning desire to save her. He felt no fear.

'What will you get by killing me, Sid?'

Sid snorted derisively. 'It would kill her from inside. She won't be able to recover from this shock all her life. That's exactly what I want. I want her life to become a hellish movie, played in slow motion.'

'And then, Sid? Will you leave her and never come back again?'

'That depends on how she takes all of this. If she ever shows signs of recovery, I will be back. And with these masks that I have, don't we know that it's possible?'

Dhruv nodded slowly. 'Okay, Sid. I choose the second option. Come, help me to the window,' he said, glancing at her.

Anuradha looked at Dhruv the way she had never done before. It was a look of fierce love, admiration, agony of separation yet fulfilment of being together in that one moment.

It was a look of a final goodbye. Dhruv didn't know what she planned to do next.

'You're an idiot, Sid,' she said.

'What did you call me?' Sid asked, getting up, tightening his grip on the bat.

'An idiot and a first class fuck-up,' she said.

'You don't know shit! You will know after this boyfriend of yours is dead!' he screamed manically.

Dhruv saw her body straightening, she was pushing herself to get up. 'You screwed up once before. And now that you've come back, you've screwed it up all over again.'

Dhruv got it. He knew what Anuradha was going to do. He also knew that he couldn't stop her from doing it.

Even as she was talking, Anuradha sprang up in a flash and hurled herself at Sid with all the strength in her drugged body. Sid, who was sitting on the sill, lost his balance with the impact and toppled backwards, head first. The baseball bat he was holding flew out of the window. His upper torso dangled outside while his legs remained inside the room. He held the window by its edge with his left hand while with the right hand, he held on to Anuradha's arm.

'Don't be fuckin' stupid!' he shouted. 'I'm not going down alone this time. You push me again and we both die together.'

Anuradha looked at him in utter disgust. Determined. 'I am not letting you go alone this time you, son of a bitch, I'm making bloody sure that you don't come back again,' she said and shoved him out of the window, taking him along with her.

It all happened in a flash before Dhruv's eyes and then all went still.

Dhruv kept staring at the flapping curtains and at the lights behind the windows that dazzled the night sky on New Year's

Eve. With trembling hands, he picked up Shiv's mask lying on the floor in front of him and shredded it with the knife that he was still holding. He gathered the pieces in his hand and flung them out of the window. They floated in the air for a couple of seconds and then disappeared. A tear escaped his eye as he fell on the floor, unconscious.

44

Dhruv

Monday, 1 January 2018
Mumbai

By the time I open my weary eyes in the hospital, a good twenty-four hours have elapsed. Everything seems hazy, but then my sight clears. My head hurts from the inside as well as at the back where Sid had hit me with that baseball bat. I spot Shalini behind the two doctors, who stare at me as if I were some kind of a laboratory specimen. My heart isn't able to conjure any emotion, it rests lifeless. I muster a weak smile at her, a little surprised that she came over so quickly. I had gone down an incomprehensible path, which Shalini could have never imagined. Seeing her here is unsettling because it means she now knows what my other life had involved. I spot Anna standing next to Shalini, a sad smile playing on her lips. I know what that smile hides—the pain of losing a colleague and a friend. The doctors nod and turn to Shalini: 'He looks fine now. The effect of the strong sedatives injected into him is wearing off. But because of the injury to his head, we'll have to keep him under observation for another twenty-four hours; it'll be okay to discharge him after that. Meanwhile I am calling the police to record his statement.'

The doctors leave. Shalini holds my hand. Her touch feels assuring. 'How are you feeling now?'

I nod slowly. 'Much better. How are the kids?'

'They're okay. They're with Mom in Delhi.'

'Are you feeling all right, Dhruv?' Anna asks. 'The cops found you in Aman's house. It was a complete mess,' she says, glancing at Shalini. The way events have unfolded, I am certain Anna knows about our affair. Perhaps everyone knows about it by now.

Shalini nods. 'It was so sweet of you, Anna, to inform me immediately and tell me all that had happened. This is the stuff of the movies. That girl went through a really bad time,' she sighs. 'Oh, I forgot to check something with the doctor. I will just go and have a quick word with him,' she says with her lips pursed.

That girl. I wish Shalini had called her by her name.

'What did you tell her?' I ask Anna after Shalini is out of earshot. I want to know what Anna knows and what she has told Shalini.

'Anuradha told me some of it when she met me yesterday and then she emailed me later.'

'Emailed you? When?' I ask.

'Half an hour after she left,' she says.

Half an hour later? She would have typed that email when she was stuck in traffic on her way back from Anna's house. What was the urgency in writing it?

'What did the email say?'

She purses her lips, shaking her head. 'Same as what happened. She wrote that Aman and his assistant had hidden cameras in her house with the sole purpose of taking objectionable videos and pictures of her and then blackmailing her. She said she feared that Aman and his assistant may try to harm you guys, because you had confronted Aman's father in the morning while Aman was away. She asked me to inform the police in an hour if I didn't hear from her within that time.'

'Did you inform the police, then?' I ask.

'Of course, I did, an hour after I received that email and when she didn't call me. Also, my calls to her went unanswered. I was already so confused ever since Ash died. I suspected Aman had a hand in his death. That is why I called Anuradha to meet me. But look what happened! Aman himself was found dead. The cops reached Cedar Grove minutes after Anuradha and that bloody murderer fell down from the tenth-floor window. The steep fall was the cause of their instant deaths. That monster Shiv, his body was completely mangled. His face was completely gone. It was unidentifiable. The police also have the same opinion about this incident. How horribly that son of a bitch hurt you! He drugged you, too! He seemed so innocuous and timid. They said it was probably a fall out between the two of them, Aman and him, over money. Which is why he first killed Aman and then his father.'

I don't believe it. This story has twisted and turned and changed course in such an unbelievable manner. Why did Anuradha write this email when she didn't know about the outcome of our encounter with Sid? Anything could have happened, so where was the urgency in emailing Anna? Perhaps it was our phone conversation that prompted her to do so, before I was hit on the head. All I remember telling her was that I was trapped in Aman's house and that it was Shiv's face that Sid was wearing.

'The cops found all the evidence from his house. The obscene pictures and videos on Aman's computer, the two hidden cameras from his assistant's room along with bottles of morphine, injections and syringes,' she pauses, 'and also the emails that Aman sent to your wife from his computer. The cops believe it's a case of blackmail that turned even more sinister because of greed. Shiv may have been demanding more money from Aman for all that he was doing for him. And when Aman refused, Shiv killed him along with his father. There was another camera they found in Anuradha's room, however its memory card is missing. Have you any idea where it can be and what it would have on it? The cops were checking with me, but I had no idea, of course.'

I know where it is, but I am not telling anyone. I don't want them to see what Aman did to Anuradha on those nights, after drugging her. There's no point. The police already have enough information about her. They have all those pictures and videos from Aman's computer as evidence. She wouldn't want anybody to see any more.

'Shiv forcibly thrust the murder weapon into my hand, the knife with which he had murdered Aman. He wanted me to look like the culprit,' I say.

Anna shakes her head. 'Well it wouldn't have worked even if he wanted it to. He had drugged both you and Anuradha. That is a sufficient reason to believe that he wanted to kill everyone. That's how the police are looking at it. Even after being drugged and attacked, Anuradha didn't give up. The police believe that a fight broke out between the two of them that led to their fall. She was a brave girl. Her email is like a confession before she died. Who can challenge it?'

That's not the truth, I want to protest, but what good will my truth do? Will it bring her back? It won't, and I don't want to open this can of worms by trying to make the world believe in the unbelievable—that a dead man came back and became the root of all problems. It would be pointless—a cock and bull story. Who would believe in our story of a dead Sid coming back with a mask and turning our lives upside down? They would scoff at both of us. That's the last thing I want to do to her memory. It's better to stay quiet, to go along with what Anna believes our story to be. What the *world* believes our story to be. *What is truth anyway?* It's merely one's version of situations and events. I would rather go with their version of the truth and let our version remain between the two of us. The real version has the potential to bring a fresh tsunami in our lives. The fact that Sid didn't die that night in Lal Tibba would have serious repercussions. If he didn't commit suicide that night, then what was it? If Sid didn't die that night, why did he come back?

I wouldn't dream of letting that truth be known to the world. She had got enough shit from this guy while he was alive. Let her not get any more now that he is dead. The world would shred her reputation without her here to defend herself. I would rather let our version stay within my heart. The last piece of evidence that was left behind by Sid, Shiv's mask, was also destroyed by me. I was in a daze when I did that. Perhaps it was the last thing Anuradha wanted me to do. Hiding the real version would be in the best interest of everyone.

'Anna, you really helped. Thank you for doing that.'

Anna sighs. 'You know, Dhruv, I hated Anuradha once, because I thought she had the man I wanted. Aman. What an asshole he turned out to be in the end! Anuradha was one of a kind. She was different. So determined and so very clear in her head.'

I nod, grasping fully why she wrote that email to Anna. Anuradha had feared the worst and she wanted to protect me from it. She manufactured a different version of the truth that she wanted the world to know in case something happened to her. She knew that it would become my version as well because it was the most appropriate one. This version was what

she wanted the world to accept. She had always protected me
fiercely, since the time we fell in love. Her writing this email
as a confession of sorts was the last thing she did for me. She
ensured that my life didn't get messed up any further. Her email
was clear: it mentioned the accused, his intent and who was to be
held responsible if something bad happened. The rest was only
between the two of us. She kept me and my life safeguarded.
What more can you do in love?

The police investigation ends after a couple of hours. Shalini
is by my side throughout. I don't think they find anything amiss
in my statement. There is nothing contrary to what they already
have evidence for and believe in. The version I give them about
the happenings is the one they want to hear. It is Anuradha's
version: about a single girl living as a tenant, being blackmailed
by the landlord and his confidant; both of them have a falling out
over money and the associate kills both his boss and his boss's
father. When the girl and I accost him to retrieve the secretly
filmed videos and pictures, he drugs and tortures us before
getting into an altercation with her. During the ensuing tussle,
both of them fall out of the tenth-floor window.

I don't hide my relationship with Anuradha because that's
the one thing they would want to probe. With Shalini around, I
confess that besides being a very close friend of hers, Anuradha
and I had an affair earlier, when she was in Delhi. I don't tell
them that it's the one relationship that will always stay with me,
strong and true, till the day I am gone.

'Extramarital?' one of them exclaims, glancing at Shalini,
as if questioning her, wondering how she could allow it. I see
Shalini squirming in her seat, but I see no point in hiding
the affair.

Later that night, when the cops have left after recording my
statement, I ask Shalini for my cell phone. She had retrieved it
from the cops, who had found it lying in Aman's house.

I scroll down the email messages on my phone absentmindedly. I stop breathing when I see an email from her in my inbox. She must have sent it around the same time she emailed Anna. My fingers tremble as I click on it.

HAPPY NEW YEAR, DHRUV. YOU KNOW I LOVE YOU, it says.

I am unable to hold back my tears. It's as if every iota of emotion I have for her hidden within me comes flowing out of my heart. Anuradha must have imagined the worst. She knew an evil soul like Sid would never leave without her. And she didn't want to go without saying her final goodbye.

I give my phone to Shalini and cry my heart out all through the night. Shalini stays awake with me, trying to comfort me.

45

Dhruv

August 2019
Bandstand, Mumbai

My head got messed up after that. When the multiple murder story broke, it created a frenzy. The media, always hungry for a juicy scandal, lapped it up greedily: the heady cocktail of blackmail, sex and crime. There wasn't any channel that didn't run this story for the next couple of weeks. I was the only surviving person in this spine-chilling incident involving a page-three restaurateur and a single girl, who was a hotshot executive from the advertising world. Yes, that's how the news channels described her. To keep my sanity, I faced the media just once in Mumbai. I mumbled a few incoherent answers to the unending questions of the waiting crowd of journalists outside the hospital. After that, Shalini and I returned to Delhi and stopped taking their calls. I was labelled 'a good friend of the deceased victim' by the media. *A good friend, that's what I was.* Vidya Apte came out and told her story. I believe she couldn't stay quiet any more. Not even Aman could stop her this time. Public verdict was unanimous—both men, Shiv and Aman, were devils in disguise and the girl, an innocent victim. The channels dug out

Anuradha's pictures from the Internet and flashed them in their telecast all day long. I stopped watching television altogether because I hated to see her like this—in the public domain.

My professional life took a beating. My affair with Anuradha was out in the open. However, C&M was kind to me as I had been their star performer throughout. I just couldn't get to work after I returned from Mumbai. Psychiatrists, like Shalini, termed it depression, a state of mind that never wants you to get back to your original self and constantly pulls you down into your own hell. I didn't go to work for three months, during which time Shalini treated me as a patient. I talked to therapists for hours in her clinic and, coupled with medication, I began to get a grip on my life again. My children played a major role in getting me back on my feet. Just being in their company every day, revelling in their innocence and love, took my mind away from the intense sadness in my heart. The branch head position at C&M was vacant again. Vikas, my boss, said that due to strategic reasons I wouldn't be handling this role for at least some time. I knew what he meant. It wasn't just my affair that had prompted them to take this step, it was the scandal that had followed. The jury was still out on the case and like any law-abiding organization, C&M wanted to wait. It was only fair. They kept my company grade and salary intact and gave me another role in customer management. There were many raised eyebrows and conversations in hushed whispers when I resumed work after three months. But I guess their attitude will change with time, and they will forget about the scandal and my affair.

The case is ongoing in the court. I have hired a bunch of good lawyers in Mumbai, and I go to attend court proceedings whenever I am required to. I don't fear the outcome of the verdict because deep in my heart I know I've done nothing wrong, except hide the real version, which is of little importance to the courts and this world. The only thing I had feared was the discovery of our hidden affair, but since that is already out in the open, I have nothing to be afraid of. As soon as we returned to Delhi, I destroyed the memory card that I had kept with me. I didn't have the courage to see Anuradha like that: walking, talking, breathing and loving me in the recording. If I had kept it with me, the depression would have killed me.

I wish I had not let people down, Shalini and the kids. To seek my own selfish happiness, I took away theirs. Over time, I realized that what I did to them was so very unfair. But then was it ever really in my control? It's useless debating the moral high ground now that our story has ended and left me wounded for life. Shalini and I are still in the process of mending our marriage. She knows that my relationship with Anuradha stretched far beyond a mere affair. It wasn't just a physical relationship. Shalini was my healer in those three months and she got to know my soul. I know what she doesn't quite like: the intensity with which I loved Anuradha. She said that she had never felt that for herself. She is at least secure now. With Anuradha gone, she knows that one vacant silo inside my heart, which was meant for Anuradha, will always remain unoccupied. She knows that no one will ever be able to fill it. She is okay as long as it is vacant. I often wonder why Shalini never left me. I had given her ample reason to do so. She is an independent woman: intellectually and financially; she could have left me any time she wanted to. I figured out the answer later. Women, generally, have a greater tenacity to hold on to their relationships than men. Their emotional investment in a relationship is so high that they rarely like to sever it. That's why both Shalini and Anuradha held on to the relationship until Anuradha killed herself and broke away. Her permanent absence from our lives was the only reason that Shalini gave me another chance.

Sometimes I wonder what if we hadn't come together again after she moved to Mumbai? Would our story have had a different ending then? But no, our story couldn't have ended in any other way. Sid was coming back for her. What could have changed except my not being there? I was glad I was with her through it. I comfort myself with this thought every time the question raises its head. I ponder a lot about our last night together. I remember I had been terribly upset with Shalini and had asked Anuradha if she wanted to have a life with me. It was the first time I had asked her this question and she had refused. Why? This has been haunting me. Perhaps by that time Anuradha had decided that she too didn't want to build her life over someone else's happiness. She probably thought it was better we part ways than continue this relationship that was leading us nowhere. Maybe Anuradha didn't want any more bad karma in her life. She had said it was a very difficult thing to erase. Sometimes I wonder what would have happened if Anuradha had lived. Would we have been able to break this relationship then? It's a futile question when one of us is not there to answer it. I know my answer though. I could have distanced myself from her and never met her again, but my heart would have never let her go. Like it can't do, even today.

I gaze at the vast Arabian Sea before me, as I sit on one of the benches at the Bandstand. It's monsoon now and the sea is in high tide. Couples are sitting on the ledge that runs along the entire length of Bandstand. The rocks that provided them with the usual privacy for their clandestine canoodling are now submerged. I keep coming to Bandstand whenever I am here. It's walking distance from Cedar Grove. I can still feel her here, somewhere around, hiding. A bunch of youngsters flock around the nearby bench; a couple of them are carrying guitars and they

start playing a tune. The song wafting through the air blends
with my being.

> *Wise men say,*
> *Only fools rush in,*
> *But I can't help falling in love with you*
> *Shall I stay?*
> *Would it be a sin?*
> *If I can't help falling in love with you*

I listen to them for a couple of minutes before looking up. It's
starting to rain; my cab waits at some distance, so I get up.

'Can you ever stop loving her?' a tiny pebble, the one with a
throaty voice, asks.

'Never,' I reply.

'Can you forget her?' they ask in unison. Tentatively.
Expectantly.

I look at them. 'Can you?' I say.

The pebbles look awkwardly at each other and lower their
eyes. Then they go silent.

I walk towards my cab glancing at the faces around me.
Anuradha comes out from hiding, dressed in a sleeveless T-shirt
and trackpants. She peeks at me and then, as I walk a few steps
ahead, I see her in her office formals and an umbrella over her
head; and then again, in a peach saree, holding the tiny fingers
of a small kid. Smiling. I am reminded again of the day it all
started, when she had first looked at me, with her big dark eyes,
inside my cabin, hiding behind Rachna. I wish I could rewind
my life back to that moment and start all over again.

But then some things are just never meant to be.

Acknowledgements

To write a sequel is a tough one. As a writer, you have to assimilate your story *once again*: the characters, the plot, the continuity, the emotional chemistry between the characters, and if the story is a thriller, you have to stay true to the plot and keep the pace of the story intact. I have invested more than four years in this story, which is a fairly long time in comparison to the independent stories that I have written. I was quite exhausted by the end of it and shall not attempt another one, soon, hopefully.

Vaishali Mathur, my commissioning editor at Penguin Random House, has been instrumental in making this book see the light of the day. She was excited about a sequel but firm when it came to pushing me to write one which also made a good stand-alone story and brought a befitting end to the first book, *You Never Know*. This book, *Only the Good Die Young*, went through multiple heart-aching ☺ revisions, but I am happy that the final result is far more exciting than what I had conceived it to be. I would also like to thank other members of the Penguin team for their professionalism and enthusiasm in making the final product worthwhile: Udyotna from the editorial team, Saloni Mital, my copy editor, for looking minutely at the manuscript and suggesting just the right changes that surprised me pleasantly many times, and the marketing team led by Neha Punj.

My family and close friends for encouraging me to write the sequel. Tulika Singh, who has always been my first editor, and has helped me fine-tune the initial drafts with her inputs.

Vijesh Kumar for his enthusiasm and confidence in the sequel and his insights into sales and distribution.

Lastly, thank you readers for your encouraging response to *You Never Know*, and picking up this sequel to finally bring an end to the story of Dhruv and Anuradha. To write a thriller, which is wound delicately around an extramarital relationship, was challenging, but for me pushing the envelope is one thing that a writer must constantly attempt. The sensitive subject of extramarital relationships has mostly been looked at flimsily in pop culture, be it films or television, where such a relationship is termed to be an outright taboo and an outcome of eroded moral values of the two people involved. However, with this story, I want to defer from the road usually taken. Treat the relationship sensitively in this thriller. How successful I have been will be decided by you once you have read it. I will eagerly look forward to your feedback.